Praise for Colin Cotterill and the Jimm Juree series

'Cotterill's fiction has been compared to Alexander McCall Smith. It is far more complex and perceptive: intelligent exotica' *Independent*

'So mordantly clever that it's a line-by-line pleasure to enjoy his phrasing' *New York Times*

'An exotic, colourful crime series' *Financial Times*

'Eccentric and sheerly enjoyable' *Good Book Guide*

'A great story, very much of the now. I laughed, I was close to tears . . . I couldn't turn the pages fast enough' *Bookbag*

'Littered with witty one-liners and razor sharp repartees in the best Raymond Chandler tradition . . . Amusing, swashbuckling and lighthearted yet tinged with touching humanity, this is an entertaining read' *Red Online*

Also by Colin Cotterill

The Dr Siri Series

The Jimm Juree Series

THE AXE FACTOR

COLIN COTTERILL

Quercus

First published in Great Britain in 2013 by Quercus Editions Ltd
This paperback edition published in 2014 by

Quercus Editions Ltd
55 Baker Street
7th Floor, South Block
London W1U 8EW

A CIP catalogue record for this book is available
from the British Library

PB ISBN 978 1 78087 700 6
EBOOK ISBN 978 1 78087 699 3

10 9 8 7 6 5 4 3 2 1

Printed and bound in Great Britain by Clays Ltd, St Ives plc

Typeset by Ellipsis Books Limited, Glasgow

Acknowledgements

With thanks to Leila, Eddy, Kyoko, Nok, Michaela, Shona, James, Janet, Dad, Mariska, Lizzie, Rachel and CG. And with extra special thanks to Gogo, Sticky, Beer, Psycho and the Williams sisters for getting me through a particularly nasty patch and asking for nothing in return but food and the odd cuddle.

UNPOSTED BLOG ENTRY 1
(found two weeks too late)

I write.

It's how I earn my living. I used to think there were those who wrote and those who performed, as separate as those who dreamed and those who lived their dreams. But tonight I stepped across that line. I graduated from writer of death, to taker of life. I've never felt as free as I do now. If they arrest me, not that they're likely to, I couldn't pretend it was spontaneous: a spur-of-the-moment red rage or passion. I'd imagined it, you see? I'd pictured it vividly in solid oils rather than washed-out watercolours. It had been a recurring multicoloured vision for so many years it was only a matter of time before it took on the grisly form of reality.

To give her credit, she hadn't deserved all this gore. She was no more annoying than most of the women I've known. Perhaps she put a little too much effort into thoughts that didn't warrant thinking. Perhaps she spoke when silence would have been the better option. But in many respects she served me well. Visitors liked her. She made a superb cup of coffee and performed her desig-nated night-time duties to the best of her ability. Were I given more to diplomacy, I might have even been able to resolve these latest troubles without the use of the axe. But there was the question of betrayal, you see? Hard to forgive. So, it had all been decided by the flip of a twenty-pence piece. Heads she lives. Tails she gets hacked to bits. Odd, you might say – the flipping, not the hacking (although perhaps you wouldn't see the hacking as particularly normal) – but in Thailand, one did not toss a coin of the realm for fear that the regent might be insulted should it land face down. The Queen of England, on the other hand, had survived far worse indignities so it was her tail that had condemned my poor woman to the fate of the blade.

And so she lies, the victim, here and there. A foot hither. An elbow thither. Like a kit – an IKEA human being. It's fascinating to look around and visualize how these parts had once fitted together so neatly. Now look at her. And look at me, all blood-spattered and sweaty. I wish I had the type of cell phone that took pictures. But what an inspiration this has been. Job done, I simply have to transcribe this recorded message to myself, made whilst the events are still fresh in my mind. While the blood is still crusted on my hands.

First, the process. Consider this a 'how to' for beginners.

The waterproof groundsheet can never be too large. Six litres of blood spreads a long way. Two layers of black plastic garbage bags upright in a bin for those butcher shop parts one might feed to one's pigs. And then the cutting order:

A. *The vertebrae of the neck to bleed her out.*

B. *Arms and legs. (Sockets put up surprisingly little resistance to a sharp axe. I'm astounded how crime writers make dismemberment seem so labour-intensive).*

C. *The legs were a little too long for the box so a couple of swift hacks to the backs of the kneecaps.*

D. *The trunk was surprisingly broad so I had a mind to slice it down the middle by chopping through the sternum then down through the ribcage. I'd imagined I might invert one side and stack them, one inside the other like swimming pool chaise-longues. But, once separated, they were uncooperative. So I ended up forming four parts by hacking across the lower trunk below the ribcage. That was a workout, I tell you.*

E. *The other slicing and dicing I have to confess was just for the fascination of it.*

To be honest it's a damned fine feeling. There was something sexual about it. Wickedly perverted. There's no doubt I shall do it again. We'll see how cleanly I get away with this one. The average policeman down here has the IQ of a sponge but I made mistakes. The most prominent was the connection between us. I'm an obvious suspect. And there's motive. They wouldn't have to dig too deep to find that. But I do have one or two things going for me. There's the fact that I'm a foreigner. A better class of foreigner than the desperate labourers from the battered countries to the north, but still an outsider. As such I can be visible and invisible at the same time. I stand out but the Thais never delve too deeply into my business. They would look for a murderer amongst their own before accusing me. Then there's the fact that there is no crime without a body. She'll fit nicely in the polystyrene ice chest now, and off she goes. They'll never find her. She had no living relatives. Nobody misses a missing person in this country.

Project proposal:

My next will be more carefully thought out. A friendship. An alibi. A glass of red with a fast dissolving opiate tranquillizer they developed up in the heroin labs across the border. And here she'll be in this perfect windowless concrete room. No sounds. No escape. The type of room the predictable authors write about where all the serial killers and child abductors take their victims. Where the screams are muffled. And like those predictable authors I shall let my next victim come around to plead and cry for mercy. Yes, the next one will be better. And the next. And the next.

C.C.

CHAPTER ONE

THE LIP AND EYE REMOVER
(brand name on bottle of make-up removal cream)

Email to Clint Eastwood

Dear Clint,

It's Jimm here, your Thai friend down on the Gulf of Siam. Merry Christmas to you and your family. It's been a while since I wrote. I hope you are well. My sister (aka brother) Sissi and I noticed that you recently fired your personal assistant, Liced. We hope it had nothing to do with us hacking into her email account and accessing private information about Malpaso Productions. Liced was a victim in all this and was virtually blackmailed into helping us. I hope you can forgive her and consider rehiring her. As we now have nobody 'on the inside' ☺, I'm sending this package to your private post office box. I promise this is the last confidential information we will take advantage of. The enclosed DVD contains recorded footage of our very exciting pursuit of Burmese slaves on the Gulf of

Thailand. As a live internet feed we attracted 1.3 million viewers for the event. Sissi and I are certain every one of them would gladly fork out fifteen dollars a ticket and watch it as a cinematic experience, especially if Natalie Portman played me. But I bow to you on casting decisions on this one. I've taken the liberty of wrapping the DVD in my screenplay adaptation of the events.

Clint, I'm sure you'll recall that this is the fourth screenplay I've sent you, each one more thrilling than the last. Although I haven't heard back from you personally (not complaining. Old age is catching up with all of us) we did intercept a message from one of your editorial reviewers that referred to serious doubts about the quality of characterization in our second manuscript. Firstly, it was heartening to know you bothered to have our work assessed internally. But we feel a need to address this issue, especially as the characters in the second screenplay are my family members. We considered the comments to be unfairly cruel and I would like to take your editor to task.

Our mother, Mair, is perhaps starting to feel the teeth of dementia nibbling at her heels, but that doesn't make her 'nutty as a fruitcake' as your reviewer described her. She has long coherent periods which do not involve wearing odd shoes or buying second-hand Cosplay rabbit suits on eBay. (She's only done that once. She wanted to bond with the dogs.) Between you and me, she was a 'flower child' for several years and did spend

6

a good deal of time in the jungle with anti-system elements and there may have been intoxicants ingested at that time. But I'd like to see them as turning her into a more whole and mellow human rather than 'a fruit basket'.

The older gentleman who was described as 'unlikeable and two-dimensional' is, in fact my Grandad Jah. I have to agree with the 'unlikeable' part, but Grandad, I have to strongly protest, is not lacking a dimension. At the very most, he may be short a sense or two. But his absence of humour and social etiquette is more than made up for by his innate skill as an investigator. One would imagine that forty years spent in the Thai Police Force, where the focus is on amassing great wealth, rather than putting oneself in harm's way, might erase a man's policing instincts. But Grandad Jah has uncanny abilities and is as honest as the day is long (which explains why he's still penniless).

This brings me to my brother, Arnon, known affectionately as Arny, after his hero Arnold Schwarzenegger. Had we not followed our mother to the northernmost southern province in Thailand for reasons that I've only recently come to understand, he would undoubtedly have been this year's Mr Chiang Mai Body Beautiful. So, the comment, 'This character has no personality, no abilities and absolutely no purpose for being in the story', is a bit like complaining that Moby Dick didn't have much of a speaking part. Everything revolves around Arny. He's the sounding board for my stories and, even though he wouldn't harm a fly, he is my protector. In the last screenplay you'll notice that he takes on a boatload of pirates all by himself. I may have exaggerated the number of opponents he faced and the injuries he inflicted, but he did make a good account of himself in front of his fiancée.

The 'Impossible Hermaphrodite Queen', is my 'sister', Sissi, who was neither born with conflicting organs, nor crowned. If your reviewer had bothered to read the character sheet, he or she would know this. I feel he or she was just being smart in an attempt to impress you. I'm sure you have a lot of people sucking up to you. Sissi is transgender and has a medical certificate to prove it. With reference to her computer skills, the Malpaso threat to 'chase you down and run you out of business', was very dramatic but I'm sure you realize she's un-chasable and un-runoutable. Our hacking has, you'll have to agree, been very friendly and, even though your accounts were wide open to access and abuse, we have not robbed you blind. And I'm sure that when we're sitting down at the negotiating table discussing the finer details of our first movie deal, we'll all look back at these days and laugh.

Which brings me to me, Jimm Juree. I should perhaps have been the most offended and hurt by your reviewer's comments but I am traditionally a punchbag for abuse. As I am only 34 and have never been in domestic service, I was forced to look up some other meaning for 'old maid'. Once found, I am obliged to protest most strongly.

I was married and had conjugal moments with my husband during our three-point-seven years of marriage. At least once a month, if I remember rightly. Not a record, I agree, but enough to disqualify me from being 'a woman who has not formed a human pair bond by the time she is approaching or has reached menopause and the end of her reproductive lifespan'. (*Wikipedia*.) My husband had been desperate to appear married and I was desperate to be asked, which may not make us a pair bond but it's a precedent. I have a good ten years of premenopausal hunting left in me.

I also take objection to the expression 'a very unlikely Thai female character'. If by this he means I don't work in a rice paddy or a go-go bar, am not listed on any internet dating sites and do not walk with tiny steps nor speak demurely when in male company, then, fair enough, he's got me. But, in fact, we Thai gals were given admittance to the twenty-first century. We're allowed to chat online and study overseas and speak foreign languages. Would you believe it? We can even run companies and stand for parliament. No, Clint, my hero, I don't believe for a second that you want movie scripts full of stereotypes and I'm sure you sent that confidential internal memo to the trash where it belonged.

Well, hey. You probably can't wait to get your teeth into the enclosed DVD and manuscript, so I'll stop here. As Sissi and I are sure the North American postal service is all but redundant since the advent of emails, we

9

decided to increase the odds of you receiving this package by making thirty-seven copies which we are sending to your work colleagues, some senior shareholders of the company, friends and family. In each one we have included a small plant pot mat hand-embroidered by Hmong hill-tribe women in the north. As I say, when we're all raking in the dollars from our first movie collaboration, you'll stop seeing this as harassment and appreciate the charming side of it. Somewhere on the director's voice-over on the DVD you'll mention how annoyed you were at first but that those goddamned crazy Thais had one hell of a product.

Have a great Christmas and may Santa bring you yet another Oscar.

Love, Jimm and Sissi

(Postal address withheld but you have our email)

CHAPTER TWO

PLEASE LEAVE YOUR VALUES AT THE FRONT DESK
(country hotel)

Ours had become a life of shoulds. My mother, Mair, should have been on duty at the inconvenience store at our family resort. Instead, she was off painting desks at her school for the children of Burmese day labourers. Arny should have been cleaning all the junk off the beach in the unlikely occurrence we'd have any guests, but he was off spotting weights for his fifty-eight-year-old bodybuilding fiancée, Gaew. Grandad Jah should have . . . well, he didn't have any role or function in the running of the Gulf Bay Lovely Resort and Restaurant, so he was sitting by the roadside watching traffic, of which there was precious little.

That just left me – who should be just about anywhere else – in charge of five bungalows, four thatched outdoor tables, a half-submerged latrine block and two cows that had wandered along the beach one day, taken a fancy to our young palms, and stayed. Oh, and there

11

were three dogs that I tend to forget because, despite what they think, I'm not a dog person. They are, in order of rescue, Gogo of the non-functioning intestines, Sticky, second name Rice, and our latest recruit, Little Beer, riddled with mange and unlikely ever to get a date. We used to have a rescue monkey as well but we sent her to Phuket for trauma rehab. All these were the result of Mair's dual conditions of early Alzheimer's and philanthropy. This was a combination which incorporated the search and recover mission for our long-lost father. Look, in fact I do have a story to tell here; a blood-and-guts tale of betrayal, sex and international intrigue, so don't let me get sidetracked talking about Captain Kow. But, just briefly, when we first arrived here in the south, Captain Kow was a local celebrity; a gap-toothed, all-knowing, squid-scented old guy with nice eyes. When we found out he was the father who'd deserted us all when I was three, at least one thing made sense. Mair had dragged us down here for a reason. There was method in her madness. We don't know how she discovered Kow's whereabouts, but she was single-minded in his pursuit. That, in a Mills and Boone kind of way, I could admire. She gave up all she had, including half her mind, to move her family to the place where her one love had settled. It would have made a good movie, but not one I'd want to be in.

Since his unmasking by my transgender sister, Sissi, the good captain had vanished again. We hadn't had a chance to ask him about our abandonment or the semi-orphanic years we'd spent rattling around in Chiang Mai with humourless Grandad Jah as the nearest thing we had to a father figure. Kow had a lot to answer for, so I could understand his disappearance. I inherited his avoidance of culpability. All right. That's all I have to say on the subject for now. As a potential award-winning crime reporter in my days at the *Chiang Mai Mail*, I am only too aware that distracting side-shows can be really annoying for a reader who just wants to get down to the murder. So, here's the lead-in.

To compensate for the fact we weren't making any money at all at the resort, I was working two outside jobs. By far the best-paying was my role as an English language doctor. During her brief visit to Maprao, Sissi had introduced me to the dongle, which turned my notebook into a loaded weapon. Suddenly I could be online without queuing for hours at the Pak Nam internet café. I couldn't afford to pay the cell-phone bills but Sissi had done something illegal to the dtac databank that automatically topped me up. I'd spent a lot of my time on the road during my working days up north and was constantly frustrated by the fact that the sign makers assumed they could translate Thai into English merely with the use of a dictionary. This led to sentences such as DO NOT USE ELEVATOR WHILE CAUSING FIRE. So I had the brilliant idea of offering my services to anyone who wanted their signs translated accurately. Sissi blitzed me all over the internet and before I knew it I was getting regular work. Local councils had me writing their signs to avoid embarrassments, such as my favourite detour sign: EVERYONE GETS OFF HERE. Hotels had me improve on warnings like DO NOT DRIVE IN THE POOL AS WATER NOT SO DEEP. Ironically, my English doctoring practice was keeping us all alive. The Chumphon Department of Highways had sent me a list of road signs to correct. I was a whizz at transcription. It was me who convinced the provincial authorities to rewrite their Chum Porn signs. I had struck gold.

My other 'job' was at the *Chumphon News*. With the advent of desktop publishing and a wealth of smart unemployed journalism graduates, it was as if almost any town with a population over fifteen boasted its own newspaper. The *News* operated out of a house beside a busy main road. Its two regular contributors had flu, so, one day, the editor asked me if I might interview a famous international writer for them. As famous writers were notoriously thin on the ground in Chumphon, I accepted with bells on. I had visions of Dan Brown on a rock-climbing vacation in Krabi, me flown business class to Bangkok for dinner with Stephen King, a weekend on Kathy Reichs' yacht off Samui. But I did not have visions of Kor Kao, a ten-minute bicycle ride down the bay from our resort. I was suspicious.

'What's his name?' I asked.

'Conrad Coralbank,' he said.

It sounded like a coastal preservation programme. I could have feigned knowledge to impress the editor but instead I asked, 'And he's famous?'

'Absolutely,' he said. He was a very literary man, but he needed to open the Word information sheet he'd put together before he could tell me what the famous author had written.

'He's won stuff,' he said. 'Awards and that. He writes –' he squinted as he read the English – 'mystery novels set in Laos.'

Laos. Great. My ardour softened to a mushy paste of uninterest. Nobody would ever become famous by writing about a place that 98.3 per cent of American high school students couldn't locate on an atlas. Not even one with the country names written on it and an index. Admittedly, 34 per cent of that sample couldn't find Canada either. Laos – and I don't want to sound racist here – is easily the most boring place on the planet. I'd been there several times on stories and it's a scientific fact that clocks move slower there. One second in Laos is the equivalent of twelve minutes over here. Getting something done was like wading waist-deep through rice porridge. This was clearly going to be one of those pump-him-up-and-make-him-look-more-interesting-than-he-actually-is pieces. Fluff. But it was work. If I did a good job they might start giving me assignments. Plus there was the bonus that I'd get to speak English. My latent second language only ever got a real run-out with Sissi in our long bilingual phone conversations. We prided ourselves on our skill at speaking English in foreign accents. I did a good Brazilian. She had Eastern Europe down pat. It didn't, however, improve the actual language.

That was another good point. It would be a boon to find a down-and-out Westerner within cycling distance who could help me with my conversation skills. He'd probably be an alcoholic with skin allergies, grateful that a voluptuously curvy young Thai girl should stop by occasionally for a chat. I'd bring him a bottle of Mekhong whisky, watch his liver-polka-dotted hands shake as he poured it neat into his cracked Amazing Thailand mug and partake of a grateful swig. Of course I'd take the mace. Western writers in Thailand drew most of their inspiration from bars. He'd assume I was as loose as all the girlies in *farang* novels. That's the problem, you see? When you have a government full of dirty old men who have more sex with professionals than with their own wives it's very difficult to dismantle a sex industry that for many years was the country's only drawing card. The US military left two-thirds of its combat pay in Pattaya. Word got around, and soon every Tom, Dick and Helmut was on a charter flight to Bangkok. A lot of powerful people here got where they are today on the back of the male libido. You see why I could never write fiction? I get too tied down with issues. Nobody wants to read all this, so . . . Conrad Coralbank. The editor allowed me to sit and look him up online. His computer was dial-up. The connection was such that I drifted into a daydream where I was a Neanderthal staring at a rectangular block of stone, occasionally hammering it with my club. Then the Wikipedia page arrived. Here's what didn't surprise me. The photo was of a fresh-faced, big-teethed, blue-eyed man – late forties according to the caption – with fashionably long hair. They do that – authors. They dig out a picture from thirty years before that they kept because, although it didn't actually look like them, it looked the way they'd willed themselves to look at the time. They send it to their publisher who airbrushes out the pimples and there it is: the jacket photo.

I was however thrown by the number of books he'd supposedly written and the awards he'd purportedly been nominated for, and by the fact he was apparently married and enjoyed cycling, kayaking, and walking the dogs on the beach. None of that sounded particularly down-and-out to me. But, hey, anyone can write themselves a Wikipedia page and, if nobody who knows any better ever looks at it, nobody will edit out your lies. The net was Club Med for the scammer. So I wasn't exactly shaken by this introduction, just a little stirred. And to stir me even more, Conrad had photos.

Conrad on the beach with his two Rottweilers. Conrad in the garden with his beautiful Thai wife, both smiling with seedlings in their hands. Conrad about to set off on a bicycle rally with the Pak Nam Mountain Bikers' Club. And in every photo he was that same airbrushed young man from the jacket photo. There was one pensive black and white picture where he leaned over his keyboard in search of adjectives, and you could see his wrinkles. But they weren't deep, merely the friendly parallel arcs of an artist's pencil.

I zoomed in to his face until his forehead and chin no longer fitted on the screen. I'd lived here a year. Spent a lot of time by the roadside praying some gypsy family might steal me away. Why had I never seen Conrad Coralbank? Why had I never seen his tall, beautiful wife? With La Mae twenty kilometres south, and Lang Suan eighteen kilometres west, Pak Nam was his nearest metropolis. He'd have to pass our resort to get there. I'd spent hours in the Pak Nam 7-Eleven, marvelling at the vast choice of potato chips, mixing myself various flavours of ice gunk, doing impersonations for the CCTV camera. Why had we never bumped into each other? Tesco Lotus? The Saturday market? Pak Nam Hospital? The two restaurants with menus? Passing on bicycles, sweaty from the climb over the Lang Suan river bridge? It seemed almost impossible not to have seen him. Good. A mystery.

18

CHAPTER THREE

MAKE YOU TEN YEARS OLDER THAN YOU LOOK
(soap ad.)

It was mid-December and I'd just been to the post office to send off my packages to California. The wind had me home in half the time it usually took on a bicycle. It was the time of year when monsoons crept up from nowhere. When rainstorms drowned your carrots. When you walked along the beach and noticed a metre's depth of sand had been slyly eaten away by the storm surges overnight. Twelve beachfront coconut palms had been whisked away since we arrived, leaving just one column of trees to protect us. The previous year the freshwater bog behind the resort had filled up with salt water and messed up the ecology. For six months there was no life there at all. Migrating birds rearranged their flight itin-eraries because there was nowhere to stop for a drink. Mair bought an inflatable paddling pool, put it on the roof of our potting shed and filled it with tap water. Birds have beaks and claws so she had Arny out there every day with his bicycle puncture repair kit until the pool was irreparable and the birds were long gone.

When I reached the resort I found Mair up a tree and the dogs below, barking. I stood with them.

'Mair,' I shouted. 'Why are you up that tree?'

'There's a cat stuck up here,' she said.

'I don't see it.'

'It's camouflaged.'

'That would make it a green cat, Mair.'

'Don't be silly, Monica. It's white.'

'And you can't see it because of the snow?'

She laughed.

'The clouds, child,' she said. 'That's why you can't see it from the ground.'

'The clouds are dark grey.'

'It's a dirty cat.'

'Of course.'

I found myself bogged in conversations like this more times than I cared to remember. She always won, because she was the mistress of her own logic. She climbed higher. One of her flip-flops fell off and the dogs gasped. Sticky ran off with it.

'Mair,' I shouted, 'have you ever seen a reasonably good-looking old *farang* with a beautiful Thai wife living over in Kor Kao?'

'That would be Conrad and Piyanart,' she replied.

Mair knew everyone by name for twenty kilometres around.

'How come I've never seen them?' I asked.

'They drive a big grey S and M. Tinted windows.'

'Would that be an SUV?'

'That might be right.'

'So, how do you know them?'

'They stop at the shop sometimes. They get their drinking water here. Catch!'

The kitten dropped between the branches, screeching and flailing her claws. As cats have nine lives I considered stepping back and letting her use one up. But Mair wouldn't have forgiven me. So, I held out my arms and steadied myself. I've never been much good at sports. If it had been a basketball I would certainly have dropped it. But that's because basketballs don't dig their claws into your forearms and hang on. Before I could scream it had disengaged, was on the ground and fleeing the dogs. I swore and held my arms out in front of me so as not to drip blood on my white shorts.

'I've never tried it myself, but they say you stand a better chance of bleeding out if you run the razor blade along the artery rather than across it.'

'What?'

'If you're going to slash your wrists.'

'I didn't . . . it isn't a suicide attempt, Da.'

'Right.'

'It isn't. A cat did it.'

'OK.'

'Really.'

'Whatever you say.'

Each district down here has a health centre. They're identical. Designed by a sadist. No matter how sick you are, you have to do a Rocky Balboa up a steep flight of steps to get to the surgery. If you make it you can't really be that sick. But that's just as well because, although technically there's supposed to be a doctor attached to each one, it's a lucky patient indeed who catches one in residence.

'Alone again?' I asked.

Da was a real nurse with a uniform and everything. She'd escaped Maprao after high school, had completed her nursing training in Bangkok, and – more fool her – had come back again. Her childhood sweetheart, Wood, had promised to wait those three years for her return. However, his mates had convinced him that a pretty young trainee nurse in Sin City would have suitors tripping over their tongues after her. So he'd given her three months and married the girl from the fluffy-stuffed-animal shop in Lang Suan. As he hadn't thought to mention this in his annual Thai New Year greetings cards, she'd returned with only his un-smudged fingerprints on her breasts and walked in on a family meal with Wood, his wife and their two toddlers. She'd stopped eating that day, moved back in with her mother and taken the only available position, at the health centre. She only had her enormous skeleton to thank for hanging on to her skin because now there was no meat on her to fill it out. You saw her type on the Fashion Channel all the time. The scarecrows of haute couture. I have no idea what kept her alive, but she exhibited no lack of energy.

'Yeah,' she said. 'The doctor's off at a conference in Chumphon. Child development. Back tomorrow. You sure this was a cat? It's really deep.'

'Small. Fluffy. Obnoxious.'

'That sounds like a cat. Was it vaccinated?'

I laughed.

'I didn't really have a chance to check its medical records.'

'Then you'll need rabies shots.'

'What? Jesus! It was just a kitten. An innocent. I doubt she'd had enough life experience to be picking up any diseases. Can't you just clean up the wound and give me a course of antibiotics?'

'It's in the blood, Jimm. She could have got it from her mother. And it's incurable. I'm giving you shots.'

'More than one?'

I hate needles.

'Four. One every three days.'

'Can I refuse?'

'Of course you can. But when you start exhibiting odd behaviours, delirium, combativeness, loss of muscle function, spasms, drooling, convulsions . . .'

'Hmm. I wonder if my grandad's got rabies.'

'. . . chronic pain and eventually death, don't say I didn't warn you.'

I rolled up the sleeve of my fashionable but sweaty cardigan while she fumbled in the drawer for the meds. I located a vein and tapped it vigorously to make it an easier target.

'It's not heroin,' she said. 'Shoulder.'

'Shoulder? Are you sure? There's nothing up there but flab. How's it going to find its way to my blood? Can't you just inject it straight into my heart?'

'I thought you didn't have one.'

See? See what happens when you befriend the natives? You assume most of what you say goes over their heads, but these people remember everything. I'm constantly disillusioned. As a city girl I'd always assumed evolution started in the sea, crawled up through the villages, and reached its peak in the coffee shops and garage music nightclubs of Chiang Mai. But I'm often presented with evidence that the suburban-ites are hoovering up plankton and the advanced life forms are living off the land and sea down here.

'I'd supposed, as a nurse, you'd have understood I was speaking metaphorically,' I told her.

She wrenched off my cardigan and exposed my bra-less Sydney Night Lice tank top. Lucky we were alone. It would have driven men insane with passion.

'So, where is Ed these days?' she asked.

She knew perfectly well where Ed was. Ed the grass

cutter. Ed the boat skipper. Ed the builder. Ed the lanky, mustachioed breaker of hearts. He was with his girl-friend, Lulu, the slutty hairdresser. If men were awarded prizes for their taste in women, Ed had a Raspberry right there in his arms. He could have had me, if only he'd been more patient. He hadn't learned the city rules. He'd expected me to agree to a date after one asking. That's the way they do it down here. If you say 'no' it means 'no'. So you give up. Ridiculous. Even then, muddled with intoxicants, before I knew about Lulu, I'd given him a second chance. I'd virtually thrown myself at him.

'You might feel a small prick,' said Da.

'What?'

She jabbed a javelin into the tender flesh of my right shoulder.

'Shit,' I said. 'That hurt.'

'Sorry,' she laughed. 'I hadn't been expecting it to go in so easily. I'm used to durian skin. You're a mango, Jimm.'

'Thanks.'

'You know? I'm worried,' she said.

'Whether you injected me with steroids by mistake?'

'About Dr Somluk. I think she might be going senile in her old age.'

Da had come to the right place. I was a child of senility.

'How old is she?' I asked.

'Sixty.'

'Da, that doesn't even count as old any more. Sixty's the new eighteen.'

'She's started with these conspiracy theories.'

She abandoned my arm and sat on the sink unit. Unlike ours at the resort, it didn't creak. She barely weighed more than her uniform.

'You know?' she said. 'All that "They're after me" stuff. "If anything happens to me, make sure they don't get my documents." "They're more powerful than you'd ever know."'

'Did she ever mention who these powerful people might be?'

'No. That's just it. She always says it'll be safer for me if I don't know.'

'So, you think she's going nuts?'

'Most of the time she's normal. You know? Friendly. Funny. Really good with the patients. The kids love her. Then, every now and then, she'll come out with one of these rants. It scares me.'

I knew exactly what she meant. My own Mair had started out like that. She'd be talking about the cost of washing powder then mention, in passing, that she'd been standing in the checkout queue behind Kim Jong Il, the North Korean tyrant, and even he was complaining about the dramatic increase in the cost of Fab. I suspected from experience that Dr Somluk was on the same slippery shopping slope.

'What should I do?' Da asked.

'Do you think it affects her work?'

'No.'

'Then ride it.'

'Really?'

'It doesn't sound like she's ready for the loony bin just yet. Maybe the sea air will clear her mind. It's helped Mair. Now, do you think I can get some Band-Aids on my bloody wrists before they get infected? I have a very serious interview to conduct this afternoon. I need to look my best.'

I had to prepare lunch before my appointment at Kor Kow. My short straw had committed me to the kitchen at the Gulf Bay Lovely Resort, but in truth, nobody else in my family could cook. Even if they worked in the Oxfam mess tent feeding the starving masses they'd get complaints. Unfortunately, I had a skill. They liked to watch me in the kitchen but deliberately failed to learn anything. I'd decided on *kanom jeen* with fish sauce that day because I'd made the sauce earlier so I just had to boil the pasta. Still they traipsed into the kitchen to look over my shoulder. Mair came first.

'Are you sure the sauce is red enough?' she asked.

'No, perhaps you'd like to make it next time?' I told her.

'I'm just saying, when Grandma made it . . .'

'When Grandma made it she used tomato ketchup. Litres of it. It was inedible.'

'She's gone, you know?'

'And I shouldn't speak ill of dead cooks?'

'I learned all my culinary skills from her.'

'I rest my case. Do you want to call the others? It's almost ready.'

'But . . . the colour.'

'I'll toss some crimson emulsion in it.'

'Yes. Good idea.'

'Mair. Where's Capt— where's Dad?'

'He's in a safe place.'

'Why don't you bring him out? Invite him for lunch.'

'Really?'

'He has to eat.'

'You don't hate him?'

'Not yet.'

'What do you mean?'

'He left you with three young children. Vanished. We're all screwed up in our own adorable ways as a result. But we met him as Captain Kow and we liked him . . . well, Grandad hated him, but he hates most people. Arny and I saw a lot in the captain to respect. He doesn't seem like the kind who'd abandon a family without a good reason. We'd like to hear what that reason was. If it turns out to have been due to, I don't know, boredom, or another woman, general irresponsibility – then we can hate him with a clear conscience. But we're prepared to give him a hearing.'

'I don't.'

'Don't what?'

'Don't think we should ask him to give his reason.'

'Why not?'

She adopted her famous everyone-else-around-me-is-going-down *Titanic* smile.

'National security,' she said.

'Mair . . . I . . .' But when I looked up from the noodles she'd already turned tail and fled.

It probably meant nothing. It had become a catch-phrase to cover a lot of ills. The six soldiers who'd turned up at Mair's Burmese school and searched the six-year-olds' satchels had cited national security as their motivation. But when Dad walked out on us there had been no such concept. Was she saying Captain Kow was a spy? Was he involved in some political intrigue? I needed to look up what was happening in the country during the period he left. Now that would make a good story. My dad – shaken martinis and a gadget-ridden Aston Martin.

Grandad Jah was next in.

'It's not red enough,' he said as he pored over my sauce.

'I'll open my wrist wounds and bleed in it,' I said. I thought I'd muttered it under my breath but he caught it, gave me that "Don't get fresh with me, girl" look and sat at the table. All the windows were open, which was unusual. The weather had been mild for the past two weeks, but not calm enough for us to venture back outside to the bamboo tables. The monsoon season liked to lull you into complacency, then blow your roof off. The Siam Commercial Bank was considering offering insurance against natural disasters but they hadn't quite got around to it. (I tried for a product placement incentive for mentioning them in my story but Mrs Doom, the manager, said there wasn't a budget for it. What she meant was that she didn't think anyone would read it.) I hadn't told the family but I'd put money aside from my modest savings and would be the first to procure said insurance. Divine intervention was our only hope. Sadly, the Gulf didn't have so much as a decent volcanic fault line. Even the disasters were dull here.

Arny sauntered into the kitchen, squeezed my flabby waist, and said, 'It's not—'

'Don't.'

'OK.'

I like my brother.

'Where's the bride to be?' I asked.

Arny's fiancée, Gaew, had been spending more time at our resort. She helped Mair in the shop. They'd become close. That wasn't such a surprise, given that they were the same age. Arny had 'saved himself' till he met the right one. He'd found her in the form of the ex-bodybuilding empress of Indochina, thirty years his senior, divorced. At first we thought it was a blessing

30

that she'd pumped so many steroids into herself that she hadn't been able to produce children. Her fallopian tubes were solid brickwork. But recently I'd been thinking it would have been nice if Arny had stepchildren his own age to hang out with.

'She's working out,' he said, with a look of pride that his elderly paramour could still bench-press sixty kilos.

'Bah!' said Grandad Jah. 'Get yourself a mindless teenaged bimbo like the rest of them. It's unnatural. A boy like you – with her.'

Arny joined him at the table. 'Have you ever loved anyone, Grandad?' he asked.

'Are you asking me if I've ever been a slave to mindless emotions?' he said. 'Whether I've ever dipped into my meagre police earnings to buy slowly decaying flowers for a woman? Whether I've been driven to write poetry or make promises of a lifetime commitment that no man on earth has ever kept?'

'No,' said Arny. 'Not the actions. Just the feeling. Have you ever had your insides melt by being near someone?'

I thought I noticed a brief hesitation before Grandad spouted, 'Don't be ridiculous.'

'Then you wouldn't know,' said Arny. 'It's attraction. It's like being a magnet that's found a refrigerator it wants to spend the rest of its life stuck to.'

Arny had inherited my mother's gift for horrible metaphors. But this was a rare moment of family

31

bonhomie. Mair, whom I'd sent off in search of the men, had presumably forgotten why. She hadn't come back. So it was a good chance to ask Grandad an uncomfortable question.

'Grandad, why do you hate our father?'

The fork he'd been juggling flew over his shoulder and missed Gogo by a whisker. She screamed.

'That isn't an appropriate topic over a meal,' he said.

'I haven't served up, yet,' I reminded him.

He looked first at the door, then the window, as if sizing up an escape route.

'Ask *him*,' he said.

'We would,' said Arny. 'But he's vanished again.'

'That'd be right,' Grandad nodded. 'He's good at that.'

'Did you know before?' I asked.

'Know what before what?'

'You know what I'm talking about. Did you know our father was here? That it was the reason Mair brought us down?'

'No. I did not,' he snapped.

'But you recognized him when we arrived?' said Arny.

'That very first day,' he said. 'I was almost on the first bus back to Chiang Mai.'

'So, why didn't you tell us?' my brother asked.

Grandad was squirming. He didn't like being cornered like this.

'I was hoping that mother of yours would come to

her senses,' he said. 'Realize what he was and leave this forsaken wilderness. But instead she ends up . . . fornicating with him. It's disgusting.'

'They're still legally married,' I told him.

'Irrelevant,' he said. 'People over forty should know better. All that physical nonsense should be out of the system long before then.'

'She's obviously forgiven him for whatever it is he did,' I said.

'If you can forgive someone for being worthless.'

We found Mair painting flowerpots. She thought she'd eaten already. We sat around the lunch table with nothing much more to say, but I watched Grandad pick at his *kanom jeen* and two things occurred to me. One: that he didn't have any more of an idea than us as to why Captain Kow had deserted us. And two: that he was a sad, grumpy, bitter old man. But it wasn't him I felt sorry for. It was Granny Noi. I would have headed off to the pyre even sooner if I'd been married to him for fifty years.

It was 1:46 when I arrived in front of the big yellow gate in the tall yellow wall that bordered the Coralbank property. It was no wonder I hadn't noticed it before. It was on a hill that formed the headland at the southern end of our bay. From the road you saw only a dirt track rising between the trees. That road eventually arrived at Kor Kow Temple, but there was a flatter path along

33

the beach that didn't put a strain on your motorcycle. Nobody took the hill road and that fact made the headland a prime piece of real estate for a writer. The tranquillity would only be disturbed by occasional temple fêtes.

The only thing that concerned me was how his pretty Thai wife might be coping with living above a temple. We have a lot of head and feet politeness issues in Thailand. It doesn't worry me because I'm culturally ambivalent. And countless condominium owners in Chiang Mai have no qualms about riding their stationary bicycles on the balcony within view of the shiny domed heads at the neighbourhood temple. But I know diehards who fear dispatch to one of the Buddhist hells for such sacrilege. What camp was Mrs Coralbank in, I wondered?

All I could see from the gate was a curved driveway flanked with bougainvilleas. In the hot season they would be a glorious explosion of colour but they didn't take kindly to being lashed by monsoon rains, so there they drooped, apologetically green. A button on the fence post had a semi-quaver logo at its centre so I pressed it. In the distance I heard the first few notes of something classical. Something a more arty person than me would be able to name to impress a famous author.

'Oh, I noticed you had Barry Mendelssohn's *Opus Four in G-strings* as your bell charm,' I would say.

But I didn't have a clue what it was. I heard a click and the gate began to slide open noiselessly. I decided to wheel my motorcycle down the slope to avoid an ungainly dismount in my little black dress. The wicked garment had already caused a smouldering in a group of house-builders I'd passed. They didn't exactly shout or wolf-whistle, but I could tell I'd excited them. It's disgusting how men can be such slaverers at the sight of an attractive woman in revealing clothing. I hoped Conrad wouldn't get the wrong idea. I do have very nice legs and my lips, as Mair is constantly reminding me, are sensuous. The bits in between could use some work but eating is one of my few pleasures.

I don't know why those thoughts were going through my head as I rounded the downward curve and came very quickly to a futuristic house. What wasn't glass was orange-rendered concrete. It was a house that would change colour with the seasons, as the rain soaked into the cement and then dried and baked. I could already see the entire living room through the glass with a full-sized pool table and a wall full of books. A cello, painted red, was suspended from the ceiling on a hangman's noose. I had most certainly left Kansas.

A small male person who looked about twelve rushed up to me, shouting something. He had a deep baritone voice. He wrestled the motorcycle from me and shouted something else. I didn't know what he was saying but I did recognize it as Burmese. I asked him in Thai where

Mr Coralbank might be and he might have told me, but I don't speak Burmese. He wheeled my motorcycle away and I was left standing on the gravel in my good shoes. Only then did I look up.

Wow.

Our Gulf Bay Lovely Resort was a motel with a two-dimensional vista. You could only attain a third dimension by climbing up a coconut tree. Ahead of me was the same murky body of water I ignored every day. It was still full of garbage the disgusting people in Lang Suan threw into the river, but from here it was the Mediterranean off the South of France. The view was majestic. You could see the beach road and the cliffs of Ny Kow. You could see the islands and the white breakers out deep in the Gulf and our home village being bombarded by the elements. Watch our palm trees topple and float away. With a high-powered telescope you might even see our family's comings and goings. Watch me step recklessly from the open-air shower.

'You must be Jimm,' came a voice.

English. I was comfortable with the language but I always seemed to lack that witty opening gambit that might establish my linguistic credentials.

'How are you?' I shouted to the breeze.

'Down here,' came the voice.

I looked down the forested slope that eventually gave in to the sea and I made out a head in a cowboy hat peeking above a bush.

'Come and join us,' he called.

A cobblestone path led down from the veranda and it was clear that there was nothing accidental about the vegetation. It was custom-designed to look aggressive and impenetrable but it was a wimp of a jungle, landscaped to within a centimetre of its natural life. Every frond fell seamlessly against the next. At the bottom of the path were four blanched coral steps leading onto a manicured lawn about the size of two good paddy fields. It was a bizarre scene.

To my left stood four watermelons on posts, like coconuts in a funfair shy. Off to one side stood a young woman, attractive in spite of a face caked in yellow paste to combat the ravages of the sun. This was not the fine-looking woman I'd seen in the internet photos. This one stood beside a heap of watermelons. She wore an ankle-length sarong, a long-sleeved shirt, a straw hat and a nasty smirk, aimed in my direction.

At the other end of the lawn, dressed in shorts and a cowboy hat, was my author. He was in good shape for an older man. He had a six-pack. Arny had – I don't know – a twelve-pack? But he was young and worked out every day. I imagined that, by fifty, my brother would have gone to flab and be embarrassed to take off his shirt. Conrad the mini-Destroyer had no such problem with his body. He was the type of man you instinctively knew would be good in bed. Here's a confession. We women know. It's an aura we can read. And don't give me that 'Decent women don't' line. Culture and tradition and religion might shut us up, but we all get the tingle. This man was ripe. The fact that he was holding an axe did nothing at all to dissuade me.

In fact, it wasn't just the one axe. He had an arsenal of them. There was a large case behind him that concertinaed open like a mobile bookcase. Except, these shelves held nothing but weapons with blades. There were knives, machetes and axes lined up according to size on a rack. It was like a golf bag for lumberjacks. My guess was that the baby he held in his hand was around a nine iron. He was swinging it back and forth beside his leg. His gaze was fixed on the line of watermelons. His stomach muscles rippled as he took in deep breaths, then, like a Russian tennis player, he grunted loudly as he let fly the axe, underarm. It seemed to somersault through the air in slow motion until the last few seconds. If watermelons had ears it would have sliced off the left one.

The powder-faced girl squealed and clapped but Conrad looked disappointed.

'Nice shot,' I said, still searching desperately for wit.

'No,' he said. 'It was supposed to go through his nose and out the back of his brain.'

'Oh.'

'Never mind,' he said, and beckoned the girl who ran over with his shirt. He didn't thank her, so I assumed she was the maid. It was sad to see his body put away.

He was over his disappointment by the time he joined me on the steps and he gave me a very polite *wai*, which I returned clumsily. Well, he'd sprung it on me. I wasn't expecting a foreigner to welcome me with a traditional salutation. I didn't get *wai*'d once all the time I was in Australia. Not even by the Thais. Conrad Coralbank was smiling at me. His teeth were too neat to be natural. His eyes were too blue to be eyes.

'Thank you for coming,' he said.

'Thank you . . . for . . . being here.'

I was doing really well. He was probably thinking the *Chumphon News* was a charity rag run by the educationally challenged. I was intimidated. I can't deny it. He even looked like a famous writer. Some people look so much like a somebody that they have no choice but to become . . . it.

'They told me you spoke English well,' he said. He walked to the steps and stopped, so I assumed I was supposed to go with him. He put a hand on the small of my back and began steering me up. Normally I'd hate that. If anyone else had tried it I would have taken a step forward and back-heeled them in the shin. But I'd seen the Duke of Edinburgh do it to Elizabeth so I assumed it was a British custom. Who was I to deny a country its culture? His hand was warm and seemed to be connected to some electrical source.

'I'm sure it wasn't a result of the Thai school system,' he said. 'Where did you pick it up?'

'Songs,' I said. 'I can't sing to save my life but I liked to memorize lyrics. And our mother spoke English. She encouraged her kids to use it. It was a sort of game. We'd watch American movies on Beta and Mair would test us at the end. She wanted us to be ready for the world outside our little shop. We weren't your typical Thai family.'

I was babbling.

'And did you see that world?' he asked.

'Only the countries on our borders, and Hong Kong and Melbourne. I did a home-stay there when I was eighteen.'

We were almost at the house. His hand was still warm on my back like a poultice.

'I was at the Sydney Writers' Festival last May,' he said. 'I'd never been to Australia before and all I knew about the place was beer and cricket. But it was a pleasant surprise. Hundreds of people paying good money to listen to authors spouting on about what fonts they preferred, and whether tight underwear restricted their creative flow. And for those not lucky enough to get tickets, there was a live audio feed for the masses outside on the lawn. I was delighted that the place was so culturally vibrant.'

We were already in the large aquarium of a living room. Glass on three sides. The gentle tickle of conditioned air, most of which was escaping through the open slide door. The girl with the powdery face either had a twin sister, or she'd beamed up to the house on the transporter. Somehow she'd arrived before us. She was at the kitchen counter pouring what looked like iced benzene into two tumblers.

'You know, in Thailand we have a sort of custom,' he said.

He was staring at my feet still resplendent in their three-centimetre heels.

'Oh, shit,' I said, kicked off my shoes and ran them back through the doorway. I could have blamed the house, him, the fact that none of this was Thailand. You didn't take your shoes off when you walked into the 7-Eleven or the airport, or Buckingham Palace.

'Sorry,' I said.

He merely laughed. It was the type of laugh you'd want to hear often. We sat at the huge table and I pulled my trusty cassette recorder from my bag.

'Ah, good,' he said. 'A fellow Luddite.'

I didn't know the word. I could have smiled and let it go but it might have been rude.

'What is that?' I asked.

'A Luddite is a person who shuns technology,' he said.

I felt insulted on behalf of my recorder.

'This is technology,' I told him.

'So was the wooden club.'

I liked him.

'I have a smartphone my sister left for me when she was here,' I said. 'It records, takes photographs, fries

41

eggs and overrides bad instructions from its owner. I still haven't worked out how to turn it on. It looked so easy when Sissi used it. My recorder here has buttons with the words, "On", "Off", "Forward", "Rewind", "Record" and "Play" written on them. There's a picture of a battery at the back so I know which way round to insert my double A. That's as technical as I want to get.'

'Then I'm surprised you don't use a pencil and notepad,' he said.

I produced the pencil and notepad from my bag and he let me have another of his laughs. The maid put the glasses on the table between us and loomed nearby like an undertaker. Her body language was rude. Conrad pushed one glass of benzene towards me.

'I suppose we'd better get started,' he said.

I pressed 'Record'.

'Then I'll begin with the obvious question,' I said.

'Where do I get my ideas from?'

'What have you got against watermelons?'

'Ah. It's research. Not the kind of information I'd find online. The effectiveness of an axe as a battlefield weapon.'

'For a book?'

'Yup. After years of begging, my publisher has finally agreed for me to step out of the series and do a one-off. Historical fiction. I haven't got a sexy title for it yet but it's coming.'

'And it's about axes?'

'And swords and daggers. I have quite a collection. Would you like to see it?'

The oldest trick in the book. 'Come upstairs and see my axe collection.'

'Do you mind if we get the interview out of the way first?' I asked.

'No problem.'

'Where are your dogs?'

'My dogs?'

'The two Rottweilers on your website.'

'That was a creation of the webmaster,' he said. 'He Photoshopped them on to a beach shot I sent him. He says being a dog lover helps sales. I'm not really that fond of them.'

My questions were all standard after that; what he did before becoming a writer (he taught English in universities); why he started to write books, (he'd read so much rubbish he decided he could most certainly do better); what his big break was (winning the Edgar Award for his fourth novel); why he moved to Thailand (cost of living, nice people, beautiful women). He answered in good humour and I was fascinated by his stories. But, to be honest, I couldn't imagine readers of the *Chumphon News* getting past the first paragraph. Not enough sex or football for most of them.

His last answer had given me an in to a subject I was particularly interested in.

'Does your wife contribute to the editing process?'

'Not any more.'

'She got bored?'

'Yes, of me. She doesn't live here any more.'

'Do you have certain hours when you— What?'

'You asked about my wife. I said she's gone.'

'When?'

'About two months ago.'

'Why?'

It wasn't my business and it had nothing to do with the interview.

'A combination of not being able to take the city out of the girl, combined with her need for a younger man,' he said. He spoke remarkably calmly.

'So you're . . . ?'

'All on my lonesome. I've filed for divorce.'

I took a sip of the benzene. It tasted vaguely metallic. I wondered whether the maid had slipped something in it. He noticed me gurning and laughed.

'It takes some getting used to,' he said. 'Some berry-leaf combination I get sent down from Laos. A shaman I know makes tonics. He says it's an aphrodisiac.'

'And you give a love potion to all your guests?'

'I think it only works on old men,' he laughed. 'For women it's supposed to beautify the skin and increase bust size.'

I took a long swig before completing my list of mundane questions, but the fact that the author's pretty wife was no longer around weighed heavily on my

frontal lobe. I'm a divorcee, you see. Since being classi-
fied as an old maid I'd become aware of my failings.
Even in my twenties when I was at my most voluptuous
and fascinating, there had been no queue of suitors.
Thai boys hoped my weirdness – my choice of clothing
based entirely on what other girls my age wouldn't be
seen dead in, my noir make-up, my penchant for dropping English words into the mix – would include my
being an easy lay. Once they found out I was saving
myself for a Westerner five times my age – Clint was
at his hunkiest in 1978. He was acting alongside an
orang-utan back then – they moved on. I had sexual
experiences, but they were of my own design. I was the
predator. My husband was disappointed when marriage
didn't tame me. During these years all I've wanted
was to be desired, just once, without having to curl-
tong my hair or slather on blood-red lipstick. So you can
probably guess where my imagination took me when
my author said, 'I've noticed you around, of course.'

'Around what?'

'Around your mother's shop. In Pak Nam. At the
Saturday market.'

I think I trembled a little at that moment.

'Should I take out a restraining order?'

That produced a full-body chuckle. I was so happy I
could make him laugh. I wished I'd memorized all
the Note Udom stand-up routines like I'd planned.

Unscripted, I didn't see myself as particularly funny or vibrant, but here I was watching my brilliance sparkle in Conrad Coralbank's eyes. Everything I said seemed to fascinate him. His fondness for me was addictive.

'I haven't seen you at all,' I told him. 'How can that be?'

'I blend in.'

'Right. All those European tour groups hanging around in the village.'

'Perhaps it helps to be in an SUV with tinted windows. I can sit and observe life and take notes and nobody feels self-conscious. In that way I see it all the way it really is. But when I saw you there was something different about you. Are you completely Thai?'

'No, my left leg is Latvian.'

He roared at that. The maid cleared her throat in the background.

'Of course I meant whether there was any foreign blood in you,' he said. 'There's something exotic about you. Something different. I was surprised when you turned out to be who you are,' he said.

'Who I are? Who are I . . . am I?'

'A journalist. I was really pleased. When I saw you before, I'd . . . and I don't want you to take this the wrong way, but, I'd imagined you to be someone's mistress.'

I almost bit the eraser off my pencil.

'You thought I was a slut?'

46

'No. Not at all. You stand out down here because you're a beautiful woman. You have class. Nobody here walks like you, carries themselves like you.'

The back door slammed, and that's when I noticed that the maid had left the building.

'You have a confidence that's hard to find in other women,' he continued. 'That's—'

'And you assumed I'd be the type of woman who'd take that walk and confidence and carry-ance and jump into bed with some rich arsehole a couple of nights a week when his wife was off playing mah-jong, just so I could make myself a few thousand *baht* extra? I can see where your mind is, Mr Coralbank. Thank you for that. The interview's over so I believe it's time I left. I've learned more than enough.'

I stood and held my chin at an indignant angle. I swept my equipment into my bag and headed for the door. I thought he might blurt out an apology, at least stand up and ask me why I was so angry. But as I leaned against the door frame putting on my shoes, I could see his reflection in the glass. He was leaning back on his chair with his tumbler in his hand. He might have even been laughing. I was rather proud of my exit. I walked around the building, expecting to have to search for my Honda Dream but there it was in the car park, washed and polished. The powdered maid was holding on to the throttle. I took hold of the other side of the handle-bar, kicked up the parking stand and said thank you.

I attempted to walk the motorbike up to the gate but the maid didn't let go. She wasn't smiling. In fact the powder cracked around her frown like a Maori Ta-moko tattoo.

'Not him,' she said, in Thai.

'What?'

'You keep away from him.'

I raised her grimace a Thai smile and wrestled the bike from her. I started to push it uphill. The driveway was a lot steeper than it looked but I'd have sooner given myself a hernia than ask her for help. She stood with her hands on her waist.

'You listen to me,' she said. 'Or you will be sorry.'

After some six metres I stopped to get my breath, put the key in the ignition and threw myself onto the seat. If you've ever had to start a motorcycle on a sixty degree incline without making a fool of yourself you'll know how important it was to get the timing right. I did kick up gravel and wobble a little but I made a good account of myself. I passed the deep-voiced child who was at the open gate smiling. How did they know when I'd be leaving?

Once I hit the dirt road outside I felt a little flutter of relief. But it was soon overtaken by a flap-flap of what could only be called elation. The Burmese maid was most definitely being seduced by the suave author. He said I was beautiful. Loudly. She obviously considered me to be a threat. I bet that was why the pretty Thai wife had left home. I liked it. It was like making a guest appearance in a daytime soap for international audiences. I was the dark stranger. It didn't matter. I had my interview. I wouldn't be *pas-de-deux*ing in their *ménage à trois*. No sir. Not me.

CHAPTER FOUR

WE WON'T LET YOU DOWN
(diving company)

'So tell me why you didn't allow yourself to be seduced. He knew he had an appointment with you but he was in the garden, shirtless and sweating and showing off with his axe. What does that all subliminally tell me? It was obviously a male courtship ritual. He'd seen you around. He liked the way you looked. He'd become bored with the maid. He wanted you. You should have gone and had a look at his collection of shafts.'

'And confirmed I was of easy virtue?'

'You'd be easy, given the chance. Tell me you weren't excited by it all.'

'Don't be . . . not excited exactly.'

'When was your last time?'

'You always ask me that. You know the answer. July the 4th, 2004. Another disappointment.'

'So don't you think it's time to get back on the bicycle before everything rusts and seizes up?'

It was remarkable how many of my phone conversations with Sissi got around to sex.

'Good advice coming from you,' I said.

'What do you mean?'

'When was your last bicycle ride?'

'That's irrelevant. My sexual organs, and I include my breasts in that category, are not given to the ravages of old age. They're still as pristine as the day they rolled off the production line. You, on the other hand, need a man every now and then so you don't become a North Pacific sponge lumpsucker fish.'

'I'm supposed to ask, right?'

'The vagina of the North Pacific sponge lumpsucker closes up once she's had her sperm intake. Sealed up for eternity. Impassable.'

'Great.'

'Tell me you aren't attracted to him.'

'It's hard not to be.'

'So, use him. Let him believe he's seducing you, whereas, in reality, you'll be taking advantage of him.'

'What about my reputation?'

'Oh, Jimm.'

'I have one.'

'You're a city girl in the country. The locals all assume you're promiscuous. So you might as well get some real loving.'

'I'm not contacting him.'

'He'll be in touch.'

'How do you know?'

'You walked out on him. You've made yourself even more desirable in his eyes. His hunter mode would have kicked in. He'll pursue you. Trust me.'

'What about the maid?'

'Now, her, you might have to keep an eye on.'

I turned up for my second rabies shot and Dr Somluk still wasn't there. Nurse Da's right hand, worryingly, the one that held the syringe, was shaking.

'Do you want to do this yourself?' she asked. 'I've got a horrible hangover. Very full-on date last night. Gogo takes his drinking very seriously.'

It concerned me that her new boyfriend had the same name as my dog.

'I thought you didn't accept anything orally,' I said.

'Liquids are fine. And whisky's an all-round meal: barley, yeast, water, sugar. That's the four food groups right there.'

'You did have to sit the exams to be a nurse, right? I mean, you didn't get a relative to take your place?'

'Jimm, I'm really worried.'

'All right. I'll come back when you get over the shakes.'

'No, I mean, I'm worried about Dr Somluk. She should have been here four days ago. She sent a message yesterday saying everything was fine but she wouldn't be back. Then she turned her phone off.'

'I expect she just got bored and moved on. Did you talk to whoever it is that hires doctors to crumble away to nothing out here at the end of the planet?'

'The Provincial Medical Placement Centre. Yeah, I called.'

'What did they say?'

'They said it was nothing to worry about. They'd find me another one. They said rural doctors quit all the time. Old Dr Prem only survived a week here.'

'There you go, then.'

'But I don't believe it. Dr Somluk isn't like that. She's dedicated. She left all her stuff here.'

Da was still leaning over me looking for a place to bury the vibrating needle.

'Hold off there, sister. You got a coffee machine here?'

'Only Medcafé.'

'In this case, that might not be such a bad thing. Let's have a couple of mugs to help us calm our nerves.'

We sat on the balcony with a steaming mug apiece and watched the pick-up trucks drift past. Like my grandad, I'd started to take notice of the details of passing vehicles. The excitement of the out-of-province plate had started to get to me. This was what living in the depths of Hades did to a girl.

'So,' I said, 'have you ever considered why your conscientious Dr Somluk is dug in at the Maprao Medical Clinic when she could have been making ten times more in a private clinic?'

'She . . . she wants to help the poor people.'

'She told you that?'

'Yes.'

'Reality check time. She's sixty. Is she married?'

'No.'

'Ever been?'

'Don't think so.'

'Kids?'

'Not that I know of.'

'So, here's my unbiased assessment of events. I only met her once. She seemed distractedly pleasant enough. No great beauty. Would never have attracted a man with her looks alone, so she would have needed an adorable personality. Especially intimidating as she's a doctor. Too smart. Thai men don't want the Dennis Thatcher role.'

'Who . . .?'

'Doesn't matter. So, she was bitter. In this country, the majority of regional administrators she'd have to work for would be male. She was probably smarter than the lot of them. She gets more and more frustrated. Despite her great doctor–patient skills she gets a reputation as "a bad team player". Gets jogged down the ranks until she finds herself in a rural clinic. Bee stings and diarrhoea and cat scratches. Anything more serious she has to refer to the hospital in Pak Nam. And she snaps. Decides she's taken enough crap and can make a better living working in telesales. No need to clear it

54

with the idiot male administrator at the Provincial Medical Placement Centre, because she has no intention of working as a doctor ever again.'

Da's mug had been getting heavier as it hovered in front of her pouty lips.

'Wow,' she said. 'That was insightful.'

'Thank you.'

'It was about you, wasn't it?'

'Me? Don't be . . . I'm talking about your boss.'

'Really?'

'Yes.'

'Then prove it. You're a journalist. Finding a lost doctor should be a piece of durian pie for you.'

'Why on earth should I?'

'I've worked with her for six months. If she'd had a bitter past I didn't see it. All I know is she's a sweet lady. And she has manners. If she was planning to flee, she would have phoned me and told me. Not sent me a message. I think she's hiding out. She knows there's somebody after her.'

'Oh, right. "Them." You do remember the last time we talked you thought she was going nuts? There never is a "Them". We create our own bogeymen because life's so boring. We need antagonists to give us a point. There's nobody after her.'

'I can pay you.'

'No, you can't.'

'I can. I have money.'

55

'I mean, you can't because I'm not a private investigator. If that's what you want you can hire a pro like Nit the plastic-awnings dealer and part-time PI. He does missing persons.'

'I get the feeling it's more than a missing person, Jimm.'

'You watch too much TV.'

'Perhaps I do, but if you were a sixty-year-old woman alone in the world, in trouble, wouldn't you like to think there was somebody concerned about you? Concerned enough to go looking for you?'

She'd hit a nerve, damn it. I'd often visualized that future world with Grandad dead, Mair in an institution, Arny domesticated and Sissi in jail. Me, alone, wheeling a Macro Supercenter trolley around the streets, wearing stockings and flip-flops, yelling at young people holding hands in the park, 'Keep your filthy habits to yourselves.'

'I don't want your money,' I told her. 'But I can do this. I have to go to the *Chumphon News* office tomorrow. You said your doctor was at a conference at the Novotel?'

'Three days. Child development.'

'OK. I'll take the Mighty X and drive down there after my meeting. I'll ask around.'

Da put down her coffee cup and wrapped her meatless arms around me. It was like being hugged by scaffolding.

*

It was, in spite of everything, almost Christmas. We celebrate this festive season along with Chinese and Hmong new years, Ramadan (although I'm not sure I haven't insulted half the world just by saying so) and the holiday of any other country that has a CD of awful songs to play on a loop. Our commercial fathers see them as opportunities to squeeze ever more money out of consumers. At our local Tesco there's hardly a gap between 'Jingle Bells' and '*Wo Ai Ni* (I Love You)', and the Thai Float Float Your *Kratong* song. Festivals promote spending. But there is something sad about the sour-faced checkout girls in their red and white pointed elf hats. One poor Muslim lass was even forced to wear one atop her hijab.

It must be said that a Tesco Christmas with its flashing Christmas tree lights and its tinsel is not for the benefit of the odd Englishman, German woman or American couple who wander in there. Expats are few in Lang Suan and their spending power is negligible. In fact, I wouldn't wonder if they'd prefer not to be reminded at all. The rather inebriated *farang* who stole into the store with a machete one afternoon and decapitated the jolly dancing Santa bears testimony to that theory.

Like Tesco, Christmas at the Gulf Bay Lovely Resort was not a celebration of Jesus getting hammered to a cross and bleeding out. But I tend to believe that most of the people who celebrate the day barely give a thought to that aspect either. No, for us it was a chance to put our predecessors' beautifully hand-crafted English sign out front:

CHRISTMAS IS A TIME OF CHAIR.
COME INSIDE AND HAVE A BEAR

I'd been tempted to fix it, but it got more responses by being wrong. Nothing delights tourists more than showing us up as ignoramuses. It really didn't make much difference to our monsoon traffic, but the odd traveller did pull up in front and take a photo of the sign, maybe even pick up a can of Leo from Mair's shop and pose beside it. And, who knew? Maybe some day in the future the photo would go viral on the net and foreigners would come homing in on us from every corner of the planet. Right. Desperate, I know. But I'd run out of marketing ploys to get us back on our feet. I had more important things to do.

Whenever the kitchen, or the climate, or the fact we were here at all depressed me, I would always flip open the last surviving menu from the old regime. I would delight at the possibility of serving CRAP FRY RICE and ROAST LAMP to be followed by SUNDAY WIPING CREAM. But the crap and the lamp and the wiping cream did little to cheer me up as I gutted mackerel for dinner that day. I looked out at the lifeless Gulf. The times that scared me the most were these, the quiet days. When the wind was low and the waves were gentle and there was a lilac tinge to the sky. They were ominous days that hinted that the next monsoon was just beyond the horizon. A raptor was skimming across the wave tips. The hawks gave me heart. They migrated from northern China to Malaysia. But it was a long flight. They got bored. Probably suffered from deep-vein thrombosis in their wings. And a lot of them would say, 'Bugger it,' and camp down behind our resort for the season. I loved watching them soar above the beach, swooping down to the surf for fish. I kept telling myself they were wise creatures and they would alert me if they sensed a hurricane coming. Our dogs, on the other paw, would be halfway to Phuket at the first hint of bad weather.

Over dinner, Gaew had told us about the Seniors' body-building tournament she'd recently attended in Hong Kong. I decided this was as good a time as any to relate my visit to Conrad Coralbank's house. I left out the part where he'd desired me with a passion and just told them about the house and the answers he'd given. We were on dessert – ordained nun banana in coconut sauce – when I dropped the bombshell that his wife had left him.

'I'm not surprised,' said Mair. 'I did notice a considerable age difference.'

According to Google the pretty wife was the same age as me.

'I don't see that age has anything to do with it,' said Gaew.

'Well, you wouldn't, would you?' said Grandad. 'You robbed the cradle yourself. Didn't you?'

'Grandad!' said Arny, almost angrily.

'What?' Grandad stuck out his grasshopper chest. 'You gonna defend your great aunt's honour? Challenge me to a duel? You're going out with a woman the same age as your own mother. Disgusting.'

'You can't—' Arny began, but Gaew put a hand on his arm.

'It's all right,' she said. 'Let it go.'

'Don't humour me,' said Grandad. 'Defend yourselves.'

Mair, who could always be counted on to inadvertently deflect tension, came out with, 'William seduced me in the classroom. On a desk, in fact.'

First there was silence, then Gaew laughed.

Grandad said, 'Oh, don't!'

'Who's William?' I asked.

'He was good-looking, too,' said Mair. 'An Irishman. Twenty years my senior. I'm not saying all British people are good-looking. Some are downright ugly. Goodness, I wouldn't touch Mark Jagger with a pool cue, but your author reminds me a lot of William. He came to Chiang Mai University for a couple of years to teach literature.'

Grandad stood up in a huff, put his bowl in the sink and left the kitchen.

'Go on,' said Gaew.

'There's no "on",' said Mair. 'William had ginger hair

and smelt of tobacco. To make matters worse he wore corduroy. I could never let myself be seduced by a man in corduroy.'

We laughed.

'So there was no seduction in the classroom?' I asked.

'Not by William, heaven bless his soul,' said Mair. 'But I knew it would shut somebody up. My father's been very testy lately. I mean, more so than usual. I think something's wrong.'

That was it with Mair. You never knew. One minute she's putting together a chain of extension cords so she can vacuum the beach, the next she's defusing volatile moments over dinner. I didn't necessarily believe there had been nothing between her and William. She was sexually active in the sixties. You see? No Thai stereotypes in our family. Good Thai girls back then didn't even let their fiancés have a peek until the honeymoon. I bet there were a lot of disappointed honeymooners. But Mair didn't give a hoot. If her recent stream of consciousness was to be believed, she'd left behind a trail of drooling lovers.

'So I think you should make a play for him,' said Mair.

'William? He's probably dead by now,' I countered.

'Conrad,' she said. 'Successful, rich, good-looking, reached an age where he probably isn't interested in sex, as long as you can keep him away from the Niagara. Sex with old men isn't really anything to write home about. He'd be perfect for you.'

'It's Viagra, and what makes you think he'd be interested in me?'

'Don't be silly. Look at you,' she said. 'Take him a pie. Englishmen like pies.'

'Where would I find a pie?'

'Bake one.'

'We don't have an oven.'

'You need an oven?'

Like I said, she wasn't spectacular in the kitchen.

'Bananas, then,' she said. 'Bananas are international. Nobody's ever disappointed with a banana. You know? I wondered where she'd gone, that wife of his. I haven't seen her for, ooh, two weeks?'

'Do you mean two months?'

'I think I know the difference between a week and a month,' she huffed. 'She was here on December the eleventh. The day they delivered the chicken manure. She had to step over the sacks to get in the shop.'

Of course, there was no way Mair could confuse November and December. She'd get my name wrong four times a day. She'd phone our old distributor in Chiang Mai and complain that we hadn't received goods from him that we hadn't actually ordered for a year. Who knows when the bride of Coralbank was actually in our shop?

'Oh, manure, that reminds me,' she said. 'I need you to take Gogo to see Dr Somboon tomorrow.'

'Can't. I'm going to Chumphon.'

'Not a problem. He has his livestock work during the day. He won't open the clinic till five. You'll be back by then.'

'What's wrong with Gogo?'

'Nothing yet. I made an appointment to have her neutered.'

'Oh no. Absolutely not.'

'I suppose you'd sooner she pumps out puppies till her tits are dragging along the ground?'

'Neuter? Objection? No. Me take her? Not on your life.'

'Why not?'

'Dr Somboon doesn't have a nurse, Mair. He makes you stand at the operating table and hold the victim down just in case she wakes up in the middle and goes nuts when she sees her insides spread out on the table. I'm not going to be a witness to the end of a woman's hopes and dreams of a happy family.'

'She's a dog, darling.'

'Dogs can be symbolic. Let Gaew take her.'

'I'm off to Petchaburi for a seminar on steroid abuse tomorrow,' said Gaew.

'Arny?'

'Blood,' he said. 'You know how I am.'

My brother was built like the Coliseum but the slightest dribble of blood and you'd need a team of paramedics to bring him round.

'Jenny, my child,' said Mair. I assumed she was talking to me. 'Gogo needs a liberationist. Someone to explain to her how she's no longer obliged to be any dog's doormat. Those little bristles on the doormat of indignity no longer have to prick her underbelly even if the word "Welcome" is spelled out beneath her.'

'That dog hates me,' I reminded her.

'Then it's your chance to bond. One female whose ovaries are in a pedal bin with one other whose reproductive system is unlikely to be put to use.'

'In that case, why don't you take her?'

'I won't be here.'

'Where are you going?'

'To see your father.'

'Oh? Where is he?'

She looked out of the small kitchen window to a point where the indigo sea met the charcoal sky. There was one green light flickering out there. We all stood up at the window.

'That's Captain Kow?' asked Arny.

'He's out there all by himself,' said Gaew. 'There isn't another boat in sight.'

'Isn't he brave?' said Mair. 'No other fisherman dares go out in this season but there he is in the sea putting rice on our table.'

'Mair,' I said. 'There's a very good reason why nobody else is out there. It's the season when little shiplets get smashed to matchsticks. You get seasick in a pedal boat on a reservoir. You are not going out there.'

'I have to.'

'Why?'

'It's all part of the process.'

'Of what?'

'Reconciliation.'

'Mair. You sold our home and dragged us kicking and screaming to this hellhole for him. Don't you think you've done enough to prove your worth? How many tests is he going to put you through?'

'There are a lot of things you don't understand. This was my idea. To live his life. See the world through his eyes. Understand the sea.'

Arny stepped in.

'Mair! That's a boat. A squid boat. It doesn't have a cabin. That's really romantic under a starry sky with no surf, but this is the monsoon season. You'll be exposed to the elements. They don't have coastal patrols out there to rescue you.'

'Fear not, little Arthur,' she said. 'I have a survival kit. It includes a waterproof groundsheet and an umbrella. I go prepared. Don't worry about me.'

'And you're planning on swimming out there?' I asked.

'I'll be getting a ride from Nu's husband,' she said. 'He goes out every morning to check his squid traps.'

I decided it was probably for the best. A couple of hours on the turbulent sea and she'd be screaming to come back. Togetherness on a wooden boat in a hostile environment was a real test of compatibility. Everyone should have to do it.

UNPOSTED BLOG ENTRY 2
(Found two weeks too late)

I've found another one. She has a family and people who'd miss her, but she's adventurous. Nobody would be surprised if she got herself into trouble, vanished one weekend. And if it doesn't work out, no problem. There are a lot of lonely women out there. She came under the pretence of an interview, but I could tell there was more. It wasn't just a job. She was lonely. She needed somebody in her life. That's why I agreed. I'm not sure I have a 'type' exactly, but if I did, she wouldn't be it. Too short. Too heavy. But I have a copy of her résumé. The internet is very accommodating like that. It yielded up an essay of her more personal thoughts. I know her desires. I can play on them. That's the modern age for you. Nobody is private any more. Social networks are dark alleyways for people like me.

I can't believe I waited this long to satisfy my urges. Now I know how frightfully simple it is I can't wait to try this new me out. I'll wait a few days before I call her. I don't want to seem too keen. I'll invite her for a meal and let her know she's the lucky candidate. She can be my next. She'll be so pleased she won't see me for what I have become, until it's too late.

C.C.

CHAPTER FIVE

LADIES ARE REQUESTED NOT TO HAVE
CHILDREN IN THE BAR
(hotel sign)

Email from Clint Eastwood to Jimm Juree

Dear Jimm and Sissi,

I'm sorry to have taken so long to reply to your many fascinating emails. Of course I'm not mad at you for hacking into our accounts here at Malpaso. It shows great initiative and drive. You were right about the jerk I hired to assess your earlier works and I apologize for any embarrassment he may have caused you and your family.

You were right too about the great material you've been sending my way. The latest really topped the lot. Man, we all adored that last screenplay. I would just love to sit down with you both to discuss rights, financing and perhaps a directorial collaboration.

I'll be passing thru Thailand over the Christmas period and it would be peachy if we could get together and discuss money. Perhaps you could give me an address so I

67

can swing by your place when I'm there. Failing that, give me your phone numbers so I can give you a call and arrange a get-together.

I'm real excited about this project and I have a strong feeling it'll work out great for all of us. I look forward to meeting two really creative people such as yourselves.

Your pal,

Clint

'OK. It's well written.'

'Thank you.'

'If you like your prose flowery and girly.'

Khun Boot, the proprietor and chief editor of the *Chumphon News*, found it impossible to give you a compliment without taking it away again. He had a complexion like a aerial photo I'd seen of Afghanistan. I'd never met him standing up. I wondered whether he'd lost his legs in a weed-whacker accident and they'd grafted a desk onto his lower torso.

'What can I say?' I said. 'I'm a flowery girl.'

'I was expecting more grit from a journalist from Chiang Mai.'

Ooh, bitchy.

'You mean more than throwing axes half-naked at watermelons?' I asked.

'That's exactly what I mean. You lead with that, so we expect you'll go on to ... to more. But we're halfway through it and you're talking about books.'

'He's a writer.'

'Our readers don't give a shit about writers.'

'Then why send me to interview—'

'They want smut. They want confirmation that *farang* living in Thailand are all losers and maniacs and mafia. They don't want nice guys being successful. Did you really not find anything sleazy about him? Abused wife? Love affair? Gay liaisons?'

I hadn't mentioned the departed wife or the horny maid. If I had, I knew Khun Boot would have led with a good old traditional Thai headline: FAMOUS FARANG WRITER KICKS OUT WIFE FOR ILLEGAL BURMESE. And I'd get the blame for both the story and the break-up. In fact, I didn't think Conrad's sex life was any business of the populace of Chumphon. I would have been happier to hope there were enough sophisticated readers to warrant an actual literary piece. I'd obviously been aiming too high.

'It's an OK start,' he said. 'Now I want it more sexy. More decadent. Dig the dirt, Juree. You're supposedly a crime reporter. Find some.'

'Is this just your sweet way of asking me to rewrite a perfectly good interview?' I asked.

'You've got it.'

'And you'll be paying me for both versions?'

'I'll pay you for the final version if you get it right. You're a freelancer. You do what I tell you. I don't need your big Chiang Mai attitude in my office. You do it right or you don't do it at all. Get it?'

69

As I was walking out of the *News'* one-room house I noticed the week's headline on the fresh batch of newspapers. It was pure class. DRUG ADDICT HAS SEX WITH DEAD GRANDMOTHER. I realized I had a long way to go.

The drive to the coast helped me focus on the decline in journalism. It wouldn't be long before the planet got its daily news in tiny boxes to one side of the celebrity scandal sites it subscribed to. Technology was making people even dumber. Moronicism was the new religion. As I drove out of the city I repeated the mantra, 'Keep it brief. Keep it vulgar.' Until I heard a *look tung* tune on Radio Chumphon that I recognized. I turned up the volume and sang along.

I'd passed the Novotel before on my way to the Ko Tao ferry. It was a vast place with its own nine-hole golf course, behind an ugly fence. Noisy road between it and the sea. No public transport into town. I'd always wondered why anyone would stay there. I parked in the car park and sought out Administration. There was one person at the front desk, who told me the manager was away. It was mid-week. There were no guests. The words 'money laundering' passed through my mind. But the receptionist, Doy, was perfectly sweet. She was pretty and delicate as a hibiscus – the way I'd always appeared in my own dreams. When she found out I was enquiring about conference facilities, she *wai*'d me respectfully and asked how she could help. I suppose I could have told her I was an unemployed journalist looking for an old doctor I wasn't particularly interested to find, but that wouldn't have got me anywhere, would it now? So I leaned across the marble counter, took hold of her arm, and said, 'Doy, I'm at my wit's end. You're my last hope.'

'Me? Why?' she said. 'I mean, what can I do to help?'

'My mother,' I said. 'She suffers from dementia. We can't find her.'

'Oh, my word.'

'The last time anyone saw her was here at your hotel at a conference.'

'Oh!'

'It's just ... it would be really bad publicity for the hotel if she's lying dead in a flower bed somewhere.'

'Well, yes. Certainly. Do you know what conference it was?'

'Child care.'

'That was just this weekend.'

'Yes.'

'I ... I should tell somebody.'

'Thank you. And perhaps they'll suggest you find the hotel reservations for a Dr Somluk Shinabut and the list of conference attendees.'

'Yes. Yes. Good idea.'

She started to rifle through a drawer.

'And perhaps you could put me in touch with someone from the hotel who attended the conference.'

She looked up.

'We . . . we don't.'

'Don't what?'

'Attend. We just rent out the space. The organizing is all up to the people who book it.'

'So, they could all be running around naked up there and you'd never know?'

'Oh, I doubt whether . . . they wouldn't do that.'

'Who was it that booked the conference room last weekend?'

'Right. I should know. There was a welcoming sign up at the front of reception. It was . . . The Bonny Baby Group. The sign said: THE BONNY BABY GROUP YOU'RE WELCOME TO MIDWIVES AND PAEDIATRIC NURSES.'

'Good. I'll look it up. But you're sure nobody from your staff dropped in to see what was happening?'

'Yes. Unless . . .'

'Yes?'

'Well, I'm not on at the weekend so I don't know, but if they wanted the event recorded, our IT person might have been there.'

'An inspired thought. And where would I find the IT department?'

'It's not a department as such. He shares a room with the chamber maids,' said Doy, as she led me along the dark corridors of the swimming pool wing. We disturbed four maids, sitting with their feet up drinking chocolate milk. They didn't jump to attention when we entered their room. In the far corner was an alcove. It was wide enough for two chairs and had high banks of shelves crammed with electrical equipment. A young man was sitting there repairing a coffee percolator. He'd allowed hair to grow wherever it wanted on his soft face and as a result he had a rambutan beard and I counted six mustache hairs. Doy left me with him and went off in search of someone who might be able to give me permission to look at the privileged hotel files. The young man was looking at me suspiciously even before I finished my story.

'You have a photo of her?' he asked.

I produced the Maprao Medical Clinic brochure open at the photo of Dr Somluk.

He sighed.

'The only photo you have of your mother is in a photocopied brochure?' he said.

'It's the most recent,' I told him.

He sighed again, as if life was a disappointment. He knew I was lying.

'You have to show me an ID,' he said.

'What for?'

'The log book. You want to look at a copy of the weekend's DVDs, you have to sign for them.'

I handed him my citizenship card. He looked at the surname and up at me.

'She remarried,' I said.

He sighed as he filled out my details in the log book. Half an hour later, I was in a hotel room with Rambutan

Chin, Doy, and a stack of DVDs. By telephone, the manager had given permission to afford me every assistance in the search for my poor mother. The 'bad publicity' gambit had worked. We skipped the bullshit opening speeches from local dignitaries and the keynote address from some renowned paediatrician from Singapore, because the camera was fixed on the podium. Rambutan wasn't big on audience shots. In fact he only bothered during the Q&A sessions at the end of each panel. That was my chance to search for my lost mother. Doy had brought me the programme for the Bonny Baby Conference and Dr Somluk was listed neither as a participant, nor a speaker.

'Are you certain she was here?' Doy asked.

'I'm certain she told her nurse she was coming,' I said. 'Oh, wait. Here.'

On the back page of the programme was a list of affiliates of the Bonny Baby Group. Half way down was Dr Somluk's name.

'Then she might have been helping to organize it,' said Doy.

'You'd think you'd know if your own mother was organizing a conference,' muttered Rambutan. I wanted to pluck out those hairs with tweezers.

It was a three-day conference. We'd been through the first two days. Doy ordered us the staff version of room service, which was tasty but classless. We'd arrived at Sunday. It was the second session of the day. The speaker was a fat woman talking on the topic BREASTS – THE MYTH. As I watched her full-body articulation played fast forward, I had to admit there was something fabulous about her enormous chest, heaving from side to side. She finished her PowerPoint. There was a Q&A session and, as the camera swung around, I thought I might have spotted someone who looked like Dr Somluk seated beside an aisle. I pressed normal playing speed on the remote. The camera had found the person asking a question and I was about to rewind to check the woman in the aisle. But there she was, standing behind the young lady at the microphone.

'I think that's her,' I said. 'Blue top.'

'You only think?' sighed Rambutan.

'I'd be sure if the camera were focused,' I said.

'There's nothing wrong with my—'

'No, that's her,' I said. She was in the queue, up next to speak. She seemed nervous. Shifting her weight from foot to foot.

'Wait. I remember this,' said Rambutan. 'It was the only highlight in a deadly boring weekend.'

'Why, what …?' I began, but at that moment the young lady stepped away from the mic and Dr Somluk took hold of it.

'Dr Aisa,' she said. 'Perhaps you can tell all the people gathered here *who* funded your trip to Chumphon and why you're rea—'

Suddenly, she was grabbed by the arm by one of two women who had been standing behind her in the queue. Both were dressed in mudmee silks and had impeccable but impossible hairstyles that stood up on their heads like Formula One helmets. The second of the two wrested the mic away from Dr Somluk and proceeded to ask a question of her own. Something about breast disease. Meanwhile, woman one was escorting Dr Somluk back down the aisle and out of shot. The doctor had been forcibly prevented from completing her question. I was delighted. It suddenly turned the whole venture from a futile favour for a skinny nurse into a fully fledged mystery. Da's concern might not have been groundless after all.

'That was weird,' said Doy.

We watched the scene again up until Dr Somluk was being frogmarched out of shot.

'Do you remember what happened to her ... my mother, after that?' I asked.

'Yeah,' said Rambutan. 'The woman in silk was joined by another woman and they walked your ... mother right out the exit. I don't remember any of them coming back in.'

We watched the rest of the day's footage and he was right. There was no more sign of Dr Somluk or her abductors. We went back to the scene. Watched it several times. In the queue, Dr Somluk was nervous. Getting more agitated the longer the girl in front hogged the mic. When she was finally nabbed she treated it like a joke, laughed and smiled. We Thais have a nasty habit of smiling to disguise what we're actually feeling. Dr Somluk's smile was vast, but it was a Band-Aid not broad enough to cover the wound. We zoomed in to her face. Her eyes were not smiling. Dr Somluk was petrified.

It was Wednesday when I got the call. I hadn't given him my cell-phone number, but in Maprao you just had to ask someone who might know you and they'd happily pass it on. What point was there in having a phone if you didn't want people to call you? My neighbours hadn't yet learned the art of caller culling.

'Hello, Jimm.'

I quite liked my name without its correct high-rising intonation. It made me sound like a Sydney bricklayer. I was, I have to admit, excited to hear Conrad's voice. But, as they'd taught me in Aussie, 'Treat 'em mean, keep 'em keen.'

'Who is this?' I asked.

'It's Conrad. Conrad Coralbank.'

'Er, how did you get this number?'

'From your mother.'

Traitoress. Happy to farm me out to any rich superstar.

'You'd rather I didn't call?' he asked.

'In fact I was about to call you.'

'Splendid.'

'My editor said you aren't interesting enough. He didn't accept my first draft. I need some dirt.'

'That's too bad. I'm clean. I could be a Sunlight-washed soup tureen.'

'I don't believe it. Everyone has dark secrets.'

'Perhaps you could hypnotize me and probe my depths.'

'You can lie if you like,' I said. 'I just need something to sell newspapers and get myself a pay packet.'

'All right,' he said. 'I'll tell you. But not on the phone.'

'Really? I'm so disappointed.'

'Why?'

'The "But I can't tell you on the phone" line was voted the worst crime novel cliché of the millennium.'

'It's unavoidable. If everyone spilled their beans over the phone there'd be no meetings in dark warehouses. No body discoveries. No arriving in a room where one entire wall was dedicated to photographs of you, illuminated by candles. No meals at the Opposite the Train Station Restaurant.'

'There's no such restaurant.'

'That might not be the name, exactly. But the sign's in Thai and I'm only up to the written character for "soldier" in my self-study programme. It really is opposite the train station. What do you say?'

'I don't have an entertainment budget.'

'My treat.'

So, that was it. The banter that led to the first date. It was lunch at the Opposite the Train Station Restaurant, and it did indeed have a view of the Lang Suan train

78

station. On a good day you might get nine passenger trains on that single track between Bangkok and the deep south. Invariably, those trains would get derailed or blown up by southern terrorists or just break down, because they were antique. If they survived all that, they could merely plough into a backhoe on one of the unmanned crossings or career down into a flooded valley like a water ride at Disney World. A five-hour delay was a good day. In fact, the only real inconvenience about Thai rail travel was on those unique occasions when the train arrived on time. You see, nobody ever turned up at the hour stated on the timetable. Those trains would leave the station empty and the railways would run at a loss. Bad scheduling made economic sense.

The reason I bother to mention all this is that our luncheon that day was accompanied by a cabaret. The eleven fifteen from Thonburi had arrived with a motorcycle entangled in its undercarriage. A shirtless, dark-brown man with a blowtorch had been entrusted with the task of removing it so the Sprinter could continue its sprint. The passengers were all out on the track giving advice, phoning ahead and smiling violently at the station staff, who were largely innocent.

'Do you suppose the motorcycle rider's under there as well?' Conrad asked.

Only a murder writer would garnish a meal with such bad taste.

'If he is, a blowtorch probably isn't going to do him much good,' I replied, kind for kind.

Conrad laughed.

'During the floods the farmers park their motor-cycles up on the embankment so they don't get bogged down in the mud,' I said. 'The train drivers usually slow down and beep their horns to give the locals time to move them. Some might just bump them off the tracks. Looks like this fellow was in a hurry.'

'How could you possibly know all this?' Conrad asked.

I smiled and took another spoonful of coconut fish soup. In my haste I accidently took in a lemon grass leaf, which was part of the debris you're supposed to leave in the bowl. I wasn't about to spit it out. I chewed it a little and swallowed it. It's probably still in my intestines.

'I'm a journalist,' I said. 'I ask the right questions of the right people.'

It was my Lois Lane line. In fact I didn't imagine for one second the farmers would be so stupid as to park on a train track. I just wanted to impress him with some local colour. I'd been prepared for the worst after his 'somebody's mistress' comment, but he'd apologized for that the moment we met in the restaurant car park. He'd offered to pick me up at the resort, but I'd made up some appointment and told him I'd meet him here. As it turned out, Grandad Jah wouldn't let me have the Mighty X so I'd arrived on our motorcycle. It's hard to look your best with insects stuck to your sweat and mud flecks on your face. The helmet plastered down my interesting spiky hairdo into a globule of fettuccini.

He'd still seemed pleased to see me when he stepped out of his SUV, Gatsby-cool even down to the brown loafers and chinos. When we'd walked past the waitresses, they must have thought I was being interviewed for a laundry position. My only saving grace was that I was wearing a dress. Scullery maids never wore dresses. The English sign over the cashier's table said WE NOT COSH CHICKS.

'I should hire you,' he said.

'What as?' I asked.

'Researcher. Cultural advisor. Odd-jobs woman.'

'You already have someone to hold your watermelons.'

'Right. That wouldn't be in the job description.'

Not a flinch. I was expecting at least a blush. Men who defile their maids usually show remorse. I decided to keep pushing.

'Your handywoman seems very content in her work.'

'You think so? I really hope you're right. I do try to keep her happy.'

Brazen.

'I'd hate to lose either of them,' he continued.

'Her and her son?'

He laughed so loud the four uniformed bank employees at the next table looked around.

'Did I say something funny?' I asked.

'No. You're right. Jo does look so young. I thought the same when I first met him and A. But he's her husband.'

'But he's . . .?'

'Twenty-four. A's twenty-seven. She graduated from Meiktila University. Literature. She spends a lot of her time typing. I gave her my old laptop. She speaks Thai and English as well as Burmese. Smart girl. And here she is, making beds and washing dishes. What a messed-up country Burma is.'

That's when it first occurred to me that he might not be diddling her after all. Especially not with her baby-faced husband walking around the grounds with a machete. So, was her warning for me to stay away from him because she had plans to get Little Jo deported and move in on her boss? Or was there something else I needed to know? I had to get her alone and find out what she meant.

Most good Thai meals give way to periods where you're enjoying the food too much to be bothered with conversation. We were in one of those vacuums. Fish *lahp*, prawns and broccoli in oyster sauce, spicy bamboo shoot and sweet basil, and cold Singha beer. He'd insisted I select the dishes. It was good to see a foreigner enjoy Thai food, even with sweat leaking out of him faster than he could throw in the beer. It was like perpetual motion. But even damp he looked adorable. With the maid issue sort of sorted out, I only had one

82

more query to address before I'd allow myself to be seduced.

'Did you beat your wife?' I asked.

Again, no twitch, no tic, just a smile.

'Would it help sales if I had?'

'Either that or a transvestite lover. The editor seems to think, as it stands, you aren't worth a headline. You promised me a dark side.'

'And you think my wife is the gateway to sensationalism.'

'Why did she leave?'

'Is this the newspaper asking, or you?'

'That depends on the answer.'

He took a few sections of tissue paper from the roll and wiped his face dry. He gently flapped his hand at the flies waiting in the wings for his leftovers.

'She wasn't ready for this life,' he said. 'She was young. Your age. So you know exactly what I'm talking about. No decent cappuccino. No bars. No pizza. No variety or stimulation. Stuck with me in Eden.'

'Did she have a lover?'

'Several, probably. Is this on the record?'

'I'm going to embellish everything you say. But, don't forget, nobody reads the *Chumphon News*.'

'Right. Then, it wasn't the lovers. The desire for sex I could forgive. Understand even. But, the deceit . . .'

A hood of gloom seemed to lower over him at that point. The toothpick snapped between his fingers.

'I'd made a commitment,' he said. 'I'd never done that before. I promised myself to her. She wasn't the easiest person to love but I worked on it. I changed . . . so it would be successful. I gave up things I thought were sacred. I refurbished my id so it could accommodate another. All this was based on the fact that she said she loved me and I valued that more than anything. A beautiful young woman loved me. So I gave her me. But that me wasn't enough for her. She deserved what she got.'

I should have taken more notice of that last comment, but I'm a non-native speaker and I assumed it was related somehow to something he'd said earlier. But there it was. Momentary loss of control. I didn't need to be native to recognize that. He looked up into my eyes, to see whether I'd noticed his nakedness. He stared into my face until it was almost uncomfortable, before his lips peeled back like mangosteen rind to show me the irresistible whiteness inside.

'What she got was a closed joint bank account,' he said. 'A studio apartment with a view of the apartment block next door, and an Italian restaurateur named Giuseppe.'

'And how do you know all this?' I asked.

'She told me a couple of weeks ago. She turned up on the doorstep with the suitcase and the foam box she'd left with. She said she'd thought it over and decided her life would be better with me. I sat her down at the kitchen table with a gin and tonic and asked her how she'd been spending her nights since I kicked her out. I recorded the whole conversation on my phone. As a writer, you can never have too much original material. She relaxed. She thought that a confession – of everything – would cleanse her. Make her pure again in my eyes. But the woman I loved was already a character in a story. And the story ended and the character stopped being real. You may fall for Gatsby while you're reading how great he is, but when you turn that last page, you have to draw the line between life and fiction. My wife had stopped existing.'

I looked into his damp blue eyes and my heart sagged. I hadn't counted on this much honesty over lunch.

'So you shot her,' I said. Well, I thought the situation could use a little levity. His eyebrows rose and seemed to nudge his mind back to the here and now. He laughed. He was a good laugher.

'Drove her to the airport and put her on the first flight,' he said.

The under-Sprinter motorcycle was being removed in small pieces. Like Conrad Coralbank's heart, I doubted they'd ever put it back together again. Beer tended to make me morose. I wanted to crawl through the empty plates and hug my old author, say 'There, there' and stroke his hair. He was perfect. All but one of the questions had been answered. His wife was a heartless wench. Mair was right. She had seen her two weeks before on her way to beg forgiveness. Conrad was telling the truth and now he was being stalked by an aggressive maid. He was doubly a victim. A poor soul. And so to the final question.

'Why did you agree to this stupid interview?' I asked.

We were sharing a plate of pineapple chunks on toothpicks at this point.

'I thought it might enhance my career,' he said, straight-faced.

I glared at him with one eyebrow raised. A month earlier he'd featured in a five-page spread in *Cosmopolitan*. The *Chumphon News* wasn't even a lifeboat on that great ocean queen.

'All right,' he confessed. 'I didn't agree. I like my anonymity. I always refuse local news and TV interviews. But your *Khun* Boot wrote back saying he had a world-class reporter named Jimm Juree who was a near neighbour of mine and she was willing to do the interview. That's when I said yes.'

'Why?'

'Because I'd—'

'Well, what a blast,' came a high-pitched squeal from somewhere behind me. Conrad's eyelids sprang open. I turned to see a slim man in the uniform of a police lieutenant mince across the restaurant floor like the opening act of Simon Transvestite cabaret. He put his hands to his cheeks.

'Jimm Juree,' he said. 'I can't believe it.'

Lieutenant Chompu was the only unashamedly camp

police officer in Thailand. He certainly wasn't the only gay policeman – not by a long pole – but his refusal to restrain his feminine side, particularly in moments of high drama, had resulted in his transfer to the last stop on the line: Pak Nam. It was a sad end for a man with keen instincts and brilliant policing skills. His timing, on the other hand. . .

He held out a limp hand to Conrad, and in surprisingly good English, said,

'How you do? I'm Chompu.'

Conrad shook the hand but was unable to retrieve his own, even as my darling policeman sat on the bench beside my would-be darling author. He was clearly drunk.

'Where you come from?' Chom asked, gazing lovingly into Conrad's eyes.

'I'm from England,' he replied with more politeness than the onslaught deserved.

'I'm come from Thailand,' said Chom. 'Please to meet you.'

'And you.'

'Do you having sex with my friend?'

An invisible axe diced my face into small croutons.

'Chompu,' I shouted from behind my unreal smile. 'What a nice surprise.' And in Thai: 'What hole did you crawl out of?'

'You didn't see me over there in the corner with my fellow crime-fighters?'

'No.'

'I've been watching your every move. You're such a vixen. And look at this . . .' He switched to English. 'Excuse me. Are you speak Thai?'

'Yes, I'm fluent,' said Conrad, his hand still a prisoner in Chom's.

'I think that means no,' said the policeman back in our own language. 'Let's test him. Sir, I would like to lick your nipples.'

'Chom?' I shouted.

'What? It's a compliment. He's just so adorable, right down to the Berluti loafers.'

He reverted his gaze into the Englishman's eyes waiting for some response. My author smiled and said something long and passionate, in what I took to be French. Chom gave him a smile of admiration.

'I thought you weren't allowed to be intoxicated whilst in uniform,' I said.

'What makes you think I'm toxilated?'

'A: You have my gentleman friend's hand in yours. B: You only attempt to speak English when you're high. And C: You didn't zip up after your last pee.'

Lieutenant Chompu imploded with embarrassment, released my author and crossed his legs.

'I not *chuck* my zip,' he said unnecessarily for the benefit of Conrad.

Conrad had started to look uncomfortable, at last.

'You have to leave us now,' I said.

'But we're—'

'Goodbye, Lieutenant.'

Chompu nodded, *wai*'d Conrad beautifully and stood to leave, his zip miraculously closed.

'Who is that over there with you getting you all sloshed?' I asked.

'We're on the job,' he slurred. 'It's the new police psychologist from Bangkok. It's a new service of the police ministry to help us poorly paid officers cope with mental stresses. She's quite remarkable. She asked the Chumphon police commander to nominate officers with a wide range of mental disorders. He came up with a chronic depressive, an alcoholic, a kleptomaniac, a bed-wetter and little old pervert me. We're sharing our intimate secrets at a group therapy lunch in a busy restaurant.'

'With whisky?'

'Johnny Black. It's her method. Alcotherapy. She's got a PhD in it so who are we to argue? And we all get three days off.'

'OK. You can go now. I'll catch up with all this craziness tomorrow. I'll give you a call.'

'Goodbye, handsome old man,' said Chompu and blew Conrad a kiss before returning to his table.

'Now that,' said Conrad, 'was particularly weird. Do you have any more friends like that?'

I was about to say, 'You should meet my family' but it might have sounded like an invitation. And he already knew Mair.

'A few,' I said.

We heard a cheer from the train station and turned in time to see one large metal train wheel abandon its colleagues, roll a few metres, then clatter against the track. The station master was furious and proceeded to stamp and whip the train with his cap.

'You know?' Conrad laughed. 'One lunch and I have enough material for two short stories. You really are quite remarkable.'

'Me? Why? You chose the place.'

'I have a feeling that anywhere you go you'd attract the bizarre.'

'You have a way with compliments, Mr Coralbank.'

'I know, look. I'm sorry. You're right. One of the reasons I wanted this lunch was to apologize for the misunderstanding at my house. I was hoping I might earn a second chance. Now here I am suggesting you're bizarre. I just find myself tongue-tied when I'm near you. You bring out the Pushkin in me.'

I had no idea what that meant but didn't want to interrupt the flow.

'I forgive you,' I said.

'Thank you.'

All the faults I'd erected around him had come tumbling down over lunch. He was a brilliant writer – I hadn't actually read anything he'd written at that point but Goodreads said he was a four star hit – he was funny, smart, disconcertingly human, handsome ...

and he liked me. How much better could it get? I had a dream once. An email arrived telling me my car registration number had won the Canadian National Sweepstake. I knew it was ridiculous but I still ran through all the things I'd do with two million dollars. I turned a blind eye to the logic of it all. Then the cheque arrived.

That's how I felt as I rode my Honda Dream back to the resort.

CHAPTER SIX

SORRY FOR THE INCONTINENCE
(condominium notice)

Gogo had reacted badly to the antibiotics and was on a drip. Her eyes didn't have pupils. They looked like steamed-up shaving mirrors. Mair was off on her second honeymoon cruise. Grandad Jah still hadn't returned with the Mighty X. It was just me, Arny and the lifeless dog. Outside, Sticky and Beer lay with their noses up against the mesh screen door.

'You think she'll die?' Arny asked.

'The vet was amazed she'd made it this far,' I told him. 'She's allergic to everything, her intestines don't work, she has a dodgy liver but has no qualms at all about eating germ-infested dead things on the beach. She has a death wish. I wouldn't be surprised if she switched the anaesthetic bottles while the doctor had his back turned. It's Munchhoundsen's.'

Arny didn't get that, but not many people would have. I have a thriving internal entertainment system.

'What do we do if she . . .?' he asked.

He had tears in his eyes.

'We bury her deep so the others don't dig her up and eat her.'

'How can you be so cold?'

'They're rescue dogs. They have a code. "Eat thy sister." It's tough out there on the streets.'

'What do you have against dogs? They have so much affection for us.'

'Right. Then what? Twelve years down the track they keel over and die. Remember Bruce?'

'No.'

'Of course you don't. You were too young. Bruce was Granny Noi's poodle. He was one of those goo-goo-eyed dogs that suck you in with their wiggly backsides and their fake smiles. You could throw the ball fifty times and he'd bring it back every damned time. Never once thought, "The girl apparently doesn't want this ball." He lay on my bed and before I went to sleep, we'd make plans for the future. World travel. Maybe open a little people/dog restaurant down near Tapae Gate. I'd hire a retired baseball pitcher to throw his damned ball as often as he liked. We were the same age, you see, and on my ninth birthday he was grey-haired and old. I threw the ball and he'd just lie there waiting for it to come back. A month later he was stiff. Such a disappointment, was Bruce.'

I tried to sleep that night, but found myself listening to the weak pants coming from Gogo on the bathroom mat. So I ended up sleeping on the floor with two fingers on her pulse. It had nothing to do with affection. It was the only way I could get to sleep. When I woke up just after five, Gogo and I were in the foetal position, she curled against my stomach. Body fluids all around. Sticky and Beer had wire mesh imprints on their noses. I took them for their early morning walk, although they were reluctant to leave the patient. A relentless wind had started up sometime in the night and it swept foam off the waves. The tide was high, and what little beach remained was piled high with bamboo and booze bottles washed downriver after the latest flash floods. I looked out across the metallic grey sea to where my mother was probably throwing up for the tenth time. The surf was over two metres and I could imagine Captain Kow saying, 'Get over it, woman, for hell's sake. It's just a wee squall.' No boat was visible now, but its grubby grey paintwork would have it camouflaged better than a white cat up a green tree. Have heart, Mother.

As it was my duty, I headed for the kitchen to make breakfast. I passed the Mighty X in the car park. On the back was a log the size of our water tank. It was so heavy the truck bed sat low on its suspension. The rear licence plate was in the sand. Grandad had brought home some serious wood. I hoped he hadn't dipped into the household kitty to buy it. Never a dull moment at our place. I was a little surprised once I reached the kitchen to find one of my meat cleavers embedded in the door. It pinned a sheet of paper there. On it was written a short message in English.

BACK OFF OR YOU WILL BE NEXT

I'd had threatening letters before. The *Chiang Mai Mail* had a noticeboard where we could all enjoy the penmanship. My favourite was from a Ukrainian paedophile I'd helped put away,

YOU BEECH. YOU WRITE BAD THINK ABOUT ME I BAT YOU.

I never did get batted. We journalists would write editorial notes recommending better grammar and less physically impossible alternatives. I'd never had a meatcleaver delivery before. And it was in so deep, the blade came clear through the other side. Somebody was pissed off. The good news was that the cleaver was in the door and not in me. None of us locked our cabins down here and the kitchen door didn't even have a latch. If anyone was so poor they'd come looking for food in our larder they were welcome to it. Then one thing occurred to me. What if the cleaver ninja *had* come to my room? What if my being curled up unseen on the floor with Gogo had saved my life?

I needed both hands to wrestle the cleaver from the door, but I'd had the foresight to put on my orange Handy Pandy washing-up gloves to preserve the evidence. At first glance, the paper had nothing more to offer up than the threat, until I turned it over. There, in the top right-hand corner, was a thumb print. It was about the same size as my own. I sniffed at the paper. I have an excellent nose. The mark was printed in neither ink nor paint. And even without the aid of a chemistry lab, I was quite certain the maroon print had been made in blood. Creepy, but cool all the same.

I had no idea what to back off from, or for whom I would be next or why, so I prepared breakfast. Once I had Grandad Jah and Arny seated with their rice porridge and homemade Chinese doughnuts in front of them, I placed the note, reattached to the cleaver, in front of them.

'What's that?' Grandad asked.

'It's a threatening note with a meat cleaver attached to it. I found it in the kitchen door when I arrived this morning. I consider myself duly threatened.'

They read it.

'What makes you think it was to you?' Grandad asked. He was great at plucking people from the centre of their universes. Of course. It wasn't always about me. Often, but not always.

'Are you involved in anything?' I asked him.

'I was a policeman,' he said. 'Twenty years in jail can make a criminal hungry for revenge.'

He was right. I'd seen De Niro in *Cape Fear*. But Grandad had been a traffic policeman. I doubted too many of his arrests for unpaid parking tickets had left jail after two nights, bent on vengeance.

'Could it have anything to do with that log on the back of the truck?' I asked.

He said 'No' through quivering lips.

'Grandad. It's time for honesty. This isn't a friendly threat. Our family's under assault. No secrets.'

'They . . . they wouldn't have known,' he said.

'Who wouldn't have known what?'

'The Forestry Department.'

'You stole a log from the Forestry Department?'

Grandad dipped the last of his doughnut into the rice porridge and sucked it till there was nothing left.

'I rescued it,' he said.

'From danger?'

'From frivolity. Abuse. Misuse. I read about it in the local paper. They were going to carve a giant squirrel out of it. Chop it down to next to nothing. That there is a chunk of prime teak. It deserves better.'

'And you have a more fitting purpose for it.'

'Yes.'

'So you stole it.'

'Rescued it. Yes.'

'And how did you get it on the truck?'

'I wore a suit.'

'And that makes you stronger?'

'It makes you powerful. Nobody questions an old man in a suit. I took the plates off the truck and told the workers to load it. They loaded it without question. I drove off.'

'Since when have you had a suit?'

'Since 1978. Granny Noi bought it for me to wear at her funeral. Said she didn't want me to look like a bum.'

'But you didn't wear it.'

'She was dead. She wouldn't have known.'

I sighed and went over the words of the note in my mind. 'Back off or you will be next.'

Even if someone had recognized Grandad and followed him home, the note was a non-sequitur, or some similar phrase to that. And I also doubted anyone at the Forestry Department could write in English. I didn't even bother to ask Arny if he was under threat. He'd never antagonized anyone. So it was at my door. I had to back off. But off what? Or did I know already?

'So, that yummy young democrat's running the show now, I see.'

'Siss, I told you—'

'Who's talking politics? Not me. I'm talking sex.'

I was determined not to waste another minute discussing my country's failure as a democracy. Not because I had no interest in the topic, but because it had all become so embarrassing. In fact I'm only prepared to give it one sentence.

In a nutshell: in the past year a rabble of yellow-shirted yuppie royalists had invaded our government house and redecorated it, an embarrassing drinking buddy of the ousted PM had been named as his successor and was subsequently kicked out for accepting a fee for regular cooking segments on national TV (the dignity of a dung beetle), to be replaced by the ousted PM's brother-in-law who – as Government House was currently running bingo nights – was forced to set up a mobile parliament in the smokers' lounge at Don Muang Airport but, not to be outsmarted by this canny move, the yellow shirts took over both Don Muang and Suvanaphum airports causing a godzillion *baht*'s worth of damage to the economy and pissing a lot of travellers off in the process, and the last thing anyone heard the brother-in-law PM was chairing cabinets in a truck stop on the Bang Na-Trat highway which gave the yellow shirts time to notice an irregularity in the voting process – one of the candidates 'looked funny' – so as December rolled around the losing democrats had been hauled out of obscurity to join one more unholy alliance of demonic political parties and their wunderkind leader miraculously became PM, returning his yellow shirt to the closet just in time.

I suppose I could have ended with, 'And they all lived happily ever after,' but trouble was brewing. The rightly aggrieved losers in this heist had donned red shirts and were seething and simmering in the background. The rural community, stirred by the ousted PM and his mates, were not going to lie down and whimper. In my sweet Buddhist country, there was nothing like a good class war to bring out the crazies. I saw nothing but bloodshed on the horizon. We were primed for a civil war.

That's why I didn't want to talk about it.

'All I said was that I reckon he'd be really hot in the sack,' said Sissi.

'I'm sure that was on his résumé. Now, to business. Sis, I need you back here.'

'I'd sooner OD on gin and paracetamol and drown in my jacuzzi.'

'Good. So you'll think about it then?'

'Never.'

'Come on. You had a good time here.'

'I had a good time at Hong Kong Disneyland, but I wouldn't want to live there.'

'You were liberated in Maprao. You shape-shifted regularly between attractive middle-aged woman and mascara-bearded, baseball-capped brother and nobody judged you.'

'Nobody noticed. They thought I was two different people.'

'Everybody noticed. It's just that nobody gave a toss. It put all this Sunset Boulevard, reclusive ex-beauty queen, locked away in her penthouse apartment in Chiang Mai into perspective. You aren't a celebrity. Nobody, and I mean nobody would remember you from your six appearances in a prime-time soap in 1994.'

'Seven appearances.'

'Sorry. But it doesn't matter if you hosted your own

show and appeared in *FHM* magazine every week and had a well-publicized affair with the prime minister. Because, two weeks after your last news byte, they'd all have forgotten you and moved on to the next star.'

There was a long silence, the type that invariably ended with her pressing 'End Call'. But I guess Maprao had toughened her up.

'It has nothing to do with fame,' she said.

'Then what?'

'Jimm, you wouldn't have experienced this but, back then, whenever I walked down a street, every man I passed wanted me.'

I loved it when she was being candid. There was no button on my phone that said 'Slap the bitch'.

'I was sexy,' she went on. 'I was desirable. Men would drive into the backs of slow-moving trucks because they couldn't take their eyes off me. Now do you know what happens when I walk down a street?'

'No, I give up.'

'Men turn their gaze from me. Nobody desires me. I'm repulsive. Nobody loves an old transsexual.'

I was surprised nobody had used that as the title of a country tune.

'I come home and cry for hours,' she confessed.

'Then why were you so happy down here?'

'Because in Coconut Grove I didn't care whether anyone found me attractive. I didn't want to be a fisherman's pin-up girl. In fact it was an advantage to be unattractive there.'

'Really? You seemed to be very fond of Ed the grass man.'

'That's just because I thought he was yours. Friendly sibling rivalry. I could have had him, of course. Down there I could have had any man.'

She'd lost her big city mojo but her little village arrogance was working fine. I knew she was just looking for a dream to hold her together. I played along.

'It's true,' I said. 'I had at least a dozen men enquire about your availability.'

'I know.'

'Should I send some up?'

'I'd never get the smell of squid out of my bedding.'

'I'll break the news to them. But, as you won't be doing any entertaining, perhaps you could do me a little favour. It may involve some illegal computer tampering.'

'Fire away.'

I told her about my missing doctor and the incident at the Chumphon conference. As I didn't have a scanner at home I told her I'd go immediately to the Pak Nam computer shop, scan the conference documents and send them to her. I often made unnecessary and complicated plans like that, forgetting I was in the twenty-first century.

'What was the name of the conference?' Sissi asked.

'Nurture and Nutrients,' I said. 'It was organized by a group called the Bonny—'

'—Baby Group. Yes, I've got it on the screen now.'

My sister typed faster than I was able to think.

'I have the speakers list here,' she said.

'And there I was looking forward to the bicycle ride. You see the paediatrician from Bumroongrat?'

'Dr Aisa Choangulia.'

'She was the one Dr Somluk asked her question to. She wanted to know who paid for her to attend the conference. Is there any way we can find that out?'

'Hmm. Too bad it was in Chumphon.'

'Why?'

'If it was somewhere with an airport I could trace her ticket back. But as Chumphon is neither here nor there, I'd guess she drove or was driven down. That's not so easy. They might have transferred her fee into her account, but banks can be a bit snotty about being hacked. It's easier here than, say, Switzerland but it still has its problems. I'd be better off going through her credit card, that way—'

'Let me put this another way,' I said. 'Is there any way we can find out who paid her and you just doing it without going through all the reasons why it's difficult?'

'Then how would you appreciate just how clever I am?'

'You know I idolize you. You make felony across borders sound so easy.'

103

CHAPTER SEVEN

PROHIBIT CARRYING DANGEROUS GERMS, PESTS AND OTHER BALEFUL BIOLOGY
(tourist attraction)

I had this idea for an informal workout DVD programme called Riding My Bicycle Into the Wind. It was full-body aerobics with bonus facelift. Or perhaps not 'lift' exactly. More of a slipstream facial. Your features get swept back over where your ears used to be. Your skin is sandpapered by the salt in the air that comes at you at 100 kph. Your underarm flaps are hardened by holding onto the handlebar for all you're worth and your bum and your thighs are so pumped, you leave a trail of liquid fat on the bitumen. All this and you don't exactly get anywhere.

I could have taken the motorcycle that day but I was in desperate need of a tone-up. I had – and, as yet there was still nothing in writing – a suitor. A celebrity stalker. Of course it would lead to nothing, but there would be no tears. It's better to have had it and lost it than never to have had it at all. I looked that up. Tennyson almost had it right. I felt an obligation to have flexed muscles and be twenty centimetres taller, but all I was getting was tired. It felt like three and a half weeks later that I reached the Lang Suan Bridge. The wind had turned into a gale and there were clumps of salty water tangled up in it. I even had to pedal on the downward slope. I crawled across the Times Square intersection and was on foot and pushing by the time I reached the local police station. The English sign beside the gate said PLICE.

There's a lot to be said about our police station but I've said it all in previous stories and, well, I have to live here and we wouldn't want to upset the gentlemen in brown, would we now? Suffice it to say that you'd have to be very naughty or lacking in faculties to be transferred to a rural station in Thailand. But every now and then you find a place that goes two years with no violent crime and that type of station attracts a softer type of policeman. A man who prefers planting poppies and training the lads' football team to chasing criminals. Such was Pak Nam. Every now and then they'd transfer a celebrity police wrongdoer from a big city station. But those thugs merely curled up and died from boredom within the month. Our Pak Nam station was so laid-back they had a timetable which listed the officers' part-time jobs and when they'd be available for duty. Such was the case with the leader of the pack, Major Mana. He was the head regional Amway direct-sales representative. He rarely left a crime scene without having sold a water purifier or anti-ageing supplements to the witnesses. Coincidentally, since my family had arrived in Maprao, there had been three murders, four unexplained deaths, a hand-grenade attack, breaking and entering on four of our unlocked cabins and a monkey-napping. Major Mana held us directly responsible for this upheaval in his crime-free precinct and also accused us of being to blame for the sudden slide of his sales unit from fifth to twenty-third on the provincial dream-team chart.

My retort was that crime had been here all the time but the police had been too busy to notice. A station that puts two months' preparation into the Lang Suan boat race procession really wasn't concentrating on crime fighting. Pak Nam's arrest record was currently 2,344th in the country. Without a shred of shame, Mana took credit for most of the crime fighting victories that should have been attributed to my family but there was still the air of 'Tell her I'm not in' whenever I stopped by.

'Ahh, Nong Jimm. Our famous reporter,' said Sergeant Phoom. 'The major says he's out.'

'How about Lieutenant Chompu?' I asked.

'He's still on his mental retardation leave.'

I'd been afraid of that.

'Can I leave you this letter to give him if he pops in?'

'No problem.'

'So, is there anyone here who . . .'

I couldn't say it with a straight face. The Pak Nam station didn't even have a functioning computer or a lock-up. What were the odds of having a crime lab?

'. . . might be able to do a DNA test on a blood sample?'

He smiled at me.

I turned to go.

'Constable Ma Yai would be your man,' he said.

I laughed. Ma Yai lived in a one room unpainted brick house along the bay from us with his wife and six children. They took in laundry.

'He's a lab technician?' I asked.

'He did a course.'

'On DNA?'

'He's our specialist.'

'In that case I'd like to file a criminal complaint and have Constable Ma Yai on my case.'

'A complaint?' said Sergeant Phoom.

'I've been threatened.'

He laughed from a place where all his cigarettes' tar had coagulated.

'I don't know,' he said. 'Disaster seems to seek you out, Jimm Juree.'

It was the second comment in two days that suggested I was a misadventure magnet. I wondered whether I really was the hub of a crime industry in Maprao, or the wiper who cleaned the windscreen so people could see what was actually there. Perhaps they didn't want to know. I felt in my back pack with my Handy Pandy and pulled out the cleaver and the still-attached note.

'Ooh,' he said, and reached for it.

I pulled it away.

It wasn't a huge police station. Sergeant Phoom shouted, 'Ma Yai! You around?'

'Out back,' came the faint reply.

'Get out here.'

Constable Ma Yai walked through from the rear of the station in shorts and a sweat-stained singlet. He was built like a ballerina.

'Hello, Nong Jimm,' he said and smiled.

'Kung Fu practice?' I asked.

'Cock fight,' he said. 'Just warming up Beauty for the bout tonight.'

It didn't surprise me. Cock fighting was against the law. That they'd be raising a fighting cock in the yard behind the police station should have been a contradiction. But I'd met Beauty, who was officially the police mascot. He was the Mickey Rourke of chickens. Beaten, bloodied and deformed but as tough as crab claws. He really gave you the impression he was fighting for the honour of the department.

I sat at one of the six empty desks while Constable Ma Yai took my statement. He took it slowly. Two fingers on the typewriter. A dog with no hair walked up the steps and lay at my feet. Birds were nesting in the corner beams. A sign beside a staff-only staircase read: PLEASE USE THE STAIRS ON YOUR BEHIND. I simplified events as much as I could and only used words I thought he wouldn't have to look up in his old battered dictionary. When I got to the part about the thumb print he stopped typing and opened the drawer. To my surprise he pulled out his own fresh pack of Handy Pandy washing-up gloves, ripped off the top and put one on. He gently flipped the note over and stared at the print.

'It could be chocolate,' he said.

'It's blood,' I assured him. 'Smell it.'

'Nong Jimm, my nose isn't my best functioning organ,' he confessed.

He had six children, so there was no doubt which organ took that prize.

'So, how do we go about analysing it?' I asked him.

He nodded, knowingly.

'I carefully put it in a zip plastic bag,' he said.

'Yes?'

'And post it to Bangkok together with this statement. There it will be analysed and we will be sent the results. But don't forget, a DNA test can only be useful if we are able to compare it with the DNA of the suspect. Do you have a suspect in mind?'

'Yes, I do.'

'That's very good news,' he said. 'I can add it to this package. Do you have any blood or body waste of the suspect?'

'Not on me,' I said. 'But I can get it really soon. Maybe a day or two. Once we've got both samples, how long will it take to get the results?'

'Hmm.'

He nodded wisely.

'Technology's come a long way,' he said. 'I wouldn't be surprised if we got a definitive answer by May.'

'May – the month?'

'Yes.'

'It's December.'

'Little cases like this aren't a priority. You'll be bumped down the queue every time a big news story comes in. It would have helped if you'd been killed.'

'Helped?'

'Hurry the lab work through.'

'Can't you do anything? I thought you were the expert here.'

'I have a certificate.'

'Right, so what did you have to do to earn that?'

'Two week course in Pattaya. All expenses paid. I tell you that was one serious booze fest. The wife was sure I'd been unfaithful. I'd thought about it but—'

'Ma Yai, two weeks of DNA methodology and all you learn is how to put evidence in a plastic bag? Didn't they even give you a station DNA testing kit as a going-away present?'

'No. But they did mail us something later.'

'Chemicals?'

'Might have been but we didn't open it.'

'Why not?'

'Terrorism. We had strict instructions. We haven't opened any parcels since they blew up New York. Plus there's no point. I don't get any financial reimbursement for being a DNA expert. Just the headache of more paperwork. And what if I made a mistake?'

'Ma Yai, you didn't actually attend any of the lectures, did you?'

'I went to the opening speech. That was compulsory. I mean, you had to sign your name. But after that there was stuff going on in two or three rooms all the time. They couldn't trace you. They had a pool.'

'Where's the kit?'

The storeroom at the Pak Nam station was a dusty museum of files, unopened packages, stolen goods and, to my surprise, three lifelike Japanese love dolls in police uniform. My guide wasn't prepared to tell me what they were doing there. He blew dust off the package he said had been sent by the DNA training organizers. I carefully slit it open with my Swiss Army knife and emptied the contents onto the table. The box inside was labelled in English: DNA HOME PATERNITY TEASING KIT. I assumed they meant TESTING.

'They sent you this?' I asked.

'Yes.'

I explained to him what it was. He didn't seem to care.

'Do you want it?' he asked.

I considered the unlikely event that I'd need to test more than one man to be sure which was the father of my child. But DNA was DNA. Why wouldn't I be able to test blood with it?

'You sure you won't get in trouble giving it to me?' I asked.

'What for?'

'I don't know. Stealing police property.'

'It wasn't sent by the police. It came directly from the sponsor.'

'Who was that?'

'Okamoto.'

'The condom people?'

'Yeah.'

The cycle ride home took about eleven seconds. Grandad Jah's plastic poncho acted like a sail. I left the ground eleven times, like Mary Poppins. When I arrived at the resort the shop shutters were down and Arny sat, head bowed, at our concrete table.

'I just flew,' I said as I dismounted.

Arny looked up and there were tears in his eyes.

'Where's Mair?' I asked.

'I don't know. Still on the boat, I guess.'

'Then . . .?'

'Gogo,' he said. 'She's gone.'

*

112

The tail end of the Mighty X made sparks on the road. The licence plate was long gone. We'd tried to remove the log but it wasn't worth the hernia. We wrapped the dog in a towel, leapt into the cab and caused untold damage to the truck in an attempt to get the body to the vet before it became a corpse. The odds were against us. Gogo was cold, her tongue was purple and she had no pulse. But I remembered once waking up at four a.m. in exactly the same condition after a night on margaritas. It was only by putting a mirror in front of her nose that I could tell she was breathing at all.

Fortunately, the doctor was in. I was shocked that, faced with a lifeless dog and two tearful owners, Dr Somboon could remain so calm. He took another sip of his beer and told us to put Gogo on the operating table.

'Is she dead?' I asked.

'Getting there,' he said.

I expected him to run over to the table with defibrillators and yell for us to get clear. But he walked casually to his medicine cabinet and took out a vial of the same drug cocktail he gave for every ailment: worms, mange, liver flukes, lice, and now, apparently, death. The only consolation was that I doubted he'd waste fifty *baht*'s worth of medicine on a dead body. He injected his home-made brew into Gogo's meatless carcass and dropped the used needle into his pedal bin. He rolled her onto her back, put his hand on her chest and slapped gently and rhythmically at her ribcage like a drummer at a wake. Arny and I backed him up by sobbing pathetically. Gogo's eyes looked like raisins glaring out of a Rastafarian fruitcake. After all we'd done for her this was how she repaid us? She didn't even give Mair a chance to say goodbye.

The vet stopped tapping and reached for his beer. I had no idea what good the tapping had done but stopping it seemed so . . . defeatist. We'd had a mechanical bathroom scale in Chiang Mai that used to lie about my weight. I'd pick it up and give it a good shake and it would turn out just fine. We're all just bathroom scales under the surface so I stepped up to the table, grabbed the little bitch and shook her like a cocktail. Those chemicals needed to get where they were going in a hurry.

'Yeah, that might work too,' said Dr Somboon.

It wasn't exactly CPR but I wasn't about to wrap my lips around her snout. Gogo didn't respond. She hung there in my arms like three-day-old spaghetti. We'd hated each other from day one. She had no manners or respect but still I fed her. I'd spent time on my balcony telling my problems to her rude backside. Tears gathered on my chin like some aqua-goatee. I pulled her body to my chest hoping I might be able to channel the last few heartbeats. The final pulse. But Gogo was gone. Until . . .

Do you remember the scene in *The Exorcist* where Linda Blair throws up in Technicolor? Well, Gogo cast out the devil from three orifices simultaneously. Most of it landed on me. She coughed, then breathed. Satan had left the body.

'That's not a bad sign,' said Dr Somboon.

My cell phone rang. It was in the front pocket of my jeans; coincidentally the pocket that most of Gogo's fluids had drained into. I put the dog onto the table. She was now panting heavily after her flight from death. I took out the phone. It was still functioning. I could see a Samsung TV ad in this. I wiped my thumb over the screen and there was his name, Conrad Coralbank. I really didn't want to put the phone up to my mouth but opportunities had been lost through a bout of squeamishness.

I splashed 'Speak'.

'Hello?'

'Jimm? It's me.'

'What a nice surprise.'

'Are you hungry?'

I looked down at the 3D art installation on my T-shirt.

'Not hugely. Why?'

'I'm making dinner.'

'You can cook?'

'That's for you to decide. Can you come over?'

'It's not English food, is it?'

He laughed.

'When you taste my mum's cooking you'll never make fun of English cuisine again. But, no. Paella.'

Had he just invited me to meet his mother?

'Oh, good. I love French food,' I said.

'Actually, paella's—'

'I know. I'm kidding. What time?'

'Sundown would be fine. It's informal. Come as you are.'

I laughed and pressed 'End'.

With Arny carrying Gogo in the towel and me wearing a white doctor's coat with my jeans and T-shirt in a plastic bag, we thanked Dr Somboon and walked through to the waiting room. There were two characters in there . . . waiting. They stood when we appeared and wagged their tails. It's difficult to hate dogs, you know? I hadn't noticed Sticky and Beer stow away on the back of the Mighty X but it was unlikely they'd chased us all the way into Lang Suan. Arny lowered Gogo for them both to get a sniff and they tongue-lashed her till her face was soggy.

UNPOSTED BLOG ENTRY 3
(found two weeks too late)

Just the thought of what I can do.

That button I have my finger on.

It's such a rush of adrenalin.

I can't look at her without the feel of the axe in my hand, her parts all around me. I'm seeing her this evening. It'll be casual. Friendly. I'm in no hurry. I'm more inclined to stretch this out, but if it happens tonight, it happens.

C.C.

CHAPTER EIGHT

INTERCOURSE FOR BEGINNER
(English language CD)

I was agonizing over how to look informal. I had all my clothes spread out on the bed. There was nothing that said 'I didn't go to any trouble'. My phone rang. I'd wiped it with Dettol antiseptic but it still stank of exorcism.

'Sissi, what should I wear?'

'Go with the gingham dress.'

'He's already seen me in dresses. Twice.'

'Jimm, whoever he is, you aren't going to do better than a dress. Your arse is too big for jeans and your tits are too small for a tank top. A dress is like a burka. He's never quite sure what he's going to get until you're unwrapped.'

'Why the gingham? It makes me look like Elly May Clampett.'

'Exactly. See what an education you got from my cable channels? Gingham's like school uniform.

Sensuality in a shroud of innocence. The clothes say virgin. The body says, don't pay any attention to the clothes. So, who is it?'

'The writer.'

'I TOLD YOU.'

'I know. It just seemed too good to be true. But I've been over all the possibilities. He isn't after me so he can get his hands on the family wealth, because I imagine his royalty cheque from Bulgaria alone is three times our gross earnings for the year. He isn't after me so he can ride my fame. He might want me for a casual fling because he misses his wife.'

'Win-win.'

'Exactly. However long it lasts, I spend time with someone who isn't preoccupied with the cost of palm oil or which domestic animal produces the best manure. Someone who's in contact with the fascinating world of literature. Who jets off for conferences in St Louis, Cape Town and Bristol, meets adorable people and drinks cocktails, none of the ingredients of which were produced in a kettle out the back of Old Winai's prawn farm. Why are you calling, by the way?'

'I've found out who paid your paediatrician's per diem and travel expenses, plus a sizeable speaker's fee.'

'Do we have to do this now?'

'There's not really a "this". I just tell you, unless I'm overwhelmed with the ingratitude, in which case I hang up.'

'No. Don't. I'm sorry. I'm just getting ready . . .'

'I know. That's why I'm forgiving you. The speaker was paid by the Thai Food Corporation.'

'Never heard of it.'

'It's an umbrella group that covers a lot of overseas companies and their local concessions. It's a sort of members' club for the multinationals. A paper partnership with a non-existent Thai sister company. They have a sort of clearing-house bank deal, so that any payments come through TFC and can't be traced back to the original company.'

'Why would they need to do that?'

'A lot of reasons: tax breaks, dishonest contracts with politicians, any dealings that might be picked up by the international press as a conflict of interest. It's a sort of money laundry. That's as far as I got. I can't seem to narrow it down to the specific company that made the payment. It's the same brick wall with the Bonny Baby NGO. As far as I can find out they're just a group of concerned doctors and health-care workers that set up training programmes in the provinces.'

I thought of my conversation with Constable Ma Yai and the DNA conference.

'I have an idea,' I said. 'Find out what they were giving away.'

'Aha.'

'There may have been a conference bag or handouts or gifts mailed to the midwives' offices.'

'And this burden is placed on me because . . .?'

'. . . it's urgent and I can't do it because I don't have the participants' addresses and I'm on my way to a killer date with a perfect man who adores me.'

'Don't get your hopes up,' she said. 'Life has a way of kneeing you in the gonads.'

'I ask you, Siss. What's the worst thing that could happen?'

Email to 'Clint Eastwood' from Jimm Juree

Dear 'Clint',

I can't tell you how excited Sissi and I were to receive your email. It was refreshing for us to see that someone of your stature is not too proud to use an internet café. We hope you weren't mobbed by fans in the cappuccino queue.

We were a little surprised that you didn't mention our 'last screenplay' by name considering you loved it so much. But perhaps you were rushed when you left your executive office in Burbank and scooted all the way up the coast to Santa Cruz, to the Mocha Rocker Coffee Lounge and forgot to take your files with you. We all suffer from absent-mindedness from time to time.

The other point that really threw us was that you seem to have forgotten you have a big family get-together planned for Christmas week and as far as Sissi could tell from the encrypted files at Jet World Travel – your regular agent – you didn't have any flight bookings purchased until the New Year. Or perhaps you were planning on coming by ship. A surprise cruise for the family?

So, you see, Liced, there were so many holes in your story, we started to wonder who might have connections to Malpaso and hate us enough to undertake such a cruel hoax. And, through the magic of the internet, we found your name on the exclusive list of Gold Blend members at the Mocha Rocker. As they say, we put two and two together. The only thing we weren't sure about was what you planned to do with us once we came out of hiding. We doubted we were a big enough threat to national security to activate the CIA Internet Crimes Division. So, on a whim, Sissi checked air bookings out of LAX. As you're currently unemployed she focused on the budget airlines and found you on a Turkish Airways flight to Bangkok stopping on every bit of dirt between there and here. Evidently, you and someone called Paco were due to arrive on the 23rd.

Although we'd like to think this is just a romantic get-away with a husky lover – we found Paco's Facebook page. He bulked up nicely during his stint in prison – there is always the chance that you are considering some sort of Guatemalan payback. You had a high-paying job you weren't exactly qualified for, but you thought your future was assured. You probably have an extended family at home relying on that income. Then, some cyber-nerd transsexual hacks into your system and screws up your world. Totally unfair.

So, here's what we've done. Sissi cancelled both your air tickets with full reimbursement. (Paco wouldn't have survived in our hood anyway.) She sent an application on your behalf to Sony Pictures with a slightly inflated résumé. All of the references will pass the standard background check. There's a glowing reference from Clint included. And, congratulations, you're on a shortlist of four to be interviewed for an executive secretary position in production. You're the only Latina applicant and Sony has just received a memo from Equal Opportunities complaining that the company has too little ethnic representation in senior positions. As long as you don't screw up the interview, we feel you'll get the job. It pays a lot more than Malpaso.

If, on the other hand, you'd prefer to beat us over the heads with a baseball bat we can arrange a meeting. Naturally we'd prefer that you were successful in your new career and let bygones be bygones. Sorry for losing your job for you.

Jimm

P.S. Clint would never use the word 'peachy'.

'It's from Aranyik near the old capital of Ayutthaya,' he said, holding up a straight-bladed sword. 'It's nothing like the swords you see in the dramas. They found that at crucial moments the curved blade would get stuck in the scabbard and you'd be run through even before you got your weapon out. The tip is flat rather than pointed to give stability to the blade. They wanted to be sure they didn't have to take too many swings to behead the prisoner at the execution.'

I never thought for a second I'd be fascinated by a knife collection. But Conrad obviously loved them. It was so much more macho than collecting stamps or *Star Wars* memorabilia. He'd built an air-conditioned concrete room with a thick door to stop the old metal ones going rusty. And he knew them. I mean, every one of them had a story attached to it. He was on to a dagger carried by the lady courtiers in Sukhothai to kill themselves, should they be overrun by randy Burmese.

His paella had been perfect and the wine washed that fancy old seafood fried rice down a treat. To my relief, the maid and gardener didn't live in. They had a hut down in the temple grounds. Temples technically weren't allowed to rent out rooms but you could make monthly donations. I'm not a person affected by alcohol but the sweetness of the wine had made me a little heady. Or perhaps it was the company. He'd loved my dress. Loved what I'd done with my hair. (I'd washed it.) Loved having laughter at the kitchen table again. I was a successful dinner guest and when he suggested we come and look at his blade collection, I'd rather been hoping he'd have them on racks around his bedroom. I know. Giving a bad impression of Thai women. Added another fifty charter flights of horny old Europeans right here. But wait, before you book, we, and by that I mean normal Thai women, are not interested in people like you. If we wanted beer-swilling, pot-bellied, stupid guys, we have a country full of them. Being sexually active doesn't mean lowering standards. If you are repulsive in Rome you'll be just as repulsive in Bangkok. Conrad, however, was classy whatever way you looked at him.

So, to cut a long story short, as we stood staring at the actual axe King Naresuan the Great had carried into battle, the weapon that cost two million *baht* at auction, I took hold of Conrad's hairy forearm and squeezed.

'I've never been this close to history,' I said. 'Not to mention two million *baht*.'

It was either the wine or the money that caused my heart to flutter and me to look up into his Manchester City blue eyes and say, 'I'd like to see the rest of the house now.'

Having sex is one thing. Describing it in writing is another. I tried. I really tried to make it sound like more than humping. But the *Guardian* Bad Sex Award was always at the back of my mind. They give an annual prize – I think it's a chastity belt – for the worst love-making description, and I didn't want to get famous for making sex sound like plumbing. But every time I tried to write what happened that night, it came out in S-bends and spurts and dribbles and suction. That's what happens when you think too much about it. When you're actually having it, when it actually works – which is rare – you aren't present at the scene. The 'doing it' becomes subliminal. Your mind is off swimming in a tub of friendly jellyfish. It is – it should be – the ultimate out-of-body experience. So I can't write about my night with Conrad Coralbank because I wasn't there.

When I got back, a jellyfish buzz the length of my body, I was in bed with him naked. He had his arms around me and the breath from his nose was blowing directly into my left ear. He was asleep and I didn't want to move. We'd done the deed and he was still there. Not even my husband had stuck around once his duty was done. He'd be over on the East Berlin side of the bolster, snoring. Most of the casuals had one leg in their jeans before the final thrust.

But my author, my old, modestly equipped, good-smelling author was holding on to me and smiling in his sleep. I wanted never to have to leave that bed. Those arms. That moment. Because deep in my stomach I felt it would never happen again.

'I didn't know whether you ate meat,' he said. 'So I had A make a few alternatives.'

When I awoke the second time, finding myself alone on the enormous bed, with a view of the entire Gulf including the Vietnamese delta and the tip of Borneo twelve thousand kilometres away, I'd walked naked through the stroll-through closet and into the black and white checked bathroom. I'd taken a rain shower, applied natural herbs, put on my crumpled gingham dress and walked down the arty staircase to breakfast. A awaited me. The look she gave me suggested she had no idea how helpful my family had been to the Burmese community. All she saw was the Jezebel whore slut descending from the love nest that should have been hers. If she'd been holding a skillet of boiling oil rather than a Scotchbrite foam pad, I was sure she would have thrown it at me.

'I eat anything,' I said so as not to appear deliberately confrontational.

In fact there were many things I didn't eat. The pork rissole A slammed down in front of me was one of them. Conrad was across the large table from me, eating muesli and drinking fresh carrot juice. His lips were orange.

'Sleep well?' he asked.

He was in a singlet and shorts and I wouldn't have been surprised if he'd been for a morning jog already. Whereas I wouldn't have a need to exercise for a very long time. The euphoria was wearing off and I could feel aches in all my muscles.

'Very well,' I said.

A full glass of orange juice sort of bounced down in front of me, spilling on the table.

'Steady, A,' said Conrad.

'Sorry,' she said in English, then in Thai she added, 'I'm a housekeeper, not a waitress in a short-time motel.'

She laughed. I laughed. Conrad laughed because he hadn't a clue what she'd just said to me. Amongst other things, I'd discovered during the night that Conrad had the type of very basic bar pidgin Thai that dispensed with grammar, pronunciation and comprehension.

'Then maybe you should get out of the kitchen and go wash some underwear,' I told her in Thai.

I laughed. She laughed. Conrad laughed.

'What are you two gossiping about?' he asked.

'She asked me how good you were in bed,' I said.

'She . . .? She did not.' He blushed. The breakfast plates clattered in the sink. I believed I'd just declared war on Burma. It wouldn't have been the first time, but Thailand had a habit of losing those wars. I wasn't about to let history repeat itself.

When I arrived back at the resort I was expecting to find a family frantic with worry that young Jimm hadn't slept in her bed the night before. Perhaps the police had been alerted. The neighbours out with bamboo sticks in a long line probing the sand for my remains. At the very least, Arny and Grandad Jah unconscious with hunger because their breakfast was half an hour late. But the Gulf Bay Lovely Resort was deserted. The night shutters were down on the shop. The Mighty X, now trunkless, was parked beside it, her rear end with an irreparable sag and no plate. I walked to the family compound. The wind was still up. Sand blew into my eyes. Through tears, I admired the line of washed-up polystyrene that gave the beach a Nordic look. We also had a nice selection of adult diapers. I wondered whether some ill-advised seniors cruise had gone down in the bay. The family bungalows were unoccupied, all but my own. The door was ajar and I found the damned dogs on my bed. Beer had turned the pillow to candy floss. Gogo looked up with a shrug. I can think of nothing worse than dogs sleeping on your bed. All right, perhaps being interrogated by the Taliban was worse, but this was unacceptable. My first instinct was to beat them with a broom but I'd had sex, so the world was a much brighter place and all the Lord's creatures deserved forgiveness.

I had to take another shower because the salt in the wind had penetrated my herb-scented skin. I dressed conservatively, black cords and a high collar, and took the truck into Lang Suan. It was like travelling by sleigh with the flatbed skimming the blacktop. I drove slowly and the only radio station I could pick up was Lang Suan City 105 FM, the never-interrupt-good-advertisements-with-music station. So I gave up and used my driving time to think about ... everything. About my mother, who was now into the second day aboard a rickety squid boat for the love of a wayward husband. They were probably out of canned sardines and living on raw mackerel by now. Wind-blistered. Sun-baked. Distilling sea water in an upturned Wall's beach umbrella. Then I wondered whether she had her cell phone with her. They were only a couple of kilometres out. I decided I'd give her a call when I got back.

With Grandad and his mysterious tree and Arny with his senior fiancée, and Sissi back in her shell in Chiang Mai, I thanked Mazu, the goddess of the sea, that there was one person in our family having a normal relationship. I imagine some women out there wouldn't consider a one-night stand to be a relationship at all. But I wager those women had never dated Mee, the airport taxi driver, out of desperation and the hope they might get a discount on airport transfers. Compared to that I was perfectly happy to be referred to as a fame groupie. I understood now why women threw themselves at heavy metal lead singers even if they looked like clams on sticks. It was the thrill of being touched by greatness. Admittedly, Conrad Coralbank was no Rong Wong-savun but he was a name and—

My thoughts were interrupted by the back axle falling off the truck.

I arrived twenty-eight minutes late for my appointment at Lang Suan Hospital and was pleased I'd decided to wear black. Twenty-eight minutes is hardly late at all in Thailand, but the woman I'd come to see made a point of looking at her watch every few minutes. Her name was Dr June and she was the head of the Regional Clinic Allocations Department. She had that rubbery Thai/Chinese look you came to expect of administrators in the south. Their ancestors had come to the wilds, toiled, and sent their children to university to become doctors and politicians. Dr June was clearly a product of those family values. She was my height, Mair's age, with a minimalist low-maintenance hairstyle and expensive glasses.

'Sorry I'm late,' I'd told her when I arrived. 'The back axle fell off my truck.'

Less serious women would have seen that as funny. She'd merely glared at the grease on my fingernails. The story had tickled a woman at a nearby table but she'd reacted to Dr June's nod by leaving the room and closing the door behind her. Dr June's gaze returned to my fingers.

'And you were attempting to reattach it?' she asked.

'No. I just felt an obligation to remove it from the poor old fellow it rolled over. He was pinned down and there was nobody else around. But from then on it was all good news. He wasn't hurt and he had a mechanic on speed dial. So they're down there now putting it all back together. I got a ride from—'

'This is fascinating,' she said, 'but I have another appointment.'

I picked up an accent. Something deep south, but I couldn't quite place it.

'Right,' I said. 'Too much information about the irrelevant. It's a bad habit of mine. Occupational hazard.'

She didn't ask what my occupation was. In fact she'd accepted my request for a meeting without asking anything about me. I'd assumed some people just craved human company, although you'd never know it in her case. She looked again at her watch, then the door, as if expecting the next appointment to walk in at any minute.

'I'll get to the point,' I said.

'Thank you.'

I wondered why she was wearing a white coat. Was she active in the wards as well as being a chief administrator? I wanted to ask her but I could tell she wasn't one for small talk.

'Dr Somluk,' I said.

'Yes?'

'She's disappeared.'

'And?'

'And I was wondering whether she officially handed in her notice. Whether she gave a reason for having to suddenly stop work.'

I was surprised that she hadn't asked me which Dr Somluk I was referring to. It was a common enough name.

'And you are?' she asked.

'Jimm,' I said. 'I'm a friend of Dr Somluk's nurse. They were close. She's afraid something might have happened to the doctor. Apart from one message, she hasn't been in touch.'

'And the message said?'

'Not to worry.'

'But you insist on worrying.'

'I'm a natural.'

Dr June looked at her watch, then reached for a file on the desk in front of her. She flipped open the cover and there was a photograph of Dr Somluk. She peeled through a few more pages, stopping here and there to extract information, then closed the file.

'In fact,' she said, still not making eye contact, 'this is a professional matter. Not an issue I'd normally wish to discuss with a lay person.'

I'd always wanted to be called a lay person. It was like a badge of non-denomination.

'But?' I said, hoping there was one.

'I think I owe it to her nurse to pass on my personal knowledge of Dr Somluk, who has had a very chequered career path. She is what I believe they refer to as a conspiracy theorist. I have her record.'

Amazing coincidence that it should just be lying there on the desk.

'Do you realize she has never stayed in a job for longer than two years?' she asked.

'I'm not really in a position to know anything,' I said. 'I'm just the messenger.'

At last, she looked at me over her glasses.

'Right,' she said. 'Dr Somluk's résumé had looked particularly promising when I first read it. But once I got to the referees, contacted them personally, it was always the same story. She was good at her job but she got a bee in her bonnet about this or that. At one hospital she was convinced the director was abusing his nurses. At another, she was convinced the pharmacy was ordering too much cold medicine and sending the bulk of it up to the border to make amphetamines. There was always something.'

'And is there no possibility there really was always something?'

'Young lady. Hospitals take these matters very seriously. They all conducted internal enquiries. Every one of her accusations was shot down. It was generally agreed she was unstable.'

'Then why would you have hired her?'

'As I say. Her doctoring was impeccable. It was only in personal conversations with her previous employers that I began to understand her character. I doubt you'd understand how hard it is to get qualified medical personnel to work in a remote outpost like Maprao. It was a question of hiring her then waiting for the references to come in. After a few months, the pattern was quite clear. She was very competent but doctoring wasn't enough for her. She needed a cause.'

'And what was her cause here?' I asked.

'Oh, I don't know. She was going on about this and

that. She submitted three or four official complaints about unrelated matters. But, by then, I'd already come to expect it.'

'Do you remember specifically what she was complaining about?'

'There was so much: inadequate treatment under the thirty *baht* low income fund, the use of interns with no experience in rural hospitals, no supervision of trainees by qualified doctors. All the things the Health Ministry and we in the field have been pushing for for years.'

'So there wasn't anything controversial?'

'What do you mean?'

'Anything that might have forced her out.'

Dr June laughed. It was a silly laugh, all big teeth and hyphenated eyes and a twittering kind of sound through her nose.

'This is medicine,' she said. 'Not the military. You don't get forced out. You get forced in. Placements in the deep provinces you'd sooner avoid. Moral pressures to do the right thing. The inborn guilt of someone who initially chose medicine for all the right, altruistic reasons. When you snare a qualified doctor to work in a place like this, she could be a part-time vampire and she wouldn't be forced out. Better to have a good doctor who's a little unstable than no doctor at all. Trust me. Dr Somluk just left. We didn't listen to her rants, so she moved on.'

'She didn't discuss it with you?'

'Not a word. It happens.'

Dr June looked at her watch for the sixtieth time.

'I really do have a—'

'I know. I'm sorry.'

I stood and *wai*'d her and she *wai*'d me back swiftly and reluctantly.

'Thank you so much for your help,' I said.

She nodded and looked down at a paper in front of her. I walked to the door but before opening it I stopped and turned back to her.

'Just one last question,' I said.

She looked at her watch. I wanted to rip it from her wrist and shove it up her nostril.

'Make it quick,' she said.

'Did you know Dr Somluk was at a conference in Chumphon just before she disappeared?'

'Goodness. There are conferences everywhere. I can't keep a check of who's off where. We leave that kind of thing to the discretion of our doctors.'

'So she wouldn't have needed permission from your office to go?'

'Absolutely not.'

'Do you know anything about that conference? It was at the Novotel last weekend. It was organized by an NGO called the Bonny Baby Group.'

'Oh, they're a very reputable group. They have seminars all over the south.'

'Dr Somluk's name was on the list of affiliates.'

'That's her business.'

'So was yours.'

She looked down at the paper, then the watch, then the door, but I was standing in front of it.

'Khun Juree,' she said. 'Doctors in this country are highly respected, which is as it should be.'

Her southern accent had become more pronounced. It annoyed me that I couldn't put a town to it.

'And a lot of charitable organizations invite doctors onto their boards,' she said. 'If we are confident that the organizations are sincere in their efforts, that their programmes will serve to benefit society, we allow our names to be added to the list of affiliates. It doesn't necessarily mean we are involved.'

'So, you didn't know that you and Dr Somluk were both on the list of affiliates of the Bonny Baby Group?'

'It wouldn't surprise me in the least.'

'But you weren't there.'

'I rarely attend conferences these days. I spend most of my weekends writing reports and journal papers. The work here at the department is time consuming.'

'She tried to ask a question,' I said.

'Who did?'

'Dr Somluk. She stood up at the end of a talk and tried to ask the speaker who her sponsors were for her trip. Then some large woman dragged the doctor away from the mic.'

Dr June laughed but with less girlish silliness, fewer teeth, bigger eyes.

'Again, I am not surprised,' she said. 'As I told you, the profession is well acquainted with your doctor friend and her wiles. I wouldn't be surprised if she was blacklisted in a number of places. I'm sure somebody recognized her and had her removed before she could start in on one of her embarrassing tirades. It can destroy the unity that's built up over a successful conference to have some maniac stand up and spout her personal grievances.'

'You're right,' I said. 'She sounds like a complete fruit loop.'

Dr June almost smiled before looking at her watch. It had been an interesting visit but the most fascinating aspect of it to me was that I'd never given her my surname.

'You do know those wheel things are supposed to go around,' I shouted.

I was on a plastic shower stool, under a beach umbrella, beside the ditch where my Mighty X had come to rest. The welder's son had kindly taken me to the hospital and brought me back. His name was Geng and he was eleven. A lot of pre-teens drove motorcycles down here.

'We're getting there,' shouted the welder who had my truck up on breeze blocks. My phone rang. The name Conrad flashed on the screen. I pressed 'Receive'.

'Jimm?' he said.

He always sounded surprised to find me at the end of the phone.

'That's me,' I said.

'What are you doing?'

'I'm sitting watching them reattach the rear axle of my truck,' I said, before realizing that the comment would fit exactly into his theory that I attracted weirdness.

'Oh, my God,' he said. 'Are you all right?'

I was crazy about him. My truck was all broken up. Any other man would have said, 'Did you get a quote?' Conrad asks me if I'm all right. My hero.

'I might have damaged my coccyx when my seat suddenly dropped onto the road,' I said, 'but apart from that I'm good.'

'Where are you? I'll come and pick you up.'

'I'm fine. Really. But thanks.'

'I've been thinking about you,' he said.

Oh my God. This was just . . . everything. More than everything. I'd had my one night. My still-around morning. And now here I was getting my 'I've been thinking about you' phone call. It didn't get any better than this.

'Who is this, again?' I asked.

He laughed.

'It's the only man in your life who ever measured your tongue with a tape measure,' he said.

I remembered that. He was amazed at how long my

139

tongue was. 'A freak of oral nature,' he'd called it. At the time it hadn't felt so strange that he'd have a six-metre retractable tape measure beside the bed. It was only on reflection . . .

'When can I see you again?' he asked.

There had to be some infirmity I hadn't yet spotted in the man. Some psychological failing. But . . . who cared? How often does chemistry with manners come along?

'I'm kind of busy,' I told him. 'I can probably fit you in around October.'

'I was thinking more this evening.'

'Oh, wait. I've had a cancellation. I might be free after all. But I have to cook.'

'Fine. Anything but Thai food.'

'I . . .?'

'Only joking. If it's not Thai food I don't want it. When can I expect you?'

'What time does your maid go home?'

'You don't like A?'

Conrad was the type of person who probably wouldn't have noticed his maid was infatuated with him. He didn't recognize his own magnetism.

'She's adorable all the way up to her powdery cheeks. But I need a kitchen to myself.'

'I understand,' he said. 'I'll have her out of here by six.'

It was two thirty by the time the welder insisted the job was done. I made him drive up and down the street a couple of times before I agreed to get in. We played the old 'How much? However much you like' to and fro for far too long. I liked the fact that in Hong Kong you'd ask how much and they'd tell you. They might have upped it 40 per cent but at least you had a figure to play with. Down here, the indecision made you want to give him a dollar and drive off. That'd cure him. Instead I gave him a thousand *baht*. My life was in his hands, after all.

I got home at three. The place was still shut down and empty. I passed an empty dog bowl I didn't recognize so I assumed someone had been by to feed the mutts. I had a task to perform before my dinner date. I went to my room and opened my Japanese DNA paternity treat. There was an instruction sheet inside. It was written in Japanese and manga. In fact, a complete imbecile could have understood the cartoons. You put a sample in plastic test tube A and another sample in plastic test tube B. You add the liquid contents of vial C and leave them in soak overnight. (Either that or you take them to the top of Mount Fuji to admire the full moon. The cartoon was esoteric.) Then you add chemical X to both samples, shake them up and use the enclosed eye-droppers to put a dab of each on the enclosed magically treated sheet. If they are a match the point at which the two dabs overlap will turn black. A child could do it.

Were I a wronged Japanese woman, my first sample would be from my baby. There was no cartoon to tell me how to get a blood sample from the womb, so I had to assume this test only worked on fully birthed babies. I had no baby so I carefully cut the bloody fingerprint from the threatening note and put it into the liquid that would go into the first test tube. All I needed then was to find something generic from A, the maid; a moustache hair, perhaps, blood spatter from a punch in the nose, a slice of skin. Then I'd be able to compare the DNA. It was almost as simple as a pregnancy test.

My phone.

'Sissi!'

'What are you doing?' she asked.

'DNA paternity test.'

'I think it might be too soon to tell. Give it a few months.'

'No. It's not that. I'm attempting to match a warning note and Conrad's maid. She's got a thing for him and I'm the femme fatale who's taken him from her.'

'You bitch.'

For some reason my mind wandered to the dog bowl in front of our shop and the fact I hadn't seen the animals since I got back.

'Siss, can I get back to you?'

'Certainly. But I do have information for you.'

'About the conference?'

'Yes.'

'That's great but I've just had a bad feeling.'

'Overuse of MSG?'

'Worse than that. I'll phone you back.'

I hung up and went to the balcony. It was unusual this close to meal time that the dogs weren't clambering around my ankles. I whistled. Nobody came. I banged a spoon on a pot – still no response. Nothing to worry about. They'd probably gone on their beach walk without me. Come across a snake. But, no. Not even tug-of-war with a snake took precedence over food. I walked to the shop. The new bowl was still lying there. I picked it up. It was the largest size you could buy. Pink with a bone motif. And there were words handwritten in magic marker around the outside.

I told you to keep off. This will happen to you if you don't.

The letters got smaller towards the end so they'd fit. The bowl was empty. My dogs – my eat-anything dogs – were missing. I put the bowl to my nose, not sure if I was mistaking new plastic for that bitter smell of poison. My stomach buckled. I called their names. They never came when I called their names, but I thought they might sense the urgency in my voice and oblige me.

I jogged around the huts, calling frantically. The strengthening wind carried my words away. I got on my knees and looked beneath the gazebo tables. I screamed above the growl of the surf for them to stop pissing me about. I'd envisioned it already, individual deaths at the hand of nature; brained by a falling coconut, liver flukes, drowning, kicked by a mad cow, but I'd never considered genocide. Not the annihilation of the entire pack. I'd never confess I was fond of them but I wouldn't wish them a slow, painful death. And Gogo had escaped the grim reaper once that week. It didn't seem fair.

I walked around the back of the coconut shed and that's where I found them. The scene was oddly ceremonial. Their bodies lay parallel like lines of coke. I sat, exhausted, on the old water pump and sighed. This was the result of a troubled mind. Why would she do this to me? To us? Could love really be this cruel? The three dogs looked up at me at the same time, as if they'd received a stage cue. They'd been staring at the dead rat, fixated. As we don't have CCTV fitted I could only guess how events had unfolded. I wrote it up later as a screenplay for a short, but I'd read how hard it was to work with animal actors – especially rats.

EXT. DAY – BESIDE THE CLOSED SHOP

A bowl of bacon slices wrapped around an unidentified substance sits in the middle of the car park. A motorcycle is driving off in the distance. STICKY, GOGO and BEER watch the motorcycle, then look to the bowl. STICKY, who has been known to eat entire cowpats, marches up to the bowl, tail wagging.

GOGO: Wait, brother. No.

STICKY (*Indignantly*): Why not? It's bacon. You know

how I've dreamed for a bowl of bacon?

GOGO: You wouldn't know pig from lizard. (*She coughs from the exertion of her recent medical traumas.*) This looks suspicious. Beer, you tell him. He never listens to me.

BEER (*Who doesn't give a hoot or a howl either way*): She says it's suspicious.

STICKY: How would she know?

GOGO: It was delivered by a stranger. You know what a stranger is? Someone who hasn't invested any time or love into our upbringing. If a rasher of bacon looks too good to be true, it's probably too good to be true.

Sticky pushes his nose against the still-warm fat.

STICKY: I'm eating it.

GOGO (*With the last of her strength*): Look, just indulge me this once. I'll make a deal with you. We sit back over here under the tree. In a few minutes the fat rat from the woodpile will get the scent. She'll come and take a bite. If she finishes that and goes for a second helping, we chase her off and you can have the entire bowl to yourself.

BEER: What about me?

GOGO: Look, you two had my back during this near-death thing. I owe you both. Bear with me on this. If I'm wrong, I'll make it up to you.

The three dogs retreat to the overhanging tree and wait.
It's only a minute before the fat rat from the woodpile
comes out of her hiding place and sniffs her way to the
bacon. She looks around, aware of some hostile scent, but
the lure of the fresh meat is too much to resist. She grabs a
bacon roll and eats it on the spot. CU STICKY salivating.
The rat finishes the entire plate, then sniffs around for
more. But suddenly her face is racked with agony. She puts
her hands to her throat and runs in panic to escape the
awful feeling of her intestines being eaten away, shredded
one agonizing centimetre at a time. An acidic foam of bile
seeps from her mouth. She makes it to the back of the
coconut shed before her entire musculature clamps shut
and she emits a blood-curdling scream, pirouettes and
crashes face down into the gravel. The dogs, following close
behind, can only stare in awe.

STICKY: Shit!

CHAPTER NINE

IT IS FORBIDDEN TO ENTER A WOMAN EVEN A FOREIGNER IF DRESSED AS A MAN
(Buddhist temple)

My second night of unprecedented bliss went pretty much the way of the first, except we skipped the axes. I'd toned down my *som tam* and spicy squid so as not confine him to several wasted minutes in the bathroom. We didn't even drink. Thai food works best with a cold glass of water. We skipped dessert.

I woke up at one stage to find him sitting up, one hand on my hip, staring at my leg. It was odd.

'Are you working out how much they'd charge per kilo?' I asked.

'What?'

'At the butcher's shop.'

It was the first joke that didn't work. It was the only time I'd seen a look of anger on his face. He pulled his hand away.

'Don't ever say anything like that,' he said. 'It's not funny.'

I rolled over and looked into his eyes. He was half-asleep but serious. Unexpected seriousness was a turn-off for me. I liked to know I didn't have to censor myself before I spoke. I raised an eyebrow and his anger dissolved so fast it could have all been in my imagination. Perhaps I'd been having a threatening dream and he was part of it. In shadows from the far light of the walk-in closet he looked stern, old.

'It's just . . .' he began. 'My grandmother.'

He looked away.

'What about her?'

'She was a naturist. She advocated every woman's right to be nude in public. Even into her forties she and her friends would go to the countryside, shed their clothes and sunbathe in the fields. But it was the dawn of the era of the combine harvester and . . . and one weekend Granny was asleep in a wheat field. The silent beast chomped effortlessly through both the wheat and, to our dismay, through Granny Green. It threw her parts in every direction. It took a week to put her together in time for the funeral. Only her right leg was missing. Later we discovered that a tramp had found it and tried to sell it to the local butcher. That's why . . .'

'Oh, look, I'm so sorry,' I said. 'I can be really insensitive at times. I didn't mea— Are you laughing?'

'Only shedding tears for the memory of Granny Green.'

'You are. You bastard. You're laughing. Your granny wasn't chopped up by a combine harvester.'

'She choked to death on a lump of shortbread.'

'I believed you . . . you . . .'

I attempted to suffocate him with the pillow which, naturally, led to what suffocating a man with a pillow invariably leads to. I was crazy about him. I was wide awake when we finished.

'You're quite a liar,' I said.

'It's my job.'

'Tell me about your axe book.'

'Certainly, at two in the morning after three rounds of passion, there's nothing I'd like more than to talk about my work.'

'Come on. Help me out here. I can't sleep. If you tell me a story I might drop off. My friends tell me your books are a bit slow.'

He smiled and punched me playfully on the nose.

'Then they obviously haven't read them. My books are a gripping combination of graphic violence and gratuitous sex.'

'In Laos?'

'It happens.'

'It wasn't happening when I went there.'

'Ah, you must have been there on a Tuesday. They have Tuesdays off.'

'So, how does the axe research fit in?'

'We really don't have to—'

'I'm interested.'

'I warn you, talking about violence gets me very excited.'

'So . . . the axes?'

'Right. But don't say I didn't warn you. I mentioned, I think, that the axe book is a one-off. I know there are a lot – I mean, an exorbitant number – of crime books featuring axe murderers. The axe has become a cliché in the genre.'

'So you want to write another one.'

'The axe and the murderer always take a back seat to the victim. Readers like the blood. The axe murderer is invariably anonymous, which adds to the tension because you never know what the maniac is capable of. But what of the skill? The training that goes into handling an axe correctly?'

He was getting excited telling me this. I mean . . . he was getting *excited*, which was a little worrying but I could handle it.

'Go on,' I said.

'Well, we never see the axe murderer from his point of view. We only get into the killer's head in the last chapter when he—'

'Or she.'

'Or she explains all the events that led up to the arrest. We rush through his—'

'Or her.'

'Or her background and uncover the awful childhood

150

she had when the stepfather made her chop the heads off live chickens or whatever. But it's too late then. I want to know the killer from page one. I want to experience this awakening in him. That moment when he makes his first kill. When he realizes how the right weapon can make easy work of both murder and dismemberment. Make it fun, even.'

I'd stopped adding 'she' by this point.

'How the hacking becomes therapeutic,' he went on. 'How the clunk of the blade against the bone and then the finale as it hits the concrete floor almost sounds out a timpani of revenge for all the horrors he experienced in his life. I want to get to the end of the book and for the readers to "feel him". Feel *for* him to the point that his kill becomes theirs. That they stop seeing only the blood and the horror and begin to see the justice of it all through his eyes.'

Well, I suppose I *had* asked. He'd become animated. He was speaking louder. He was as awake now as me. There was a fire in his eyes. I recognized it as the passion that authors, I mean, real authors, have to feel in order to be truly great. I smiled and for a few seconds he hovered over me not knowing where he was. He'd entered that fiction/reality realm where the characters were more real than the woman in his bed. I could never force myself to be excited about making things up. Not when there was so much in the real world to be horrified by – to dedicate myself to.

'So,' I said, 'you decided you couldn't introduce this element of your personality into those gentle Lao books.'

'What?'

'Laos?'

He was back in the bedroom with me. He lowered himself to the mattress and let his head sink into the soft pillow. He smiled and ran a hand through my short, wild hair like the hairdressers on TV who point out there's no hope for such a thatch.

'Right,' he said. 'I sent a plot outline for the latest Lao book to my editor. In it, the entire cast is wiped out in an axe attack. The marketing people suggested it might tarnish the franchise.'

'That surprises me.'

'I think that was why they agreed to the one-off. They thought I was going mad, afraid they wouldn't get any more of their beloved Lao books. They made one proviso, that I had to write under a pseudonym. And, Jimm, do you know what? Suddenly having that new name was an excuse to be a different person. It was like my evil twin had made a belated exit from the womb.'

'What's his name?'

'Myster Egal.'

'Mister as in the adjective?'

'No. It's a first name. Myster. The marketeers loved it. Short for mystery. The surname sounds like "Eagle". But could, in this enlightened age of the international crime novel, be a translation of the work of a Lithuanian writer. And anyone hearing it would assume it was just "Mr" and say, "That's really cool." They'd never forget it. It has everything. It's brilliant.'

'And your idea, of course.'

'Of course. Marketing people don't come up with new ideas. They just steal other people's.'

'And is Mr Eagle around right now?' I asked, running my hand down his chest. 'I could use a little . . . evil.'

'He's out of the office at the moment,' said Conrad. 'But if you give me a few hours' sleep I'll see what I can come up with. I think he'd be delighted to meet you. You're exactly his type.'

I'm sure he was asleep even before the end of the ensuing kiss. I was almost unconscious as well when A, the maid, crept stealthily into my mind – with a knife. Nobody locked their doors down here. It would be the simplest thing for her to sneak into the master bed-room and dice my intestines. With that thought firmly in place, there was no hope of me getting back to sleep. I left the bed and walked around the house – wondering where a maid might leave bodily traces. The place was lit by the moon skipping from cloud to cloud. When it was eclipsed it was so dark I had to stop and wait. I used those moments to gather my thoughts. I doubted she'd use the bathroom to groom herself so hairs on the brush wouldn't work. I looked in the kitchen for onion-cutting, finger-nick blood stains, but it was spotless. I was starting to think I might have to go down to the temple and clip a toenail as she slept. But then I remembered the day of the watermelons. She'd been wearing a silly hat with a neck flap. There had to be a shed for the hoes and the hoses and the hats.

It was disappointingly easy to find. The garden apparatus was in a small alcove behind the laundry. There was no window so I shut the door and flicked on the light. A's hat was on a hook on the wall. At first glance it appeared to be devoid of forensic evidence. But there was an inner towelling sweatband, the kind you'd sew in yourself if you were anal. Tucked in the crease of that was a hair about three centimetres long. It had to be hers. I wrapped it in a tissue and put it in the pocket of my *yukata*. I turned off the light and went back into the living room, with the intention of returning to bed and the anticipation of meeting Mr Eagle the next morning. But, for a moment, I sat on the vast comfy sofa and looked out at the Gulf. I could see Captain Kow's squid-boat light, still the only one on the horizon. The moon, appearing sheepishly from the next cloud, leaked a carpet of yellow light across the sea. It was better than Cable. I decided to go to the fridge and get myself a beer and watch the show. The moonlight on the designer forest exposed all the creepy shadows and nooks in which any psychopathic maid might lurk.

I was on my second gulp of Heineken when the moon vanished again. But, just before the cloud swallowed it,

I thought I saw movement in the garden. A figure stepped out from behind a candlestick bush, then disappeared in the blackness. I might have seen its shadow pass in front of the glass doors, right to left, but, in truth, I probably didn't see anything. I walked to the doors and stood close enough to the glass to feel my breath bounce back at me. I remained as still as I could wondering whether I'd been visible to the intruder. The beer was in my hand, but I didn't dare take a sip in case the figure on the other side of the glass saw me. That stalemate and the accompanying knot in my gut, continued for . . . I don't know . . . some very long minutes. And then, that quirky old moon peekabooed from its hideout and the garden was illuminated like a stage show – there was nobody there. But still I couldn't move. The room all around me was clear as day but I couldn't tell what effect the reflection on the tinted glass might have from the outside. I was either spotlit by the moon or masked behind a mirror.

I counted my breaths.

There were lots of them.

Then, I saw him. Left to right now. Walking confidently. Shirtless. Sweat gleaming on his dark skin. A's husband, Jo, still retained that boyish grin even though in one hand he held a machete. It's hard to pick out colours at night but the blade dripped with something dark. Something fresh. And in his other hand he held a small sack by the neck. It was half full. He stopped about three metres from where I stood and turned his head and looked directly at me. I was a statue. All my oxygen had been used up and I felt I was turning blue. If he could see me I must have looked really stupid. My robe had fallen open to reveal a long strip of naked me. I wondered if waving would help. I mean, I wasn't exactly doing anything wrong.

But Jo turned to face the window and flexed his muscles, as if in a mirror. I was used to it. Arny did it all the time. Men were so vain. Jo couldn't see me. He smiled at himself and walked on. When he was out of sight I returned to the sofa and chugged my beer. What gardener worked at two a.m.? What could he possibly be cutting down . . .? Or chopping up?

The can dropped to my feet. There were external steps to Conrad's office and paper *shoji* sliding doors to his bedroom. An assassin wouldn't need to pass through the house. I tied my robe as I ran to the interior staircase. My feet got tangled in the *yukata* hem when I tried to take too many steps at a time. The house was open plan and the stairs gave directly onto the upstairs sleeping space. Those last few steps I took slowly. The bed was in shadow now with only the dim light from the closet. I could barely make out the figure of a sleeper. If there was blood I'd need to turn on the main light to see it and I wasn't ready to do that. The *shoji* door to the office was open. I couldn't recall whether it had been so when I'd gone downstairs.

I knelt at the foot of the bed.

'Conrad,' I whispered.

No answer. No snoring. No loud breaths.

'Conrad?' I tried louder. 'Conrad, don't be dead.'

I was about to go to the bedside lamp when I heard a distinctive sign of life. I'd need to look it up later, but I was reasonably certain that dead men didn't fart. Good old *som tham*. I was so delighted I jumped onto the bed and fell on top of my author. He grunted.

'What? What?' he said.

'You farted,' I said with undisguised joy.

'You don't say. Can we discuss that in the morning?'

'Certainly.'

And he was asleep again.

CHAPTER TEN

FRESH GRAVE JUICE
(restaurant menu)

I skipped breakfast at the Coralbank mansion for two reasons. Firstly, I didn't want to be served impolitely, or be macheted on my way out of the gate. Secondly, because I had a lot to do back at home. My schedule was:

1. Text Sissi to let her know I'd done it again.
2. Make sure the dogs were still alive and give them a walk.
3. Conduct a search for Grandad Jah and force him to eat something.
4. Phone Mair on her cell and tell her to come home.
5. Work on my DNA comparison.
6. Get my next rabies shot.
7. Follow up on Dr Somluk's disappearance.

In fact, the last item became the first. As I drove into

our little car park I saw a tall man in luminous green Bermuda shorts, pink Crocs and a Kylie Minogue T-shirt sitting at our concrete picnic table. Our palms were being battered by the wind all around him. Three potted plants were on their sides. The Mighty X shuddered to a stop and I barged open the door.

'Well, Lieutenant,' I said. 'I can only assume you're undercover.'

My sweet Chompu *wai*'d me as if I were a duchess.

'I'm hiding out,' he said. 'I can't take any more caring and sharing.'

'Have you been here all night?'

'Yes. I hope you don't mind.'

'What happened to your clandestine love nest over-looking Pitak Island?'

'I rented it out to an old gay couple. I needed some spending money.'

'So, where did you sleep?'

'Your room. And I think we need to take a little time to discuss personal hygiene.'

'Don't bother. Our drug-challenged dog slept and emptied her bowels there. It needs fumigating. I haven't had a chance to clean up. I keep forgetting. I haven't slept there.'

'Why not?'

'None of your business.'

'The ancient foreigner?'

'He's forty-eight. Same age as Boy George.'

'Don't get me started. Talk about letting yourself go. And I didn't say ancient was a bad thing. So . . .?'

'So what?'

'How is he?'

I blushed.

'He's very well, thank you.'

Chompu let out one of his raving queen squeals and all the dogs came running because they thought it was a downed heron. That took care of item two on the agenda.

'I'm so proud of you,' he said, taking my hand. 'Is this a relationship or are you merely taking advantage until you tire of him?'

'I don't know, Chom. He has an estranged wife who looks like a fashion model. He makes more money than Boon Rawd Brewery, and he's gorgeous.'

'And the problem is?'

'Why does he want me? Even for a quickie. He can have his choice.'

'There you go throwing mud at yourself again. Look at you. You're stuntedly beautiful, pleasantly breasted, you have legs I'd die for and you're funny. If this psychologist cures me of my horrible affliction, you'll be the first girl I bed. I swear it.'

'You're a darling. Thanks. Did you manage to . . .'

'Your enquiry? It was a pleasure to have an excuse to dodge Madame Freud.'

'Great. What did you get?'

'Your Dr Somluk has nobody to miss her, and don't I know how that feels. No brothers or sisters. Parents long gone. Friends scattered here and there haven't heard from her for a long time. I could find nobody who's seen her since the conference. She was booked into the hotel for three nights but didn't stay there. If only I'd known. They have such yummy cocktails at the Novotel. It appears she didn't show up until an hour before her appearance on the video. So it looks like she went there specifically to embarrass the speaker or the organizers. They have no cameras in the car park but the front gate logged her car in at eleven a.m. and out again at three p.m. The attendant didn't notice who was in the car.'

'Anything on the speaker? Dr Aisa Choangulia?'

'Not a tinkle. She's as clean as a whistle – although I've had a lot of whistles in my mouth that weren't particularly clean, and I'm not speaking metaphorically. They give us training courses on—'

'Chom.'

'Sorry. She's a top paediatrician, thirty years' service to the hospital, good but humble family, father dead, ageing mother in a hospice. Plus she's a Christian and I'm told they aren't allowed to do anything wrong.'

'I wonder if she had any private dealings with Dr Somluk.'

'No. I called her.'

'The paediatrician? You did?'

'Well it seemed a better option than just guessing.'

'Right. And?'

'Said she'd never seen the woman before in her life. She'd been surprised by the fuss. She was later told that the questioner had mental problems and had embarrassed a number of speakers during the conference. That's why they felt they had to remove her.'

'Which wasn't true because she'd just arrived.'

'Quite. Look, I don't suppose I could get something to eat, could I? You had nothing but stale M&Ms in your room.'

'You ate them?'

'My stomach was rumbling.'

I walked Chompu to the kitchen having decided it was best not to tell him those M&Ms were Gogo's antidiarrhoeals. I made him a breakfast that promised to be with him for a long time.

'I went to see Dr Somluk's boss at the hospital,' he said.

'Dr June? Gee, you're thorough. You must have got there just after me. I hope you weren't dressed like this. She wouldn't have seen the funny side of it.'

'No problem. I have a lot of dress-ups in the back of the car. But, as it turned out, she wasn't there. She had some function or other. I did talk to her colleague, a Dr something-beginning-with M. I forgot to write it down.'

'There's the mind of a great detective.'

'Look, honey, I'd just arrived from one of our Mekhong

whisky therapy sessions. I had to put the siren on just so I wouldn't be pulled over for drunk driving. I reeked of peppermint. But over tea and coconut macaroons I did manage to pick up one or two delightful snippets from Dr M. Firstly, were you aware that your Dr June, the head of the Regional Clinic Allocations Department, was at the conference in Chumphon for the entire three days?'

'The lying cow.'

'She told you she wasn't there?'

'She . . . no, not exactly. But she pretended to be vague about it.'

'Not vague at all, it seems. She was one of the organizers.'

'You don't say? Huh! She certainly didn't tell me that.'

'Well, in fairness, she didn't have to tell you anything at all. You weren't there in any official capacity.'

'I went as a friend of Dr Somluk's nurse, Da.'

'And she saw you and answered the questions she thought were relevant to Dr Somluk's disappearance.'

'No, she was being sneaky.'

'You're right. What time is it?'

'Eight.'

'Doctors get up early, don't they?'

He took out his phone and speed-dialled.

'Hello,' he said. 'This is Lieutenant Chompu. I talked to . . . Yes, me too. I was wondering . . .'

While Chompu yakked, I fed the dogs. I couldn't be bothered to fight the wind on a morning walk. They could go themselves if it was important. When I returned to the kitchen, Chom was smiling.

'It looks like there's something else Dr June didn't tell you. I phoned my doctor friend from yesterday whose name began with M, but turned out to be called Niramon.'

'Close enough.'

'Who do you suppose Dr Niramon has just recently been drafted in to replace?'

'You've got me.'

'Your own Dr Somluk.'

'No.'

'Dr Somluk worked in the Regional Clinic Allocations Department for nine months before she was moved down to the Maprao clinic.'

'Why wouldn't the director have told me that?'

'Did you ask?'

'No.'

'Then, that's why.'

'No. This is all wrong. Director June was organizing the conference but her name didn't appear in the programme or on the list of speakers. Dr Somluk turns up and tries to ask a question in a room full of health professionals but is dragged away from the microphone. She subsequently vanishes.'

'Her car left at three.'

'But we don't know who drove it. Everything revolves around what answer Dr Somluk was expecting to get to her question in the conference hall. When you spoke to Dr Aisa in Bangkok, did she mention who funded her appearance?'

'She said she paid out of pocket. A charitable act.'

'No sponsor?'

'She said she often agreed to public appearances as a public service. She sounds like a saint.'

'Drives four hundred kilometres, puts herself up in a four star hotel to talk to a couple of hundred rural health workers, most of whom are only there to stay in a fancy hotel and claim overtime? Call me cynical but that doesn't sound very likely to me.'

'I doubt there's any way we can prove her a liar.'

'Yes. There's a way,' I said.

With Chompu sitting opposite me at the kitchen table, belting down French toast, which he found terribly exotic, I called Sissi.

'I was just about to call you,' she said.

'Why?'

'Surely you don't think a text stating "I did it again" is going to satisfy the curiosity of a retired sex goddess like me.'

'What is it with you confused gender people?'

'Hi, Sissi!' Chompu shouted.

'Is that the fairy policeman I hear?' Sissi asked, then shouted, 'Yoohoo!'

'We're working on the missing doctor case together,' I told her. 'We're at a juncture where your input could be vital.'

'Oh, marvellous. I phoned you last night full of excitement to pass on the news, and you turned off your phone so you could run off and have geriatric sex. Yes, I do have some information.'

'About the free gifts at the conference?'

'Yes.'

'Let's hear it.'

'It'll cost.'

'You're charging your own relatives for information now?'

'Not money. I want a blow-by-blow of your nights with the writer.'

'That would be very tacky of me, don't you think?'

'Non-compliance would be a deal breaker.'

I confess I'd had my sister tell me the details of all her conquests when she was still the conquistadora.

'All right, but you first.'

'Hold on to your hat. All the conference participants got . . . *dadarada* . . . a carton of chocolate milk.'

'That's all?'

'Yup.'

'I take back my offer.'

'You can't.'

'What brand was it?'

'Medley.'

I had to think about it. Medley the multinational milk and coffee people. Why would they be interested in a little conference in the Thai outback?

'Are they one of the companies in the Thai Food Group?' I asked.

'They are.'

'Why would they be sponsoring a medical convention?'

'Ah. So it wasn't just the pert buttocks and the looks in our family that went to me. And I thought you were a journalist.'

'It's easy, is it? OK. Don't tell me. Doctors . . . are up all night so they need Medcafé to stay awake.'

'I think you're toying with me.'

'No? All right. Milk. Babies drink milk.'

'Bravo.'

'But they drink breast milk.'

'They used to.'

'They gave it up?'

'Don't you notice anything on your supermarket adventures?'

I'd noticed they play Christmas carols ad nauseam until you'd want to run out into the car park and scream. But that didn't seem relevant.

'I'm still not getting it,' I said.

'You haven't spotted there's an entire aisle dedicated to babies?'

'Milk?'

'Formula. Cocaine for the under-twos. It outsells Pepsi and Coca-Cola combined.'

I could see I'd been in denial for too long. I'd noticed the aisle but never ventured through it. All those grinning fat baby faces and blue teddy bears. I knew nothing at all about formula.

'Medley make it?' I asked.

'They are the brew-meisters. The witches who stir the cauldron. A blend of vitamins and minerals and rapid-growth fertilizer all mixed together with milk powder to spare Mummy the inconvenience of flopping out her titty on the bus.'

'So, it's not healthy?'

'It would appear to be astoundingly healthy.'

'So . . . it's a good thing.'

'Perhaps. I don't know. That's as far as I got on my internet trek. A lot of people appear to be against it. But I've found that multinationals do attract more than their fair share of weirdos like your Dr Somluk. Just the fact that they're ginormous and successful and rich is often reason enough to hate them.'

'But I wonder why Dr Aisa's appearance at the conference being sponsored by Medley would upset our Dr Somluk so much. I mean, she obviously asked the question because she knew the answer. She wanted all the participants to hear it. What was so important that Somluk would be dragged away from the mic?'

'Right. And these are questions you can ask yourself on your own time.'

'That's true.'

'So now it's my turn.'

'I don't know, Siss. Do I strike you as the type of person who'd describe intimate details of the two most passionate nights of her life on an insecure phone line?'

'Absolutely.'

'Well, it all started with cocktails . . .'

With that case simmering nicely at the back of the gas range, I left Chompu to his Sudoku and went in search of Grandad Jah . . . or his body. I stopped off at my cabin and put A's hair in test tube B before heading for the beach. Very little happened down here that every man, woman, and child of speaking age didn't learn about in the space of half a day. It was either the worst or the best thing about Maprao. The first person I met on the beach was Uncle Rip who collected plastic bottles. This was his high season. I used to think it was desperation until I found out you could make more out of recycled plastic in a month than you could working on a building site.

'Uncle Rip,' I said.

Only his eyes and the top of his nose were visible through his ski mask. Locals here dressed for the season rather than the temperature. He was the type of person who jumped with surprise whenever you spoke to him.

'Is that Jimm?' he said.

He wasn't blind and it wasn't dark, so I don't know why he asked.

'Yeah,' I said. 'Have you seen my grandad?'

'Oh, yes,' he said, and tried to walk on. Only the dog barricade forced him to turn back. He was petrified of our dogs and they knew it.

'Where is he?' I asked.

'I'm not sure you'd want to know,' he said.

'Would I have asked if I didn't?'

'Ah, no tricking me with your clever newspaper-reporter questions.'

'Uncle Rip. Don't make me set the dogs on you. Where is he?'

The ripple of fear that ran through him caused to dogs to growl.

'All right. All right,' he said. 'But you didn't hear it from me. He's at the boat yard at Jamook Prong.'

'Really? He wouldn't have a big chunk of wood there with him, would he?'

'That's all I'm saying. Now, call them off.'

The dogs were so busy rooting out putrid fish from the garbage that they'd completely forgotten him. He gave chase to a water bottle that was being tumbled along the beach by the wind. I wondered when my grandad had developed an interest in boat building. I picked my way through the bamboo and the broken beer bottles and bloated blowfish and looked out at a surf that, to a city girl, was formidable. I knew even the most incompetent surfer would laugh at the little waves. But Mair was a city girl too. I took out my phone and called her. Some canary-voiced recorded idiot told me the number wasn't in service. I called Arny.

'Arny, what are you doing?'

'Watching *Terminator Two*.'

'Can you get out of it?'

'I guess.'

'Right. Arrange a boat. I'm worried about Mair. It's been three days at sea and it's rough out there. I'm getting nervous.'

'How will we know where to find her?'

'They've been moored at the same spot since she left. I see the light every night. But I keep thinking about that Nicole Kidman movie when she was still earthy and Australian and a maniac got on her boat and ravaged her. What was the name of that . . .?'

'I don't think anyone would ravage Mair.'

'You watch your mouth. That's our mother you're talking about. There's a strong movement towards elderly women on internet porn. She is highly ravageable.'

'That's not what I meant. I'm just saying that Dad will take care of her.'

Arny was the only one calling him 'Dad'. I think he'd always been desperate to have a father. It didn't matter if he turned up thirty-two years late.

'Just organize the boat, Arny.'

'Why can't you?'

'Look, anything I'm doing has to be more taxing and valuable than watching *Terminator Two*. I happen to be in search of Grandad Jah.'

Arny was silent.

'What?'

'Just, don't get mad when you find him.'

'Why should . . .? What do you know?'

'I'll get a boat,' he said, and hung up.

What a bloody family. I seemed to be the only clueless member.

Jamook Prong was just the fancy name for a tiny jetty where all the local squid boats tied up. In the monsoons, the high tides banked up the sand and they couldn't get out without a backhoe. So here they rocked idly for weeks at a time. It was ten a.m. and the harbour was deserted. I heard the buzz of an electric sander. They always reminded me of a sadistic dentist's drill fitted with an outboard motor. The 'boatyard' was actually a slight sandy incline, up which the fishermen dragged their vessels to make repairs or chip off barnacles or paint fortuitous but culturally inappropriate names like 'Ronaldo'. This was where I found Grandad Jah and his log. He had his shirt off and his back to me. At first I thought he was an untidy stack of CDs draped in damp tissue paper. Grandad was a man who should have always worn a shirt or a sheet . . . anything.

The log had been sawn lengthwise into two parts, the smaller of which leaned against a nearby tree. The larger portion had been partly hollowed out and the corners rounded. It looked like an attempt by a crocodile to make a canoe with its teeth. Like plumbing, electronics, building, and child-rearing, woodwork was not my grandad's strong point. I sat and watched until the local power supply, not for the first time, went off. It did so whenever there was a huge storm, a moderate wind, or if somebody sneezed within forty metres of the generator. Grandad Jah uttered a good number of words we would have been severely reprimanded for using as children. The rant ended with, 'Can't these hillbillies do anything right?'

'Grandad Jah,' I said.

He turned and saw me and, for some unfathomable reason, he covered his nipples with his index fingers.

'What are you doing here?' he snapped.

'I haven't seen you at breakfast for two days.'

'Well perhaps you would have if you hadn't been out canoodling with the international community, instead of being in the kitchen where you belong.'

See what I mean about word getting around?

'Where have you been eating?' I asked.

'Not that you care.'

'I care because if you've found an alternative venue for breakfast, I can stop ordering all that expensive high-fibre stuff that keeps your haemorrhoids in check.'

'Right. Shout it to the world.'

'Grandad, there's nobody else here. There's just you and me and your canoe.'

'Canoe? I don't see a canoe. Are you referring to this? Have you ever seen a canoe that looks like this?'

'I assumed it isn't finished.'

'Of course it isn't. But it will be extremely splendid when I'm done with it.'

I walked up to the project and looked at the gnawed-out interior and the unevenly sanded exterior. And I turned to the skinny surfboard of lumber by the tree and, probably much slower than any of you, I got it.

'Grandad, are you making a coffin?'

'As if you need to ask.'

'But for twenty years you've been describing how we should carry your body to the local pyre, lay your tired bones on the recently lopped branches of still living trees and set fire to you – al fresco. That your soul should be able to rise up on the flames without it having to fight its way out of a box.'

'And none of those plans have changed.'

'So, why do you need a teak coffin?'

'Because I refuse to spend a fortune on one of those crappy paint and plaster efforts they sell down in Pak Nam.'

'No, I mean, why do you need a coffin at all?'

'As a statement.'

'Of . . . ?'

'That I'll go when I damned well please.'

I vaguely remembered a Thai movie about a man who spent a night in a coffin, in order to cheat death and put to rest the bad luck he'd experienced in his life. The movie was probably based on some Thai tradition I didn't know about, and Grandad was more likely to have heard the myth than to have seen the movie because I doubt he ever went to a cinema in his life. But, either way, movie or myth, this was a lot of work to go to for nothing.

'Are you planning to sleep in this?' I asked.

'Just the four nights. That should be enough.'

'You'll get splinters.'

'It'll be smooth as a virgin's thighs when I've finished with it.'

The way he was going, I could imagine it chopped smaller and smaller until there was nothing left but a small heap of sawdust and woodchips. But it was a good workout and better than getting into drugs and criminal activities, so I didn't dissuade him, but I did have a more urgent job for him.

'Grandad,' I said, 'do you remember the note that was attached to our kitchen door with a cleaver?'

'It's hardly something that happens every day.'

'Well, somebody tried to poison the dogs. I think it was the same person.'

'Why didn't you tell me this?'

'Because you were off whittling with no forwarding address.'

'You know who did it?'

'Yes. I mean, I think so.'

He reached for his shirt.

'I'll get Captain Waew down here.'

'No, don't. Not yet. You two old cops always resort to violence.'

'That doesn't make us thugs. We're avengers. Those that the stupid laws excuse will have to undergo a retrial with the upholders of social justice.'

Yes, he was being serious, and I'd seen the results of his social justice.

'When I get home I'll take out Mair's sewing machine and run you up a couple of suits with capes. But, in the meantime, we aren't going to beat anyone up because we need evidence. I have a small DNA test on the boil at home. But even if it's a match it won't be admissible in court. We need some old-fashioned policing.'

I knew that would get his attention.

'What do we have to go on?' he asked.

'I'm quite sure it's a woman, Burmese. Conrad's maid. Perhaps her husband's involved somehow. It's weird. She's clearly jealous of me and wants me to stay away. Or there may be some other reason they don't want me hanging around. Last night I saw the husband at two a.m. carrying what might have been a bloody machete and something in an old sack. It's got me wondering about a lot of things.'

'And what do you want me to do?'

'What you do best. Investigate.'

He looked over his shoulder.

'I am a little busy.'

'Grandad, the coffin can wait. You won't be dying for

at least a month. This woman invaded our home and tried to kill our dogs.'

He thought about it.

'I'm not that fond of dogs.'

'I know. Me neither. But it's the principle of the thing. A crime has been committed and social and legal justice needs to be upheld.'

His chin rose.

'I'll look into it.'

'Can you start now?'

Grandad looked at the lifeless sander at his feet and nodded.

I was on my porch staring at the magic of Japanese DNA testing. There was nothing I could do for twelve hours. But I imagined I could see the little DNA molecules breaking down and swimming around and reassembling to recreate their history. I looked up to see Arny standing there. He'd just appeared like a genie.

'I've got a boat,' he said.

'Well done,' I told him. 'Whose is it?'

'Ed's.'

My stomach always rolled over when I heard the name Ed. Ed the grassman, Ed the boat skipper, Ed the bimbo hairdresser fancier. Everything always came back to Ed.

'He doesn't mind us using his boat?' I asked.

'No.'

'That's nice of him.'

'Because he's in it.'

'What?'

'He said he doesn't trust us to use it on a rough sea so he'll take us out.'

'Oh, God. All right.'

I followed Arny to the thin sliver of beach and there on the garbage was what looked like a plastic bathtub, with a long-tail boat engine strapped on the back. Ed was posing beside it in his standard fisherman gear; shorts and a T-shirt. I hadn't seen him for a while. He looked great. If I didn't have a steady boyfriend who happened to be a world famous writer and rich, I'd have allowed myself a little heart flutter.

'Hello, Ed,' I said.

'Jimm.'

'Haven't you got anything bigger than this?'

'I'm not taking out the squid boat in this squall. The waves are two metres out there. I don't know what Kow thinks he's playing at.'

Two metres? I suddenly remembered a hairdresser's appointment.

'Here, put this on,' he said, throwing a grubby life jacket at me.

'Haven't you got one in pink?' I asked. He didn't laugh. 'What about Arny? Doesn't he get one?'

'He can't come,' said Ed.

'Why not?' I squealed, thinking what a bad time this

was to get me alone in a boat in order to tell me how much he cared for me.

'With Arny's weight at 105 kilograms plus mine at fifty-seven,' said Ed. 'And what are you? Fifty-five?'

'Fifty, thank you,' I replied, although fifty-five was closer.

'That's 217 kilos,' he said. 'Not counting the motor, this boat can take two hundred.'

'Well that's just a fraction over,' I argued.

'Right, but if the purpose is to rescue your mother from Captain Kow's boat and bring her home, one of us would have to stay out there.'

I saw his point, considered staying on the beach and sending Arny in my place, but it might have needed a woman's voice of reason to wake her from her trance. So Ed and I set out for the deep ocean. Actually, the Gulf was only eighty metres at its deepest. In the calm season you could walk a kilometre out and the water still wouldn't be over your head. My hair whipped into my eyes. We'd only been out five minutes and I was already feeling nauseous from the roll. Distraction helps in moments of impending seasickness.

'So, you're sleeping with the *farang*,' he said, one hand on his long-tail, the other in the pocket of his shorts.

How the hell did . . .?

'Oh? What makes you think that?' I said as nonchalantly as I could, whilst yelling at the top of my voice

179

above the sound of the engine. 'And, in fact, what business is it of yours?'

'None.'

'Good. End of discussion.'

'I just don't think it's appropriate,' he said. His gaze all this time hadn't left the horizon.

'Appropriate for who?'

'You.'

'I'm perfectly able to decide what's appropriate for me, thank you, Ed. And, at this time in my life, having a nice, honest, faithful boyfriend seems most appropriate.'

I believe he aimed deliberately at a big wave and bounced me on the plastic seat.

'He's married,' said Ed.

'She left him.'

'There'd be a reason.'

I smiled at him.

'It's very sweet of you to be jealous, Ed. Thank you. Oh, and how's the hairdresser? I heard she's a good stylist but she won't get her licence until she turns fifteen.'

'She's twenty-two.'

'Really? So that's as developed as her body's going to get?'

That put an end to the none-of-your-business stuff. In fact we didn't speak again for ten minutes. Finally, I asked, 'How do you know where you're going?'

'When Kow dropped anchor two days ago he radioed in his position,' said Ed. 'It's tradition. We have customs down here we adhere to. We look out for each other. Kow's one of us.'

'Did you know he was my father?'

'What?'

'Before Sissi came down and exposed him. Did you know that Captain Kow had a family he'd deserted thirty-four years ago?'

'No.'

'Then I guess you aren't as close-knit as you think you are. When did he come here?'

'What do you mean?'

'I mean, how many years has he lived here?'

'He's always been here. His family's from here. He went to school here. Apart from those four or five missing years he hasn't been away.'

'So he just decided to take a short hiatus, father three children and leave the mother to raise them?'

'It's really not my business.'

'Don't you think that's a bit irresponsible?'

'He'd have his reasons. He's a good man.'

'He'd have . . .? Bloody hell. Why couldn't I have been born a man so I could get my non-accountability licence too? I wish I'd brought Grandad's gun. Rid the world of two more chauvinists in one . . .'

Ed turned off the engine.

'Look,' he said.

'What is it?'

Bobbing jauntily on the brine was a large block of polystyrene with a small generator and a green light bulb.

'It's Kow's position,' said Ed.

'It's a block of foam.'

'It's a fishing method. There's a fine mesh net under the float. The fish are attracted to the light and get tangled in the net. The sea used to be peppered with them until they were banned. It's still not legal but it beats sitting out here night after night getting pummelled by the surf. You just sail out when it's calm and see what you've collected.'

'So, the light I've been seeing the past two nights . . .?'

'Was this.'

'So, where . . .?'

'Your guess is as good as mine, Jimm.'

UNPOSTED BLOG ENTRY 4
(found two weeks too late)

I think this weekend would be as good a time as any.
She's in awe of me. She needs a figurehead in her life.
She'd probably do anything I told her right now. I need
time to prepare. To establish an alibi. I'm going to do it
right this time. The first dismemberment was too rushed.
This one I'll savour. Why did it take me so long to discover
this feeling?
   C.C.

CHAPTER ELEVEN

KINDLY WATCH YOUR HANDS BEFORE OR
AFTER USING COMPUTER
(Java Coffee Shop)

While Arny was off in search of Mair and Captain Kow's boat, I was back staring at the DNA equipment, which was a little bit like staring at a chair wondering who might sit in it some day. I was thinking about Conrad and Ed and how poorly the latter stacked up against the former. There was no competition really, which made me wonder why I was thinking about Ed at all. I wondered what Conrad might be doing at that moment. Wondered if I'd seem too keen if I phoned him and invited him down to the Gulf Bay Lovely Resort. Give him mildew and bedbug experiences he wouldn't get in his glass castle on the bluff.

And the phone rang.

And it was him.

'I miss you,' was the first thing he said. I couldn't remember how much time had passed since anyone had said that to me. I mean, anyone who wasn't obliged to say it due to family ties. He was such a romantic.

'Oh, Steven, I miss you too,' I said.

'Who is this Steven?' he said. 'Bring him to me.'

'I'll organize a joust,' I said.

'How on earth would you know a word like "joust"?'

'*A Knight's Tale*. Heath Ledger. And they say there's nothing to be learned from cinema and TV.'

'You really are remarkable, in so many ways. What are you doing on Saturday?'

'Well, there's the ladies' darts tournament.'

'Do you feel like a drive and a night out?'

'With you?'

'Yes, of course with me.'

'Where are we going?'

'It's a surprise. But I promise you it's something you'll never forget. I'll be away in Bangkok for a few days, but I'll give you a call on Friday to confirm the details. I wish I could be with you sooner.'

'Me too,' I said, and I meant it. Although I'd told Ed otherwise, I knew one lunch and two nights of satisfying sex did not make a relationship. But they were a lot closer to it than anything else I'd been through in recent history. I tried to force images of attending crime-writing conferences and book readings out of my mind. My hand on the crook of his elbow as we chatted amiably with Salman Rushdie. But those past few days had infused me with confidence. I was better than I'd given myself credit for. That alone was worth the price of admission to the 'other woman' stable. Who cared what Ed, and Grandad and half the damned province thought? I wanted to write Conrad's name in fancy letters on my school exercise book. Put his photo in my underwear drawer. Write him little rhyming sonnets. It was a really strong 'like'.

I went to see Da for my rabies shot and to confirm that Dr Somluk hadn't returned. The skinny nurse seemed a lot chirpier than she had been during my previous visits. I asked her what she was smiling about.

'Gogo's talking about getting engaged.'

'Wow. Now that's serious.'

Actually, talking about getting engaged was just like talking about world peace. Much easier than actually doing it.

'So, tell me about him,' I said.

'No, Jimm. I wish I could. But this is a small town. I know what it's like here. I don't want everyone knowing my business. Especially if it doesn't work out.'

Romance had steadied Da's hand. I hardly felt the shot. We talked about Dr Somluk and I told her all the news I'd gathered from my meeting with Dr June and the conference.

'Any idea why she would have singled out the paediatrician from Bangkok at the conference?' I asked.

'Do you know what subject she was speaking on?'

'Something about breasts being a figment of our imagination, which in my case . . .'

'Ah, well. That's why,' said Da. 'Breastfeeding was one of the doctor's pet subjects. It wouldn't surprise me if the Bangkok woman was encouraging mothers to shift over to formula.'

'See? I still don't get this. If formula's as healthy as they say, why shouldn't they switch?'

'Right. Dr Somluk's argument was that formula's a poor substitute for breastfeeding, but the company promotes it as a healthy alternative. It's cleaner, they say. Easier to use. It turns your kid into some preschool genius. She agreed there were times it was necessary if the mother can't breastfeed for any reason, but basically it's only healthy in the same way that vitamins are healthy. No doctor's going to recommend people give up food and live on vitamins.'

'So you're saying that mothers aren't using formula as a supplement.'

'We're in the countryside. Mums see the healthy chubby babies on TV and they start thinking they've done their babies wrong by giving them breast milk. Formula babies do get fat faster but big isn't necessarily a positive thing. The doctor said that these babies are more likely to become obese when they get older. But the companies convince mothers that suckling is old-fashioned. You never see the high society divas on TV giving babies the nipple. Mothers figure the more formula they give, the more healthy, happy and smart their babies will be. So they spend money they haven't got on the products. Then, when the money runs out, they water down the formula.'

'And babies are getting sick?'

'The doctor had all the figures. She said that twenty-something per cent of babies that didn't get breastfed between one and twelve months were toast. She might have phrased that a different way, mind you. No antibodies in formula, you see, so no natural ability to fight diseases. She said that worldwide, optimal breast-feeding up to two years of age would prevent over a million deaths a year. Then there were the stats on child deaths in the region due to mothers confusing the packaging on formula and coffee creamer.'

'And where does she keep her figures?'

'On her laptop. In her room, with her stuff.'

'She left it behind?'

'She left everything. I got another text yesterday saying she'd come by to pick it up later.'

'She texted you?'

'Telling me not to worry about her. That's the third time.'

'That's weird. She can text but she can't talk? Can I look at her things?'

'OK.'

We walked to a low building with a corrugated roof behind the main complex. Dr Somluk's room was closed and padlocked.

'Has anyone been here since she left?' I asked.

'Only the policeman as far as I know.'

'Tall? Gay?'

'That's the one. The way he was dressed, I didn't believe he was a policeman. I asked him to show me some ID. He whipped out his Thai Savings Bank ATM card.'

'And that got him into this room?'

'He said he was a friend of yours.'

'I'll have to get him to stop doing that.'

Da found the room key on a ring of twenty or so similar keys and opened the padlock. The room was sparse and tiny. There was one small bed and a foldable plastic closet with a zip door. In my mind there were two types of doctors; those who died of malaria working for the natives and those that drove Mercedes and had air-conditioned toilets. This was a jungle doctor. I unzipped the closet. Her clothes were piled in two neat stacks. Hanging from loops were two white coats and a funeral dress. Below were two pairs of shoes, one black, one white, a small selection of books and a laptop. I took out the books and the computer, which didn't seem to have a lead. I hoped there'd be enough power in the battery to show me what was stored there. I turned it on and thumbed through the books while I was waiting. They were all medical apart from one which was titled *Advertising Practices in the Twenty-first Century*.

'This is all she has?' I asked.

'I guess.'

'No TV. What did she do in the evenings?'

'I don't know. I went back to my room in the village as soon as the clinic closed. There's a TV in the main building. She might have watched that although I never saw the lights on over there if I passed by at night. She stayed here all the time.'

'Anyone living in the other rooms?'

'No. Just her.'

'Did you ever see her using this laptop?'

'Yeah. All the time. She had a lot of down time.'

'Do you recall seeing a little rectangular gadget sticking out of the side of it?'

'Do you mean a dongle?'

Once Sissi had taught me how to use a dongle, I thought it would be very cool to spread the word to the locals. 'White man in big city, he make big magic. Small gadget put in computer. Pick up cell-phone signal.' But they all reacted with, 'You mean a dongle?' as if I were the last person to have heard of one. And they'd add insult to injury by saying, 'We had one last year but we upgraded to MiFi.'

'Yeah, a dongle,' I said.

'She was online, if that's what you're asking.'

'Thanks.'

The computer sang its annoying, 'New York, New York' ditty and the screen came to life. I went digging. The desktop had no files saved for easy reference. 'My documents' was empty. C drive was empty. The machine might as well have been straight from the shop.

'It's been wiped,' I said.

'I know,' said Da, who sat on the bed behind me looking over my shoulder.

'How do you know?'

'Your policeman checked it. In fact he asked all the same questions you just did.'

'Well, thanks for that information. What else did he ask?'

'If anyone else had a key to this room.'

'And you said . . .?'

'Just me and Dr Somluk. And he said somebody could easily have taken her key when she was abducted and come here in the dead of night and removed any evidence she had stored away.'

'Right. Anything else?'

'He asked if she had an external hard drive, or access to another computer and I said I'd seen her on the clinic's desktop computer from time to time.'

'You know you could have saved us a trip to this room if you'd told me all this in the beginning.'

'Sorry.'

'And I'm assuming you went to the clinic's computer and he turned it on and that was empty too.'

'Right.'

'And he went home.'

'No, I think he said he was heading back to the bar.'

'One more honest policeman. I suppose I'd better stay faithful to the joint investigation and take a look at that computer too.'

We returned to the surgery, where a very large mother was sitting patiently beside a red-welted child. I counted some thirty stings on him.

'Why isn't he crying?' I asked the mother.

'*Bai dteui*,' she said. It was a local version of betel leaves that slowed down reaction time and numbed the senses.

'Hornets?' Da asked. The mother nodded.

'He was up a tree and knocked it down by accident,' she said. 'He would of got bitten worse if he hadn't fell out the tree.'

'How did you get here?' said Da, opening the medicine cabinet.

'Motorcycle.'

'OK. I'm allowed to give him an oral dose of antihistamine,' said Da. 'Then we rush him down to the bike and you ride as fast as you can to Pak Nam hospital. Take him straight into Emergency.'

'All right,' said the mother, who had apparently chewed a few leaves herself.

After the shot, Da and the mother raced the boy downstairs. I turned on the clinic computer and found nothing but government training programmes and reference material. It was a nice machine, a Dell Optiplex; Thailand, with its ex-communications tsar PM, was big at dropping lumps of IT here and there for show without explaining how they might be best utilized. It was not online and apparently never had been, which posed an interesting question. If Dr Somluk had her own computer and was online, why would she bother with the desktop at all? And the answer was pretty damned obvious.

Nurse Da returned from her race, shaking her head.

'See?' she said. 'I could have fixed that myself. We've got all the right drugs here but I'm just a nurse. There are restrictions on what I'm allowed to do, which include saving a patient's life. I've got a cupboard full of adrenalin up here that would work instantaneously. But I'd be fired if I gave him a shot. That's why we have to have a doctor here. Then, if she screws up and the patient dies, the clinic has insurance cover. They might as well just employ a traffic cop to redirect emergencies from here to Pak Nam.'

'Feeling better now?'

'Yeah. I'm probably just worked up because Gogo got to see me flustered.'

'Gogo was here?'

'He just arrived downstairs.'

'I missed Gogo? Damn.'

'He dropped by to remind me of our date tonight. I invited him up to meet a real newspaper reporter but he couldn't stop. He said to say hello.'

'I've probably seen him around. What does he look like?'

'I'm not telling you.'

'One hint.'

'He's big. More than twice my weight. Eighty-five kilos. That's all I'm telling you.'

I had to smile at the image of skinny Da walking around with her fat Thai boyfriend. Still, whatever makes a girl happy. But that led my mind to the looks I got when I walked into the restaurant with Conrad. They were probably thinking, 'There's no accounting for taste.'

'So, anyway. Do you have a music system here?' I asked.

'What?'

'Somewhere you can rest after your busy day and listen to music, read magazines?'

'We've got a staffroom.'

'Lead me there.'

We walked to the end of the corridor to a room labelled STAFF RELAXATION CENTRE. It was furnished with comfortable chairs, a carpet of all things, and a flat screen TV. The whole centre was typical of big-country politics on small-town pockets. Buy things. Build things. Re-lay perfectly good roads. But take a lot of pictures. Political advancement was about buying favours and my modern nation's elders had decided country people were easily swayed by the sight of shiny beads. You couldn't take photos of human development so it took a back seat. Nurse Da had a shiny white health centre all to herself with a glass cabinet, a DVD player and a stack of music and movies.

I got to my knees, opened the smoked glass doors of the cabinet and thumbed through the discs. The one I was looking for was at the back. There was nothing written on it.

'Did Lieutenant Chompu get this far?' I asked, gloating slightly and waving the unmarked CD.

'No. Looks like you win,' said Da.

We returned to the office, put the CD in the computer drawer and I found it on the menu. There was one Word folder on it. When I clicked it some thirty or forty Word files came up with names like *Letter One to Medley. Reply to Letter Four from Medley.* The first letter was dated April. That would have been two months before Dr Somluk first started working at the Maprao clinic. When she was still at the Regional Clinic Allocations Department with Dr June. I opened that first letter to Medley and Da leaned over my shoulder to read it.

To Medley Regional Office, Bangkok

Dear Sirs,

My name is Dr Somluk Shinabut and I am working at the Chumphon Regional Clinic Allocations Department based at the Lang Suan hospital in the south of Thailand. I have recently become aware, through my work here, that your rather forceful advertising campaigns on our national television stations and in the popular press are having a negating effect on our rural efforts to encourage women to provide breast milk for their infants.

I am enthusiastic about the use of your product (budget permitting) when, due to extreme conditions, a woman is unable to breastfeed. But even using your product as a supplement interferes with the natural process of suckling. Your company continues to promote formula as a supplement because you know that formula babies stop taking mother's milk and the supply dries up sooner as a result. I am concerned that an increasing number of mothers are getting the wrong message from your ambiguous advertisements – that they should abandon breastfeeding in order to give their babies a better chance to be strong and healthy. You make astounding claims that formula babies have a higher IQ, are stronger and have better digestion and immune systems. As you know, this is clearly not the case.

I also remind you that your formula needs to be mixed with water, and many rural communities still rely on well- or river-water and live in unhygienic conditions. This is clearly far more dangerous for babies than taking mother's milk regularly.

In 1981, your company signed the International Code on the Marketing of Breast Milk Substitutes, which was drafted to protect the culture of breastfeeding by controlling the marketing of formula products throughout the world. You are clearly not operating under the spirit of that agreement. In fact, you seem to have refocused your

efforts on Third World countries where you believe health
workers are easier to manipulate. Well, health workers in
Thailand are neither gullible nor stupid and we will not
allow you to endanger the health of our children in your
quest for higher profits.

   Sincerely
   Dr Somluk Shinabut

I scrolled down to find a reasonable English translation of the same letter addressed to Medley's head office in Switzerland.

'Wow,' said Da. 'She was. . .? Wow. And she sent that to Europe?'

'Looks like it.'

'She's got balls.'

'She certainly has. And I doubt whether this stock reply from the Bangkok office shrank those danglers even the slightest.'

To Dr Somluk Shinabut

Dear Doctor,

   We at Medley always appreciate comments and opin-
ions from health professionals in the field. We may be a
multinational corporation but one valuable suggestion
from a doctor in even the smallest village in a developing
country has the power to change an entire national
policy.

We have noted your comments and our Public Relations department is, at this very moment, making enquiries into the practices in your region and will pursue every effort to address any misunderstandings or misrepresentations.

As a result of this, we trust that matters will be resolved to your satisfaction in the very near future.

Yours sincerely

Medley Customer Relations Department, Bangkok.

'It was nice that they wrote back,' said Da.

'Da, are you kidding? They didn't write back. They just cut and pasted Dr Somluk's name and the date on their form letter and returned it. I doubt anyone even bothered to read it. And Europe would leave these regional hiccups for their regional office to take care of. It was a bullshit response and Somluk knew it.'

I opened a later correspondence and scanned through it.

'Huh! And so we get to letter number thirteen,' I said. 'She's already left the regional office and been transferred down here to Maprao. And poor old Dr Somluk knows that she still hasn't been referred to an actual person who gives a monkey's bum. She knows she can discard the politeness and be reckless. Perhaps then someone might take notice.'

I smiled as I imagined her typing this.

Dear Idiots at Medley,

Thank you for not replying in person to any of my letters, which have articulated why children in my region have been dying unnecessarily as a result of your illegal and irresponsible misrepresentation of facts. I thought you might enjoy one more anecdote from an insignificant rural doctor. Now that I'm working directly in the field I see even more clearly how evil you are.

In the same aisle as your life-giving, godforsaken formula, are your own dairy creamers, coffee whiteners with the same grinning teddy bear on the packet. The same packaging. But so much cheaper than formula, and such a better option. And, congratulations. Word is out that children given coffee creamer from an early age are fatter and jollier than kids that aren't. I even saw a TV spot from a famous actress who held up her bloated baby to the camera. And I see them here in the villages. They really are round and chubby and every one of them is undernourished and suffering from anaemia.

You are so clever. You're getting away with murder. But I'm not going to rest until I let the world know how despicable you are. I'll stop you, I swear I will. I have become involved with a number of online organizations that already know what you're doing. My experiences have been posted there. Soon, everyone will know. Remember this name. You'll be hearing a lot of it.

Dr Somluk Shinabut

'She's starting to sound a bit . . .'

'Fanatical?'

'Yes,' said Da. 'Paranoid, even.'

'Paranoid doesn't always mean wrong,' I said, although that was probably an oxymoron.

'You'd have dealings with local health workers,' I said. 'What do they say about all this?'

'They're all really big on formula.'

'You think this is just another one of your Dr Somluk's mental symptoms?'

Da thought about it for a while.

'No. I don't know,' she said. 'She's a troubled woman for sure, but she has a good heart. Ooh.'

'What?'

'Do you think she might be on the run from the Medley people?'

'I doubt multinational milk companies hire hitmen to deal with troublesome correspondents. But I guess they could make life uncomfortable. Look at this last letter from the Medley Legal Department.'

Attention: Dr Somluk Shinabut

The Medley Corporation and its associates take personal threats very seriously. We would prefer to avoid pursuing legal proceedings against you but if you continue with this personal vendetta based on groundless accusations and insinuations we will have no choice other than to lodge libel charges with the police and pursue the matter in court.

'Looks like the doctor got somebody's attention after all,' I said.

'She hit a nerve, right enough,' said Da.

'The internet,' I said. 'It can make a lion of the tiniest ant.'

That wasn't my line. I think Donald Trump or somebody said it.

'Can I take the disc and go through it at home?' I asked.

'No problem.'

Back at the resort, I saw a familiar motorcycle sidecar combo in the car park. Captain Kow had presumably removed the fried-fish ball attachment to make space for his beloved to sit. Now that was class. I found the happy couple on Mair's veranda, holding hands. Mair was gloriously pretty in a hibiscus print frock and an unashamed beaming smile. Sitting opposite were Arny and Grandad Jah.

'Well, at last you bother to show up,' said Grandad.

'Hello, Mair,' I said. 'Sea too rough for you, was it?'

'I could have handled it,' said Mair. 'But your father insisted I come ashore.'

I still couldn't get used to that 'Father' tag.

'How long did you last?' I asked.

'Half an hour,' said Grandad. 'Some tough fisherman, he is.'

'So, where have you been?' I asked.

'The One Hotel in Surat,' said Mair. 'It was a first honeymoon. We never did have one back then.'

'And here we were worried frantic about you and there you were fornicating on a bed in a sleazy motel,' said Grandad.

I don't recall Grandad worrying, or even mentioning Mair in all the time she was gone. But he did have a point.

'Couldn't you have phoned?' I asked.

'I told her she should,' said the captain. 'But you know what she's like.'

I knew less and less what she was like.

'I wanted you all to get used to not having me around,' said Mair. 'It's like the mother hen leaving the hive and all the workers having to sort out where to store the honey without a technical advisor. And certainly without jars. It was such a lovely place and the staff were so polite.'

I assumed she'd stopped referring to the chicken hive.

'So, are we having our family powwow at last?' I asked, and speed-dialled Sissi for the quorum. It was one of the few things I'd learned to do on that phone.

'Not exactly,' said Mair. 'There's just the one thing that I need to clear up.'

'Hang on,' I said. The phone took its time. 'Siss? You busy? The seafaring mother has returned and she's got an announcement to make.'

'If she's pregnant I'm putting myself up for adoption,' said Sissi.

'Wait, I'm putting you on Skype and sitting you on a nice chair so you can see everyone. Comfortable?'

'Very. Hello, Mair.'

'Hello, darling,' said Mair. 'Now, isn't this lovely. We're all here together. It's quite exciting. Children, there's something I need to tell you about your father.'

'Huh. Some father,' said Grandad Jah.

Mair steeled herself and took a deep breath, like a gymnast before a floor routine. There was no *Titanic* smile.

'Well, that's just it, you see?' said Mair. 'Here you all are having bad thoughts about poor Captain Kow when it's me you should be blaming. The truth is I first met Kow here in Maprao thirty-eight years ago. Oh my. He was handsome and so virile. He could—'

'Mair, can we skip the details?' said the cell phone.

'I was so in love with him,' Mair continued, 'but he was a common fisherman and I was a university graduate. He was terribly unworldly.'

Captain Kow's face hardly changed its expression this whole time. There was still a slight crack of a smile between his lips. The merest shadow of the gap between his teeth.

203

'I thought how beautiful my children would be if he fathered them,' Mair continued. 'But I didn't want to live here. Oh my. If you think this is backward now, imagine what it was like thirty-eight years ago. It was prehysterical.'

I had visions of mad dinosaurs queuing up at the 7-Eleven.

'I wanted my children to grow up cultured,' Mair said. 'To give them a good, international upbringing. And I wanted you all to grow up in Chiang Mai. I frankly didn't think Kow would be able to advance you the way I hoped. I had your upbringings all worked out. Sissi, darling, I'm sorry you turned out female. I hadn't reckoned that into my calculations.'

'That's OK,' said the cell phone.

'If I'd married an educated man in the north, he would have insisted on a traditional upbringing for you. Whereas I wanted you to be children of the world. So . . . I hired Kow to come to Chiang Mai and be your father.'

'You what?'

On reflection, I think we all may have said that at the same time. It was the only instance I can recall us being coordinated as a family.

'Three years or three children. Whichever came first,' she said. 'That was the deal.'

'Oh, say this isn't happening,' said Grandad.

'I didn't want him around after three years, you see?'

said Mair. 'And he was really itching to get back to his sea and his squids. So it worked out quite well. You were his life experience – like Peace Crops. He took odd jobs in Chiang Mai, mostly labouring, just to keep himself from getting bored. Producing children isn't exactly an occupation, you see. Not for a man. Three ten-second spurts at the most. But I confess I did insist on a lot of practice. And we needed him around for signing documents and the like.'

I remember being speechless just four times in my life but never like this with my mouth open and my eyes bulging like an ornamental goldfish.

'Where did you get all this ... this procurement money from?' asked Grandad.

'Oh, he wasn't that expensive,' said Mair, the way you'd discuss a second-hand bicycle. 'And I'd put away quite a bit from when I was selling marijuana at the university.'

'You what?' said Grandad.

'Don't worry, Father. They still sold it at country markets back then. It wasn't actually illegal. And I only dealt to students. No chance of undercover cops spoiling that gig.'

Arny and I put our heads in our hands and the little screen Sissi was doing the same in Chiang Mai. Mair just rattled on as if she wasn't unleashing the dragons.

'And you all had a legal father without the negatives,' she said. 'When it was all over, we had one last night of

205

passion, I took him to the train station on my bicycle ...
actually he pedalled us there and I pedalled back alone.
And I thought that was that. Everything had gone so
smoothly.

'But then he started to write. That really wasn't part
of the deal. I supposed he must have jotted down the
address from the postal box, and once a month I'd get a
few lines telling me about Maprao and asking after you
lot. I didn't want to encourage him so I didn't reply.'

'What, never?' Sissi shouted.

'Not for the first twenty years,' she said.

I found my voice.

'And you kept writing, Captain Kow?' I asked.

'Every month. Regular as clockwork,' he said and
smiled so wide I could see his tonsils through the gap.

'Why?' asked Arny.

The captain leaned back on his chair, almost buck-
ling the plastic legs. He looked at us all in turn with an
expression of ... I suppose it was pride.

'Sometime in those three years I was up there in the
north, I fell in love with your mother,' he said. 'I knew
she didn't want me in her life but, well, it's like when
you've got a big fish on a fragile line. You can't give it
one big yank 'cause you know it'll snap. So you tug
gently and often and it tires the fish out.'

He grinned and I had a ghost image of those beautiful missing teeth.

'Isn't that romantic?' said Mair. 'He tugged on me till

I was completely tuckered out. The hook bloody inside my mouth to the point that I could only ingest passing plankton, because I couldn't chew on say, mackerel or sandfish. But whales . . . I mean look how big they grow on tiny little water vermin. If I'd been—'

'Mair!' Sissi shouted. 'Enough with the fish.'

'No need to shout,' said Mair.

'Go on,' I told her.

'It was the day Arny finished high school,' she said, 'and started his physical trainer's course. I felt . . . I felt that in your own unique ways you had excelled. I had produced three remarkable children. Not counting steroids, none of you were on drugs. No criminal records. You were all independent and so not main-stream, it made me cry with pride. So, I wrote to Kow to let him know. It was rather a long letter.'

'One hundred and thirty-four pages,' said Kow. 'A4.'

'Well, I had a lot to tell him,' said Mair. 'Sissi, your rise in show business and leanings towards severing your links to manhood. Jimm and your remarkable intelligence and language skills. Arny's magnificent body. I wanted Kow to see how beautiful you'd all turned out. So I sent photos.'

'Two hundred and sixty-one,' said the captain. 'Taken from the day I left through every birthday and school award and beauty competition and hospital visit.'

'And so we became penfriends,' said Mair. 'And after all those years of hearing about Maprao, I started to fall

207

in love with the place and, very slowly, with the man who'd tugged on me all that time. And when I found that my mind was starting to go, all I could think of was for all of us to be together here in the place that Sissi was conceived.'

'Wait!' shouted the cell phone. 'I'm a bastard?'

'Of course you aren't,' said Mair. 'We tied the knot right here at the Ny Kow Temple. You were the result of that blessed, star-filled wedding night on the beach, right here when it was still deserted and unpolluted and startlingly beautiful. Just like you.'

She squeezed Captain Kow's hand and they stared into each other's eyes like models in an ancient chocolate commercial.

There was nothing more to be said. It was hard to decide who to hate first; my mother, who'd hired a fisherman's son to fertilize her, or the squid boy for agreeing to . . . damn, there wasn't even a word for it. We all walked away from that meeting in zombie silence. The cell phone was speechless in my hand. I waded through the beach garbage down to the angry surf and squinted into the salt wind. It was a long while before I raised Sissi to my ear.

'You still there, Sis?'

'Just.'

'Can we . . .?'

'Not talk about it?'

'I think I need time for this one.'

'We all do.'

'I'll call you later.'

'All right.'

I sat on a Brother printer, circa 1980, and was wondering whether there were entire reefs of discarded IT equipment down in the Gulf that would one day regenerate the fish stocks, when the phone vibrated in my hand.

'No, wait. I have information,' said my sister. 'Sorry, I forgot.'

A distraction. Perfect.

'Your conference in Chumphon,' she said. 'You were wondering why your Dr Somluk was so upset about who sponsored Dr Bangkok?'

'Right.'

'Well, I'm thinking she just targeted the biggest name as an example.'

'What does that mean?'

'It means I went through the accounts of all the speakers at that conference. Locals and overseas experts. And you know what? Every last one of them was paid to be there by the Medley umbrella organization, the TFG. And I looked at the papers. Virtually all of them dealt with the inherent dangers of breastfeeding in rural communities. They had scientific data to support their arguments. And you know who comprised eighty per cent of the participants?'

'Midwives?'

'And nursery school teachers,' she said.

'So, it was a set-up,' I said. 'Select your speakers. Tell 'em what to say. Fill the place with professionals who work directly with mothers and mail them a lot of free samples to get them hooked on the product. Off they go to spread the word. Formula is the future. Mother Nature got it wrong. This is what the Lord Buddha would have given pregnant women if only he'd had access to a clean chemistry lab. But I still don't understand why the experts would be so easily lured into the honeytrap, Sis. Don't any of them have morals?'

'There are things more important than morals, Jimm.'

'Like money?'

'Like how to take care of an elderly mother.'

'You found something?'

'Dr Aisa, your Bangkok specialist. She has a mother in a hospice. Cancer. She's been hanging on for almost two years. Up until a year ago, Dr Bangkok was a prominent voice against the abuse of formula. She was the same type of thorn in the side of Medley that your Dr Somluk is threatening to be. Then, quite out of the blue, she had a change of heart. New research findings. Improved production methods. New additives. Perhaps formula wasn't quite as bad as she'd thought.'

'And her mother's hospice care is miraculously taken care of.'

'You've got it.'

'That's why Dr Somluk targeted Dr B. These people are monsters. We have to find Somluk. She's hiding out somewhere in need of friends. She's too afraid of her phone being tapped to call old colleagues. I reckon she's been threatened to keep her mouth shut.'

'Or someone's already shut it for her.'

I shuddered at that possibility.

'I'm into Dr Somluk's email account,' said Sissi. 'There have been no sent messages for seven days. You might be right. She might be playing it cool. As soon as she feels confident enough to get in touch with anyone I'll be on it.'

'I just . . .'

'What?'

'I just wonder whether big business might be on it too. Maybe they really are looking for her.'

I was on my way back to my cabin when Grandad Jah popped out from behind a hedge like an anorexic mugger. I was afraid he might want to engage me in a debate on why none of us look like Captain Kow . . . or each other. But like all of us he was opting to keep quiet on the subject.

'I've been watching your Burmese,' he said.

'Good man.'

'They're both illegal.'

'You can tell that just by watching them?'

'They live in a room in Kor Kow Temple, just down from your elderly boyfriend's place. He pays protection money to the nun there.'

'So she doesn't beat them up?'

'So she doesn't report them to the police. I went through their belongings while they were up at the house. They are not married.'

'Wow. All this in one day? I'm impressed. Are they living in sin?'

'They're brother and sister.'

'What? The nun told you?'

'There were photographs of the pair of them from a young age. With parents. Progressing through school. It was a rural school where all the pupils studied in one room. There was a photo with the kids' names written in English. Your Burmese have the same surname. I rather doubt they got married when they were five.'

'So, why would they pretend to be married now?'

'As yet I do not have an answer to that question.'

'Any insights into the machete or the sack?'

'No indications from their room. They may have a hiding place. I shall endeavour to find it. Do you happen to know when your author might be away from home?'

'He's in Bangkok.'

'Perfect. A rowing boat, a pair of binoculars and the property without its master could yield up a vast array of data. People in glass houses should not expect to keep secrets.'

CHAPTER TWELVE

IT IS OUR PRESSURE IF YOU COME AGAIN
(guest house sign)

Given her less-than-truthful replies to my earlier questions, I decided to pay another visit to Dr June, the head of the Regional Clinic Allocations Department at Lang Suan Hospital. To add weight to this second interview I took my own policeman. Lieutenant Chompu, on day five of his programme to recover from homosexuality, was still hiding from the psychologist in one of our cabins. Even though the income at our resort in the monsoon season was approximately zero, I hadn't charged him for the room, so he owed me. He was miffed that I'd aced him on the CD clue so he'd been particularly pedantic going through Dr Somluk's files. She was a one-woman campaign. If you believed everything she wrote, you'd have to think Medley had shares in the Thai Ministry of Health. The company sponsored doctor fact-finding missions and mother-and-child picnics and half a dozen TV spots on childcare issues. Medley incarnate was a six-foot blue teddy bear who cuddled overweight toddlers in shopping malls all over the country. The world according to Dr Somluk was snowing formula. The new operating theatre at the Lang Suan hospital had been funded quite unashamedly by Medcafé. The blue bear would be appearing in person next month to cut the ribbon and officially open this state-of-the-art medical facility. A five-metre-high poster to that effect had been erected on the highway in front of the hospital.

Chompu and I had come to discuss this and other matters. We were directed towards the new building, latticed with bamboo scaffolding that tentatively supported a dozen painters arranged like shelf ornaments. We found Dr June inside haranguing the foreman of the work team. She was not leaning on the side of diplomacy and her regional accent became more pronounced the louder she shouted.

'Because this isn't a brothel,' she said. 'If I'd wanted red floor tiles I would have ordered red floor tiles. Did you ever consider that?'

The southern building contractor smiled angrily.

'We just thought it wouldn't show the blood so much,' he said.

'Oh, that's so considerate of you,' said Dr June. 'Goodness knows we wouldn't want to know where the blood was so we could clean it up.'

'But—'

'White,' she yelled. 'Tear up these ridiculous things and find me some white ones. Either that or I'll find a foreman who knows how to read plans and follow instructions.'

Chompu and I had been standing in the ante-room during this exchange. A lot of money had been pumped into the space where the surgeons would wash and have a quick bite to eat before heading into the cutting arena. It contained splendid stainless steel sink units, an off-suite shower stall and toilet, an air-conditioning unit the size of Norway, and a fully equipped emergency firefighting cabinet with, amongst other things, a fifty metre hose. There was a flat-screen computer, and a large refrigerator. As often happens, the equipment for the theatre itself had arrived long before the room was completed, so it was still packaged and piled up to the ceiling.

Dr June turned and saw us in the doorway. She closed her eyes as if to say 'Haven't I had enough to deal with for one day?'

'I take it you haven't found her,' she said, walking between us and not stopping. We followed her out of the new building and across the car park.

'I'm not surprised,' she continued. 'People like Dr Somluk make enemies. Eventually she'll push just a bit too far.'

'There are one or two things we need to discuss with you,' said Chompu in his rehearsed baritone.

She stopped and turned to us.

'We?' she said. 'Has the police force adopted a community buddy system I haven't heard about?'

'If we could go to your office . . .' he said.

'I'm sorry. I have no time for this,' she replied.

'Doctor,' he said, 'we can either talk here, or I'll have no choice but to take you to the police station and get a statement from you there.'

Chom and I had once discussed the dropping of that line. It only ever worked in the movies. Most people knew you weren't obliged to go to the police station just because a policeman told you to.

'Are you arresting me?' she asked.

'I'm asking you . . . nicely.'

She looked at her damned watch.

'You can have ten minutes.'

'Thank you.'

We passed Dr Niramon whose name began with M as we neared the office. Dr June became a much nicer person when she saw her. They smiled and joked and Dr June even gave her a little squeeze on the arm. Dr Niramon said hello to Chompu and skipped off down the corridor.

'She seems happy in her work,' said Chompu.

'She's new,' said Dr June. 'They all start off enthusiastic. She'll leave soon enough. They all do. She's already been hinting at a move.'

She sat at her desk. The guest chair had vanished,

leaving a two-seater couch against the far wall. Without any discussion Chom and I grabbed an end each and carried it to Dr June's desk.

'Feel free to rearrange my furniture,' she said.

'Thank you,' I replied.

We sat. Dr June looked at her watch. Our time had begun.

'Firstly,' said Chompu, 'I need to point out that withholding information from a police officer is a criminal offence.'

'I'll bear that in mind if ever I find myself doing it,' she said.

'But you've already done it,' said Chompu.

'I most certainly have not.'

'You led me to believe that you weren't at the conference in Chumphon,' he said.

'As I never commented on my attendance, one would have to conclude that you led yourself.'

'You failed to mention that you organized the conference.'

'You didn't ask.'

'You failed to mention you were in attendance when Dr Somluk was forcibly removed from the microphone and dragged out of the conference room.'

Me and Chom had talked about this too. It was a bit of a bluff. We weren't to know whether she was in the room at the time, but conference organizers are never far away from events.

'Again,' she said. 'You didn't ask.'

'Did you order her removal from the microphone?'

'We had ushers who had been briefed to limit microphone time for troublemakers.'

'Dr Somluk had been there for no longer than ten seconds. She'd barely had time to ask her question before the bouncers were on her,' I said, even though I'd promised to keep my mouth shut.

'I . . . I had been expecting trouble from Dr Somluk,' she said.

'Why?' Chompu asked.

'Because she's intent on being confrontational.'

'But why were you expecting her to be trouble at that particular conference?'

'She'd announced to her fellow conspiracy theorists that she would interrupt us.'

'And where did she announce this?'

'On the internet. Any number of misguided people can find companionship there.'

'How do you know?'

'Know what?'

'About her internet activities.'

'The internet is available to everyone.'

'So you Googled her? Checked all the websites to see if she'd written to them?'

'No, I'm not . . . I'm not obsessed with her.'

My turn.

'So, accidentally, you're surfing the net for surgical

trusses and you come across Dr Somluk's announcement to a subversive site?'

So much for me keeping my mouth shut.

'No.'

'Then how did you find this announcement?' I asked.

'Somebody sent it to me.'

'Who?'

'I don't believe I'm obliged to be interrogated by a holiday resort cook,' she said.

Ooh. That hurt.

'Then you can tell me,' said Chompu. 'Who sent you Dr Somluk's announcement?'

'A friend.'

'A friend with a team of employees with nothing to do but name-search?' I said.

'Just a friend,' she said and turned to Chompu. 'Look, what is this? You can't just bring your girlfriend along on a police enquiry, you know?'

'I'm gay,' he smiled, which completely derailed her.

'Why didn't you tell me Dr Somluk was working here with you?' I asked while she was still off the track.

'It wasn't relevant.'

'Why would you work alongside someone who so violently disagreed with your policies?'

Dr June breathed deeply to compose herself.

'In the beginning there were no conflicts,' she said. 'I admired her spirit, her attitude. She worked hard. We soon became close. I'd taken note of the lack of longevity in her job records, but I chose to put that down to the spirit of adventure. New thrills and experiences. I'm an administrator. I sit. I write miserable papers on child morbidity for paediatric journals. She was different. She went out and did things. I respected that. It was six months before she started her rants.'

'Her tirade against Medley?'

'Yes. But I got the feeling if it hadn't been that, it would have been something else. Medley has been indispensable for rural health centres and hospitals like this. If it hadn't been for them, a lot of smaller clinics would have been forced to close down. They sponsor training for nurses. They buy us equipment.'

'And ask nothing in return but for you to convince nursing mothers to keep their bras on,' I said.

'There is nothing unhealthy about formula,' she said.

'Dr Somluk didn't think so.'

'Which is why we parted company. I was sorry to lose her, an able deputy. But she deserted the team. If she'd merely put it down as a difference of opinion we could have remained friends. But there was the campaign. We've already lost sponsorship deals as a result of it. You have to recognize this as what it is. A bitter woman looking to rock whatever boat she happened to be riding on.'

'Do you have any idea where she might be?' Chompu asked.

'I haven't a clue,' she said. 'On that Sunday, my ushers

escorted her to her car and she drove off. She didn't go back to the Maprao clinic. I haven't heard from her since.'

'Why did you think it necessary to keep quiet about all this?' he asked.

She looked down at her desk and shook her head.

'Lieutenant,' she said. 'Despite everything she'd done, I . . . I didn't want to be the one to end her livelihood. I still believed her career was salvageable. If she could have just accepted some help – I mean some professional, psychological help – I believe she could have had many productive years ahead of her. And, to tell the truth, she really was a lovely person. A good heart. You know? That's hard to find these days.'

We drove away from the hospital in Chom's airconditioned, SUV police Batmobile. Our police force allows officers to use their private vehicles on the job as long as they look ominous and have enough roof space to attach a flashing light. Chom had wealthy parents so the SUV was the least they could do. Donna Summers blasted from the quad speakers. I turned her down.

'Did you notice the switch to past tense there at the end?' I said.

'It could just mean Dr Somluk stopped being lovely. It happens.'

'Or she stopped being Dr Somluk,' I said. 'I need Sissi.'

I speed-dialled my sister on my smartphone. While I waited, Chom said, 'If you're going to suggest anything illegal I can't be a part of it. I'm going to put my fingers in my ears.'

'And steer with what?'

'Have you never watched the monkeys unscrew the coconuts from the trees with their tails?'

'You wish . . . Siss?'

'Hello, my lovely one,' came my sister's voice.

'You sound chirpy.'

'I just traced an Estonian computer dating scammer all the way back to his living room. I arranged for a couple of hoods I know in Tallinn to go there and beat him up.'

'You're such a romantic.'

'I have no pity for men who break hearts. So, what unpaid task do you have for me now?'

'We're still looking for Dr Somluk. She posted her intention to disrupt the Chumphon conference on some website. No idea where. How hard would it be to find that site and trace back anyone who accessed it and read her post?'

'For a human being? Virtually impossible. But me . . .?'

'Great.'

'You wouldn't be searching for the Medley Mobster Department by any chance?'

'I think someone at Medley found Dr Somluk's threat and passed the information on to Dr June. If you can use your magic to locate that communiqué, it would be very useful to know what other messages passed between them.'

'You do realize any dirty stuff would never be traceable back to Medley? These people invest a lot of money in covering their tracks. They've probably outsourced their threats and intimidation to Mumbai.'

'I don't care for now. I just want to see what instructions were passed along to shut Dr Somluk up.'

'You surely don't think Dr June buried her in cement?'

'No. But half of her programmes are sponsored by Medley so it's quite possible she's sold her soul to formula like all the doctors at the conference. I think her reputation rests on her good relations with her sponsor. Maprao would be a very small blip on the Medley radar but the web makes heroes of blips. They could see Dr Somluk getting bigger. They might have dug the dirt and found something in her past to shut her up. Wherever it is, she's gone to ground. I want to root her out and make this all right.'

'My little sister. The Aung San Suu Kyi of breast milk.'

'Er . . . thanks?'

I turned off the phone and had one other thought.

'Chom?'

'Yes?'

'How do you think Dr June knew I was a cook in a resort?'

Chompu and I drove directly to the resort car park and covered the SUV with a tarpaulin. I doubted the psychologist from the police ministry was cruising the streets looking for him, but he'd decided to play it safe, especially as my name had come up in group therapy. The shrink had asked him to name a male and female role model in his life. He'd cited Bird McIntyre, the singer, and me. When asked to hypothetically make the choice as to which he would sooner be he'd chosen me. But that was only because Bird was too gay even for him. The police psych department probably had my address on file.

Captain Kow was sitting on a fold-up chair at the edge of the car park, looking out to sea. I wanted to ignore him but Chompu stopped and stood beside him. He hadn't yet heard of our tainted rent-a-dad history.

'See anything?' he asked.

'Storm,' said the captain. 'Big one. Tomorrow. Maybe the next day. Not violent but significant. Could be the highest tide we've seen down here for a long time.'

'Awesome,' said Chom. 'That you can tell all that just by studying the whitecaps, the scent of the brine, the mauve clouds gathering on the horizon.'

The captain reached into his right ear and pulled out the earphone connected to the transistor radio in his jacket pocket.

'Government weather report,' said Kow and laughed. 'There was a time we could predict the weather to

224

within a centimetre of rain. I could have told you the height and shape of tomorrow's waves but we've screwed it all up. You and me and the lords of development. We take from nature and give nothing back. Ten years ago we'd listen to weather broadcasts and have a good laugh. We knew they made it up as they went along. Then all the natural indicators vanished: the ants' nests, the early blooms, the migrations, the revolving seasons of sea life. It all went arse upward. Now the radio's the nearest we can get to knowing what to expect. We deserve whatever Mother Nature chucks at us.'

That was him. That was the Captain Kow I'd grown to respect before I knew he'd sired me. Honest. Knowledgeable. Tied to the sea. He must have had a miserable time in landlocked Chiang Mai. He didn't do it for the money. I knew that much. He followed my mother. He'd always loved her. A man doesn't give up all this for a contract. It was at that moment I decided to cancel my hatred of him. I thought I might even try to call him Dad.

A text message tinkled from my phone.

Bangkok boring. Looking forward to Saturday. Conrad.

It was astounding how – all right, not love, but romance – scented everything around you. How the fact that somebody attractive found you interesting made even the most mundane activities fascinating. I descaled our lunch mackerel and laughed as the scales sprang into the air and fell like snowdrops to the ground. I'd never before noticed anything erotic about slicing open a fish and removing its intestines. Never spent so long staring at a carrot before slicing it. This was what – not love, but romance – did to you. Trust Grandad to bring you back to earth.

'You put any more MSG in there and I'll be preserved for life.'

He was leaning over my shoulder in the kitchen. I hated it when he did that.

'Isn't that what you've been hoping for?' I asked.

'I want to be preserved as a living person, not a dead one.'

'Shouldn't you be in a rowing boat spying on the glass house?'

'Not much to be learned there.'

'Why not?'

'Your Burmese aren't likely to get up to anything until your writer leaves for Bangkok.'

'He's already in Bangkok.'

'Not as of half an hour ago he wasn't.'

CHAPTER THIRTEEN

ROOM FOR RANT
(real estate)

I sat with the dogs on my veranda. Gogo was almost back to her old disagreeable self, growling at the other two. Sticky was chewing a shoe I didn't recognize. Lieutenant Chompu was seated opposite me, raising his feet every time mange-ridden Beer nuzzled up to him.

'Just kick her, Chom,' I said. 'She's a Thai dog. She'd appreciate the discipline.'

'Right. And get mange-foot and have it slowly fall off.'

'That's leprosy. It's one of the few diseases she hasn't got.'

'It's nice to see you're feeling chirpier.'

It was three p.m. and we were on our second glass of Chilean red. The wind had died down and we were in another one of those ominous lulls. The prediction of a storm surge in our area had even made a TV appearance.

'No,' I said. 'Even before the wine I was fine. I mean, I don't have any claim over him. He can go where he likes whenever he wants. I just don't see any point in pretending he's in Bangkok when he's actually here at his house.'

'There could be any number of reasons,' said Chom. 'He didn't like you in the first place. He's gone off you. He started to notice your annoying habits. He doe—'

'All right. Thanks.'

'You know I'm teasing. He probably came back early because he misses you.'

'Then why doesn't he phone me?'

'Call him.'

'I don't want to sound like a desperate girlfriend.'

'You don't have to. Lie. You're a grand mistress at that. Ask him if he can pick you something up in Bangkok.'

'Like what?'

'Something you can't get down here.'

'Well that's just about everything, Chom.'

'All right. Ask him for pizza. They sell it at Suvanaphum Airport.'

'If they believe you can hijack an aircraft with nail clippers, just think how much mayhem you could cause with hot cheese. They wouldn't let him on the flight.'

'Jimm, it doesn't matter. He's here.'

'Right.'

So I called his number, or at least the number he'd

texted me from, but that same silly-voiced mutant insisted it didn't exist. I've always wanted someone to invent a cell-phone avatar who could take on those annoying recorded messages. Engage them in a dialogue. Slap 'em around the head. But I was probably just venting my ire. On reflection, that was probably the moment I slammed my phone down on the side table and didn't notice Sticky sneak up behind me and run off with it in his mouth. I should have known better than to think he wouldn't have been fascinated by a smartphone. If I'd just been a little bit more careful all the subsequent misunderstandings and disasters could have been averted. And one more person might still have been alive at the end of it all. That's a lot of responsibility on the shoulders of one fat puppy, but theft is a crime against society and he has to accept the consequences of his actions.

'No answer?' Chompu asked, unnecessarily.

'It's not a big deal,' I said, and quaffed my mid-afternoon red.

'There is one eventuality we haven't taken into account,' said Chompu.

'That we're figures in a computer game and none of us is real?'

'How old is your grandad?'

'Two . . . maybe three hundred.'

'Well, we're trusting his word that he saw your author in his house from however many metres whilst in a rowing boat on the high sea. It could have been the maid's brother, for all we know, or a house guest, or some full-length cardboard cut-out of the writer for tourists to take photos with. Did Grandad Jah ever meet Coralbank?'

'Not that I know.'

'There you go then. We're relying on the word of a senile, coffin-carving ex-cop. Perhaps we should give your man some leeway. Innocent until proven guilty. At least long enough to squeeze in one more session of scrumptious loving.'

I suddenly felt a whole lot better. I smiled. From my balcony we could see Mair planting potatoes on the beach. She argued that potatoes needed water to grow and salt to taste. She cited potato chips and French fries as evidence. So the logical place to plant them was in a spot where they'd get both. Damn, I wanted to blame her for depriving us of a real father but, although she was in there somewhere – that open-minded, independent, hippy single-mother – we could no longer untangle her from all the other Mairs she'd become.

'A bit early to start drinking, isn't it?' came a voice.

The dogs barked half-heartedly, despite the fact out-siders had snuck up on us from the rear. Chompu and I looked back to see Ed the grass man with a small ver-sion of Shrek in a blue waistcoat.

'My fault entirely,' said Chompu, who had long

230

adored Ed and was convinced the man's infatuation with women was a phase he'd get over.

'We're celebrating,' he continued. 'Today was the final day of my course. I passed.'

'Congratulations,' said Ed. 'What are you now?'

'Unambiguous. Second grade.'

Ed didn't seem to understand or care.

'Who's your friend, Ed?' I asked.

'This is Ad,' said Ed. 'As you see from his waistcoat, he's a motorcycle taxi driver. Ad's got a sidecar so he gets all the big jobs, the removals and family excursions. Ad's got a story I think you'd be interested to hear.'

'Ooh, good. A story,' said Chompu. 'I love stories.'

We unstacked two more plastic chairs and sat in a circle. Ad cleared his throat.

'I got a call on my cell,' he said. 'Asking me to go up to that house up by Kor Kow Temple. Pick something up. It was a girl that called. Not Thai. Had trouble understanding her at first. Then I got it. I rode there at about eight. Dark as shit up there and me with only a tail light to see by. Then I reached the lights on the gate and some little boy was waving me in. I went in and down to the house and there was the woman standing in the driveway. Burmese, she was. She had two polystyrene ice chests wrapped up with masking tape. There was a smell. My nose is messed up after all them years in the methylated spirit factory but that I could smell.

Horrible, it was. Sweet and sour, like a dead body sprayed with air freshener.'

Me and Chompu sat spellbound.

'But money's money,' said Ad, 'and they helped me lug the chests onto the side car and told me to take them down to Uaychai bus terminal. Someone would meet me there and take possession, they told me. There weren't any buses due so the place was deserted. I did a circuit around the terminal and suddenly this grubby-looking guy steps out of the shadows and jumps in front of me like he was going to rob me. I stopped and he handed me an envelope with money in it. The fee I'd agreed with the woman at the house. He unloaded the chests and I drove off. I could still smell the stink on me a week after.'

'Do you recall what date this was?' I asked.

'December the thirteenth. Birthday of Ban Sipan, national team midfielder.'

I thanked Ad, gave him petrol money for his trouble and he rode off. That left me and Chompu and Ed staring at each other. A cold wind had just risen from the Gulf and Mair was no longer down on the beach.

'Don't be ridiculous,' I said.

'Your mother said she saw the writer's wife on the eleventh,' said Ed. 'Nobody saw her leave the house.'

'Of course not,' I argued. 'He would have taken her to the station or the airport in his truck.'

'Or sent her to the bus terminal in ice chests,' said Chompu.

232

'Oh, don't you start,' I said. 'Ed, shame on you for even suggesting it. I know what brought all this on.'

'And what would that be?' he asked.

'You're jealous. You wouldn't have gone to all this trouble if you weren't.'

'I am not. He's bad news, Jimm. He's dangerous.'

'And what evidence do you have to support that claim?'

'I can tell you things about him.'

'You know? I think I've heard more than enough already.'

'He's had—'

'Like I say, Ed. You aren't welcome here any more. Go and get yourself a free perm or something.'

He looked at me as if I'd run over his favourite cat with a steamroller. He stood and the plastic chair fell backwards. He didn't bother to pick it up. He stepped off the balcony and seemed to be carried off in a gust of wind.

'That was dramatic,' said Chompu, helping himself to another glass of red.

'Men!' I said.

'He went to a lot of trouble.'

'You only want the ones that you can't get,' I reminded him.

'"Desperado". Eagles. Timeless,' he said. 'But what if he's right?'

'You know what the only relevant part of that story was?'

'All of it?'

'No. The characters. Did you see Conrad in it? No. The Burmese. They called the taxi. They loaded the chests. If there's anything dodgy going on up in that house, that's where we should be looking. What if the pretty wife went down to the temple to say hello to her faithful staff and A brained her with a hammer? If Conrad had done it, why would he get the staff to clean up after him? He'd just drive her body off in his tinted SUV and dump her somewhere. No, it's her, A. She's the one who threatened me. Tried to poison our beloved dogs. If anyone did away with Conrad's wife she's the one we should be looking at. The second threat said "I told you to keep off. This will happen to you if you don't." What if A and her brother are clearing the field so A can move in? She's educated. She's probably attractive under all that powder gunk. And I have no doubt she's fallen in love with him.'

'And you have evidence that connects her to all of this?'

'Almost.'

Mair's arrival on the veranda changed the mood somewhat. The dogs went nuts with excitement.

'Who's for a naked swim?' she said.

She was dressed in a white towelling robe with the words *The One Hotel* embroidered on the pocket.

'Mair,' I said. 'If you take off that robe I'll shoot you.'

'It's getting really choppy out there,' Chompu told her.

234

'You youngsters,' she said. 'You've lost the spark. In Portugal I was bodysurfing waves taller than these coconut trees.'

As far as I knew she'd never been to Europe.

'There's a lot of sea junk flying around out there, Mair,' I said. 'You might get crushed under a discarded tool shed.'

'Nobody discards tool sheds,' she said. 'Tools are very expensive and you need a dry environment with a sturdy roof to keep them in good condition. And I didn't come all this way to discuss such nonsense. I have something to tell you.'

'What?'

'Well, if you hadn't tossed my mind around this way and that I'd remember, wouldn't I? Still, it will come to me eventually.'

She turned to go, then stopped.

'No. I have it. There's a message to Miss Jimm, in English, pinned to the front of the shop. That was it. Now. The captain's waiting for me.'

She went off to join Captain Kow in the high tide garbage swill and I did my lumpy version of 'jogging' down to our shop. Chompu followed. The note delivery had been comparatively dull. There was no cleaver attached, just a single thumb tack. I looked for wires that might trigger underground mines but there were none. It appeared to be just a note flapping in the wind. I took it down and read it.

Darling Jimm,

This is my surprise. I came back early because I couldn't stand being away from you. Don't tell anyone. You'll see why later. Bring this note with you so I can translate the words on the back for you.

I turned it over and there was what looked like a poem in French. Even illegible, it was terribly romantic. I turned back.

I'll pick you up at the 21 kilometre marker at seven-thirty.
I've arranged something very special.
    Your lover,
    CC.

I was excited and confused all at once. How could I ever have doubted him? How could I ever, even briefly, have conjured that image in my mind of him holding King Naresuan's axe in his hand as he stood over his pretty wife?

'So?' said Chompu.

'So what?'

'What does it say?'

'Oh. False alarm. Nui the used-car guy wants us to pick up brown rice next time we go to Tesco.'

I put the note in the pocket of my shorts and walked past him. I should have known he wasn't fooled. He followed me silently back to the veranda and into my cabin. The DNA test equipment was lined up on the shelf.

'This should prove it one way or the other,' I told him.

Following the manga instructions carefully, I took the two drippers and sucked up a small sample from each test tube. I laid the chemical blotter on the table and squeezed both drippers at the same time. They each made a blot that spread outward like fast-acting viruses. And where the two blots met ... nothing happened.

'What does it mean?' Chompu asked.

'That I made a mistake somewhere. The point where the two meet is supposed to turn black.'

'And if it doesn't?'

'It's not a match.'

'Or, in other words, the maid's innocent.'

'It can't b— no, wait. Of course. She didn't use her own blood to make the fingerprint. She used the blood from the pretty dead wife. Wouldn't surprise me if she hacked off the finger and used it like a rubber stamp.'

'I get the teeniest feeling you've become obsessed.'

'I have not. She did it. I'm certain she did. All we need is a sample from the wife. I'll find something tonight. I can do this test again.'

'I can make an appointment with my psychologist for you.'

'I'm not—'

'And what are you two lovebirds doing?' came a voice.

I looked up to see Mair and Captain Kow standing arm in arm in the doorway in their matching bathrobes, their hair wet from the sea. It was like a commercial for a seniors' spa.

'I'm making cocktails,' I said.

'Don't you go drinking too much before your date,' she said and they turned to go.

'My . . .?'

I ran after them.

'Mair!' I called. 'You stop right there.'

The happy couple turned around to look at me.

'Did you read my personal note?' I asked.

She did her *Titanic* smile.

'There was nothing personal about it,' she said. 'Your name was on the front, that's all.'

They marched off to her cabin. Leaves were being ripped off the bushes by the wind. The door slammed behind her.

'All right, hand it over,' said Chompu. 'You know lying to a police officer is a criminal offence.'

I dug the note out of my pocket and handed it to him. He read it.

'It's too bad Ed isn't here to see it,' I said.

'This rather supports his case,' said Chompu.

'Of course it doesn't. It means Conrad hasn't deceived me. The text about being in Bangkok was all part of his surprise.'

'So why the note? And why the "Don't tell anyone"? It looks suspicious to me.'

'He's a mystery writer. He's playing a game. What's so suspicious about that?'

The lieutenant grabbed his chin 'twixt thumb and index finger the way a television detective might do.

'It could be perceived as the establishment of an alibi,' he said. 'As far as any electronic records show he's still in Bangkok. By leaving a paper note and asking you to bring it with you he could be cleaning up the paper trail. There would be no evidence that he invited you to his house today.'

'And I'm supposed to be the paranoid one.'

'Not at all. Why didn't he phone to invite you? Or send another text?'

'Perhaps he did. Let's see,' I said, searching around for my phone. 'Perhaps that's exactly why he left the note – because he wasn't able to get my attention on my cell. Where is the bloody thing?'

Sticky Rice looked up with that familiar, Sim-cards-wouldn't-melt-in-my-mouth expression. I'd seen it too often to ignore it.

'Dog, if you ate my phone,' I said, 'I'm going to deworm you twice a day till it comes out.'

He crawled under the table.

'Chom, have you got your phone with you?'

'Yes.'

'Call me.'

Chompu obliged but 'Mamma Mia' did not ring out from Sticky's belly.

'Then he's buried it,' I said. 'The runt. But that's it. That's exactly why Conrad couldn't get through. OK, I'm not playing any more. It's all quite simple. There is no missing person. His wife ran off with a younger man. He's cool about it. There's nothing suspicious about him. Now, if you'll excuse me, I have to prepare dinner before my date.'

I stomped off towards the kitchen with the wind buffeting me left and right like a dim sum in a pinball machine. Chompu held his ground and, as I discovered later, that was the moment a nefarious plot was hatched in my absence. According to my policeman, he had heard a commotion in the bougainvilleas beside the cabin and Grandad Jah emerged from the bush doing the St Vitus's dance, slapping his bare head, stamping his feet. Red ants were very fond of bougainvilleas. His arrival on the veranda was greeted by a distant roll of thunder and a slither of lightning that snaked across the sky.

'It's coming,' he said. 'It's going to be a big one.'

'Have you been hiding in the bushes listening to our conversation?' Chompu asked.

'Yes.'

'Very well.'

'The girl can't see what's clearly there in front of her face. Love does that to women. It turns them into bigger idiots than they already are. I suggest we set up a surveillance operation. Here's what we'll do . . .'

'I'm the policeman,' said Chompu.

'Have you got a plan?'

'I don't even have a crime.'

'Prevention's better than cure, young fellow.'

CHAPTER FOURTEEN

DON'T SCREW UP
(self-assembled furniture instructions)

Translation of Grandad Jah's Surveillance Operation Notes

Hypotheses

1. *Conrad Coralbank killed his wife.*
2. *The Burmese servants were in on it.*

Supporting Facts

  i. *The note inviting Jimm for her date had to have been delivered by someone else. If Coralbank went to the trouble of setting up this alibi he wouldn't risk being seen putting the note on the door. The maid or her brother wouldn't have been noticed. Nobody looks twice at Burmese.*

  ii. *The Burmese were complicit in the dispatch of the wife's body.*

3. *They plan to make Jimm their next victim.*
   Supporting Facts

i. A rich guy who could get himself any woman he wants is seducing a plain girl that he can't possibly find attractive. So there has to be another reason. As he is a crazed killer there is no need for motive beyond blood lust. I know these types.

ii. He's established an elaborate alibi.

iii. He collects weapons.

Methodology

The young fellow was right. We don't have any concrete evidence of a crime. So we need to play along and let them make the mistakes. For that we need more warm bodies on the ground. Reluctantly, as time was pressing, I called my good-for-nothing grandson, Arny, who was off with his old lady. Also, I had no choice but to recruit Kow.

Coralbank will be picking up Jimm on the main road, which is why he had arranged to meet her out of sight at the top of the lane. We do not alert her that we are observing as she may spill the beans to her 'lover'. The policeman will follow at a safe distance to make sure Coralbank takes her to the house. With a storm coming it should be overcast at six p.m. Kow will approach the property from the bottom of the hill at Coralbank's land and establish a beachhead with a view of the house from the grounds. He will be equipped with a cell phone. I will be at the top of the hill near the gate ready to enter the property over the wall when Kow gives the word (map attached). As Arny is next to useless in combat situations, he will be

based at the resort where he will answer the telephone and
make us sandwiches for when it's all over.

N.B. Killers prefer to torment their victims. We will catch
him in the act, hopefully before he's murdered my grand-
daughter.

It was five. I'd prepared dinner and taken the dogs on a blustery walk along what was left of the beach. Mair's salted potato plantation was already under water. The sky was invigorating, charcoal grey with spits of lightning. Whatever was on its way would be a classic. Our gulf, geographically speaking, was a paddling pool with no extreme underground activity so the worst we could expect was a lashing. No waves had ever exceeded four metres and that had been way out at sea.

I was in my room preparing my wardrobe for the night. I wanted something sheer and playful that could slip off one shoulder as we lay in bed laughing about Ed's theory that Conrad had killed his wife. We'd reach a peak of mirth when I added Chom's 'perfect alibi' theory for my own demise. Conrad would be excited by all this talk of murder and roll onto me, rip off my chemise and we'd make love through the night. The only obstacle I could see in this pleasurable night was the maid. I'd make sure the house was locked and bolted before we retired to the bedroom.

It occurred to me that I didn't have a silk chemise so

I put my white cotton singlet in my overnight bag and opted for jeans and a T-shirt for the journey over there. He'd seen everything already, so there was no need to be mysterious. The rain had started to blow against my window, so I knew I'd be soaked before I made it to the end of the lane. I took my pink plastic poncho from the closet. I was way too early. I looked at myself in the mirror and decided a touch of lipstick wouldn't come amiss. I didn't have any so I put on the cape, pulled up the hood, and went down to the shop. The moisture in the air took my breath away. Mair was counting the forty-seven *baht* she'd made for the day. The sign beside the till – a legacy from the previous owners – in Thai said, *No Change Given*. The English said *No Chance*, which I supposed wasn't so far wrong.

'Mair,' I said, taking her hand.

'Yes, Davinda.'

'I forgive you.'

'Oh? And what have I done now?'

'I forgive you for turning my upbringing into a New Age experiment.'

'That's sweet of you, darling. If it ever bothers you again you should consider what you'd be like today if I hadn't taken charge of your upbringing.'

I needed to sit outside under the canopy on the concrete bench at the concrete table to consider such a thing. The sky was heavy. There were lumps of salt in the wind. The sea, silent for so many months, was growling from the depths of its belly. Nature was in control again. If Mair hadn't taken charge . . .? I gave it thought. I wouldn't have been here for sure. Captain Kow wouldn't have fathered me. I wouldn't have been an outcast at school. Wouldn't have found solace in the English language. Wouldn't have gone to Australia and learned how to drink wine directly from a box. Wouldn't have become a journalist. Probably wouldn't have eaten so much at the urging of a mother who considered trimness a sin. Damn it. I would have become a Thai Airways flight attendant. I'd be groomed and polite and neat and married to a pilot.

I was awoken from that nightmare by the beep-beep of a motorcycle horn. I looked up to see Nurse Da ride up the kerb and under the canopy beside me. Her white uniform seemed preserved beneath a transparent cape but her hair had been plastered flat by the rain. She switched off her engine.

'Don't you answer your cell phone any more?' she asked.

'My dog buried it. What's up?'

'Dr Somluk, she's back.'

'Well, that's . . . I suppose it's good news as long as she recognizes how much trouble she's put everyone through. I'm relieved. Is she OK?'

'Seems to be.'

'Seems? You haven't seen her?'

'I just got back from a couple of naughty days with Gogo. She texted. She wants to see both of us.'

'She wants to see me? Why?'

'I've been texting her about you and your help from the beginning. Keeping her up on the news. I suppose she wants to – you know – thank you or something. Give you an exclusive story? I don't know.'

'When?'

'Now. Have you got a few minutes?'

I looked at my wrist where I used to wear a watch before I became unemployed.

'What time is it?' I asked.

'Five-thirty.'

I wasn't meeting Conrad till seven-thirty. I had time.

'Where is she?' I asked.

'She said she'd meet you at the health centre.'

That was a few minutes down the road.

'I can see her,' I said.

'Great. Give her my love.'

'You aren't coming?'

'Nah. I said I'd see her tomorrow. All I'm fit for at the moment is bed. That man of mine is an animal, Jimm. I've had barely an hour's sleep in the last twenty-four.'

She blushed.

'Wait!' I said. 'You haven't been working for twenty-four hours?'

'That's right. I took compassionate leave. With no doctor in residence I had to shut the clinic.'

'Then . . . why . . .?'

'The uniform?'

247

'Yes.'

'He's a devil, isn't he?'

I got it. I had to confess a fat man with a nurse uniform fetish wasn't what I'd call the optimum life partner, but who was I to complain?

The health centre was only five minutes from the resort, but the rain was coming down in carafes. I didn't want to make the trip twice, so I went back to my cabin to put on my lipstick. Mair had already shut the shop when I got back to the car park and I didn't see anyone else. I shrouded myself in my poncho and cycled down to the intersection. There was already a three centimetre top layer of water on the road flowing towards the sea. I hoped the lipstick was waterproof. I was the only one silly enough to be on the road. I'd never been that fond of cycling in the rain in Chiang Mai but it was one of the few thrills down on the Gulf so I'd learned to see it as a hobby. That and hanging up damp laundry.

The gate to the health centre was open as usual, but the clinic appeared to be locked up and dark, as were the rooms at the back. The only light pushed through the rain from the road out front. I parked the bicycle around the side and walked up the concrete steps. The centre was blocked at street level by a line of bushes. I sat on the top step and watched the rain gush in parallel lines from the corrugated roof. And I wondered whether Dr Somluk might be hiding somewhere in the shadows, still afraid of the boogie men. But after five minutes she still hadn't emerged and I was wondering whether to go home.

Then a truck, an old beaten-up Datsun with a clunky exhaust pipe, drove into the compound at speed, did a noisy U-turn on the wet gravel and stopped just below my perch. The driver's window squeaked slowly down. I was as surprised to see the woman sitting there as I was to see the smile on her face.

'Dr June?'

'Hello, Jimm,' she shouted above the storm. 'Hop in.'

'I'm here to meet—'

'I know. She's with me. We've got a lot to tell you.'

The passenger door swung open. All I could think about was not being late to meet Conrad.

'Come on,' she said. 'The rain's getting in.'

'I have a date,' I shouted as I walked down the steps.

'What time?' she asked.

'Seven-thirty.'

She looked at her watch.

'Oh, no problem,' she said. 'Somluk and I just need to clear a few things up and I'll have you back with your lover long before then.'

I stepped out into the rain and ran for the open door. The seat was already soaked so I didn't bother to take off my cape. I had to slam the door three times before it would close properly. Dr June smiled at me again, then gunned the engine.

'Where is she?' I asked.

'In a safe place. At the hospital.'

She pulled out into the road without stopping at the entrance. We kicked up a wall of water.

'I have to apologize to you,' she said.

'You do?'

'Yes. I was extremely rude to you when you came to the hospital.'

'I hadn't noticed.'

'Yes you had. But there was a reason, you see? Somluk and I didn't know who to trust. Back then I didn't realize you'd been helping us. I was afraid you might have been one of them. Somluk will explain it all. We really need your help.'

She rested her gear hand on my thigh and I felt a jolt of unease. She was driving faster than the conditions warranted.

'Nice truck,' I said, looking for a seat belt that didn't appear to be there.

'Hospital maintenance,' she laughed. 'It was the first piece of shit I could find the key for. I'm sure this thing causes half the accidents we treat in Emergency.'

She was chatty and friendly all the way to the hospital. A different person. But still she wouldn't answer any of my questions about Dr Somluk.

'I think she'd like to tell you all this herself,' was all I got.

We entered the hospital through the rear gate and parked away from the car park under a sprawling duckfoot tree. The sun had yet to go down behind the mountains of Phato but it might as well have been midnight. The clouds were black. We ran together to the door of the administration building, which was unlit. Not even a light on the porch. Inside, all the office doors were closed apart from that of Dr June.

'Dr Somluk,' she called out. 'Jimm's here.'

There was no reply. She waited till we were inside her office before she turned on the light. There was nobody in the room although on the coffee table in front of the small couch were two used coffee cups, two glasses, and half a bottle of wine.

'She must be in the bathroom,' she said. 'She never could hold her wine. I do hope you won't tell anyone.'

'Tell them what?'

'A registered doctor driving under the influence of alcohol.'

'It doesn't look like you drank that much,' I said.

'After everything we've been through, we both needed it,' she said. 'Once you hear what's happened, you'll probably need one too. In fact . . .'

She went to the wall cabinet and took out a clean glass.

'Oh, I don't think . . .' I began, but on a night like this a glass of red was exactly what I needed.

'Don't make me drink alone,' she said, poured a few fingers of wine into the glass, then the same amount into her own. She didn't wait to salute me, just threw hers back and poured another.

'Don't you go thinking I'm a drunkard,' she said. 'These are extreme times. I have to confess I am terribly nervous.'

She looked at her watch and the door at the same time, which seemed impossible. She was making me nervous too.

'What is keeping her?' she said.

If the wine was to calm her nerves, it wasn't working. I wondered why Dr Somluk would turn out the light in the office and go to the bathroom in the dark. Or perhaps it was lighter when she ... I took a couple of mouthfuls of my wine. It was a little bitter for a Shiraz, but I felt the bite of the alcohol at the back of my throat. Another half-dozen of these, I thought, and I'd be ready for anything.

Or ...

Perhaps I wouldn't.

Dr June put down her glass and smiled at me. It was a smile I would never forget.

CHAPTER FIFTEEN

HAVE A GOOD FRIGHT
(Nok Air)

'Where in heck is she?' asked Grandad Jah, not for the first time.

The surveillance was all primed. Captain Kow had phoned Lieutenant Chompu from the rocks below Coralbank's garden. He was being battered by the rain and buffeted by the wind, but he was a man of the sea so what did he care? He said the main lights in the house were on but, as yet, he'd seen no movement inside. Chompu's SUV was parked at a spot near Mair's shop that had a view of the 21 kilometre marker on the main road interrupted only by sheets of rain. Chompu's car was unlit and invisible in the dark. His nose pointed towards the road, ready to fall in pursuit when the *farang* picked up his prey. But the bait had vanished. They'd looked for Jimm in her room, the shop and the kitchen, but she was nowhere to be seen.

'I don't like this,' said brother Arny, who had been recruited out of desperation. 'What time is it?'

253

All cell phones were on conference. Grandad Jah was above the house not far from the gate, waiting for the arrival of Coralbank's car.

'Seven fifteen,' said Chompu. 'And no sign of anyone.'

'The bicycle's gone,' said Arny. 'In this weather she couldn't have ridden far.'

'But why didn't she tell anyone where she was going?' asked Chompu.

'What if . . .?' said Grandad Jah. 'What if he came early? What if she was down at the shop and he drove past, said he just happened to be passing and she might as well come before the allotted time? Left her bike at the store.'

'You've been there half an hour,' said Chompu. 'And you didn't see anyone come.'

'Who said he'd have to bring her to the house?' snapped Grandad. 'He could have taken her anywhere.'

Chompu clicked on his service radio and called the Pak Nam station. He told the desk sergeant to put out an APB and gave the registration number of Coralbank's car. It sounded very impressive but there was just the one police truck out after dark and it spent most of its time parked in front of the 7-Eleven. The duty officer was very fond of microwave tuna pie. There would only be a make on Coralbank's car if the writer decided to stop by there and pick up the daily newspaper.

'Arny?' said Chompu.

'Yes, sir?'

'See if you can find the bicycle.'

'Yes, sir,' said Arny, and everyone visualized him saluting down the phone line.

Arny took his duty seriously. Once he was sure the bike wasn't leaning against a wall anywhere at the resort, he jumped in the Mighty X and began a slow search of the few places his sister might have ridden to in the pouring rain in the dark. Once you were away from the seven street lights, darkness was all-consuming in Maprao and the bike didn't have a lamp.

Grandad Jah and Ed were contemplating their next move – although there wasn't one – when Chompu, in a whisper, reported a sighting.

'Men,' he said. 'A scruffy, country-singer type on a motorcycle has just stopped in front of the road sign. I think I recognize him. He's one of the Pak Nam motor-cycle taxi drivers.'

'What's he doing?' asked Grandad.

'He's just sitting there.'

'In the rain?'

'Wait. He's started up the motorcycle,' said the policeman, 'and he's coming this way. I mean, precisely this way.'

The motorcyclist made a beeline for the lieutenant's parked car and tapped on the window.

'Hello, General,' said the taxi man, and saluted.

Chompu wound down his window and was immediately splattered by the swirling rain.

'What are you doing here, Anot?'

'Here to pick up a Miss Jimm,' he said. 'I was waiting at the 21 kilometre marker as instructed, but she's not there. So, my next instruction was to come to the resort and look for her here. Naturally, I'm not expecting any extra fee for this diversion which is eating up even more gasoline than the original agreement covered.'

'It's two hundred metres.'

'It all adds up. So, where is she?'

'Who hired you?'

'I'm sworn by motorcycle taxi driver confidentiality not to pass on that information.'

'Fair enough. Let's see your licence.'

Anot spat out an imaginary wad of tobacco.

'A Burmese. Female. Speaks Thai. I didn't ask her name. Told me to pick up this Miss Jimm at seven-thirty.'

'And take her where?'

'The big house on the headland.'

'All right. Sorry. Your job's cancelled.'

'Oh, no, General. It was COD. I can't lose this gig. I have a family of eight to feed. Little Noo is on his last legs with diphtheria as it is.'

'You live alone, Anot. Nobody in their right mind would let you father children with them.'

'Be that as it may, I was promised. Look at this night.'

Chompu reached into his pocket.

'How much did she agree?'

'A thousand dollars, US. Large bills.'

The policeman gave him a hundred *baht*. Anot held it up to the light above Mair's shop to see if it was real.

'Better than nothing,' he said, and rode off.

Everyone had heard the exchange.

'What do you fellows see up there?' Chompu asked.

'Still no movement,' said Captain Kow. 'All the lights on downstairs. No lights upstairs.'

'I bet she rode up here on her bike,' said Kow.

'She'd do that just to be difficult,' said Grandad. 'I say we storm the place. I've got my pistol.'

'Wait,' said Chompu. 'There's no way Jimm could make it up there on a bicycle. He's expecting her to arrive on a motorcycle. So this is what we'll do. I'll drive over to the temple and meet you at the main road. We'll take your Honda Dream to the gate. They might open up when they hear the motor. If they let us in, that's an invitation. No need for a warrant.'

'What about Jimm?' said Kow.

'She's best out of it. She probably got a flat tyre somewhere. Or she's waiting out the storm. Either way, Arny will find her.'

Arny had been to the two shops that didn't belong to Mair and therefore had goods for sale. The girls in the shops fell into little pieces at the sight of him and he had to wade through a lot of flirtatious banter before they'd tell him they hadn't seen his sister. The bicycle

257

was nowhere to be found. He was on his way to ask at Headman Beung's place when his cell phone rang out the theme from *Rocky*.

'Arny?'

'Sissi?'

'Has Jimm lost her phone again?'

'I hear the dog buried it.'

'Is she around?'

'No, Sissi. I'm worried to death. We can't find her.'

'Is there anyone else there I can talk to?'

'No. I'm by myself.'

'Then listen. This is serious. I got into—'

'Wait. Let me get under cover so I can hear you. It's raining really hard down here.'

A couple of minutes passed as he pulled into a public gazebo beside the road.

'OK,' he said.

'All right. Has she told you about the missing doctor?'

'Yeah.'

'I got into the emails between Dr June at the hospital and the Medley people. Like I suspected, they were all sent via some proxy address in India. But it's all traceable back to Europe. The people . . . Are you listening?'

'You hacked into someone's account?'

'I . . . you . . . look, we'll get into the morality of all this later. Right now, Jimm's in trouble. Dr June is the rep for Medley for the whole of the south of Thailand. She's the one who's responsible for spreading the word that formula is stardust. Everything that's happened down there she's reported to her minder in Switzerland. I traced him to a freelance business agency. The staff roster there looks like roll call at the penitentiary. All seedy guys and gals with records and fake CVs. I've got a printout of the correspondence between W, that's the code name of the minder, and Dr Seuss, that's your Dr June. Are you getting all this?'

'You have to stop treating me like I'm stupid.'

'All right. I'm sorry. The highlights of the emails are these: "W. Dr S is getting troublesome. I'm not sure I know how to shut her up." "Thanks, Seuss. We're all sympathetic to your problem. We're sure you'll find a way to reduce the doctor's influence. In fact, your bonus depends on it."

'And later: "Seuss. Congratulations. We were confident you'd find a way to nullify Doctor S. Your new problem seems to be equally annoying. But journalists in Thailand have proven to be easily influenced away from a story. One or two threats should be enough. We support whatever method you adopt. Good luck."

'And then later, "W. The journalist is still pushing. Threats ignored. Any suggestions?"

'"Seuss. Whatever approach you used to shut up Dr S would appear to have worked just fine. We suggest you repeat that with the journalist."

'So, Arny. I know it doesn't actually say how they plan to shut Jimm up, but I don't like it.'

'I don't either,' said Arny.

He floored the accelerator, which made a lot of noise but didn't actually start the truck moving. Then he remembered the gears. The truck lurched out of the shelter and into the rain.

'Are you still there, little brother?'

'Yes, Sissi.'

'Good. I did research on Dr June. Do you want to hear it?'

'Yes.'

'She was born in Malaysia to Chinese parents. The parents split up and June moved to Thailand with her father. He stuck her in international schools, and went through most of the family wealth on a parade of girlfriends and drink and drugs. June already spoke English and Malay and Hokkien so picking up Thai wasn't such a problem. She was fluent by the time she was seventeen. She applied for Thai citizenship four times before it was approved. She had the money and the determination, so by the time she was nineteen she had a Thai passport and a Thai surname. She took the name Chantavath. June was her original given name but, although she kept it as a nickname when she arrived here, she stated her given name as Chani. With her language ability and excellent grades in the entrance examination she registered to study medicine at Mahidol.

'She passed all the exams without remarkable distinction, as one would expect from a foreigner studying in Thai, and after an internship at the Bangkok Christian Hospital she worked in general practice. From there she took a modest interest in child health, for which she became relatively well known. She authored a lot of journal papers. Depressing subjects. Child mortality and incurable diseases. She moved into administration and spent more time writing about health than practising it. But it wasn't until five years ago that she rose from this unspectacular career and became a minor celebrity in the south. Her name was suddenly a buzzword for advancements in rural development in children's issues. No husband. No children of her own. In later interviews she claimed to be married to her work. Although she "would have relished the opportunity to have children", she never found a man who could accept her devotion to her causes and her energy. You still listening?'

'I'm listening. Sissi? All that was in her immigration file?'

'That and her police record.'

'Police record?'

'She apparently has harassment issues. Twice she's been taken to court by people who claimed she'd threatened them. One younger intern made a complaint that she was being harassed sexually. Dr June got off both times.'

'All right. I get it. But my priority right now is to find Jimm and get her home.'

'But you will tell her everything I've said here?'

'Of course.'

The boys on surveillance had turned off their cell phones before they approached the open gates of the Coralbank mansion. They stopped at the top of the hill. Grandad climbed from the motorcycle and Chompu drove back down to give the impression of a taxi man dropping off a passenger. In the house, they'd assume that Jimm had paid the fare. Chompu jogged back up to join Grandad, bemoaning the fact that he'd given up Pilates and had suffered accordingly. He was running on adrenalin and soaked to the bone. He and Grandad kept to the shadows of the flailing bushes and edged down the driveway to the house. Tall palms leaned away from the sea and clapped their fronds as a warning of things to come.

Before it was snatched by a gust of wind, they saw a note pinned to a tree with the word *Jimm* and an arrow pointing to the house. Chompu and Grandad reached the back wall just as the power went off. They were immediately lost in a velvet maze. They were close enough to hear one another's breaths.

'You bring a flashlight?' Chompu asked.

'You're the policeman.'

'You're the organizer.'

As they were men, albeit elderly or gay, neither would admit to being petrified at that moment. There was a mechanical cough from somewhere off to their right and the sound of a generator coming to life. The house-lights were ignited almost immediately, the only illumination for twenty kilometres around. Maprao was blacked out. The two men squeezed themselves into the last of the shadows. Even though they were close enough to speak without being heard, Grandad Jah insisted on employing the nifty hand signals the SWAT teams used. He'd picked them up from DVDs. Chompu disliked violent movies so he'd never learned them. He had no idea what the old man was trying to tell him, so he walked down the driveway without crouching or zigzagging to avoid gunfire. When the old man scurried to a damp spot beneath a sprawling hibiscus, Chompu walked up to the nearest glass door and slid it open. He was only too pleased to step inside, out of the relentless rain. Grandad followed him in.

'What are you doing?' he whispered. 'The door could have been wired to an alarm.'

'I knew it was safe.'

'How?'

Chompu pointed to the note taped to the inside of the glass. It read: *Jimm. This door's open.*

'We're lit up like the Royal Palace here,' whispered Grandad.

But Chompu drew solace from the fact that they had Kow watching their backs from the bushes below. He took the cell phone off his belt.

'Kow,' he said. 'See anything?'

'I see you two,' came the reply.

'Nothing else?'

'No.'

'I'll keep this channel open. Shout if anything comes up . . . Kow? You're supposed to say, "Roger" or something. Kow? Kow?'

There was nothing but static.

'The useless lump's probably dropped his phone down a crack in the rocks,' said Grandad. 'Worthless. I tell you.'

'There's no need for—' Chompu began but he was interrupted by a man's voice from the stairwell behind them.

'I know you're down there.'

Grandad's heart flipped over like a pancake. Chompu's legs turned to agar. The voice was followed by what could only be described as a soundtrack, the type in movies that accompanies a lone female on a walk through a haunted house, all singing saws and piano strings.

'Come on up,' said the voice. 'Don't be afraid. I have something for you. Something you'll never forget.'

This time it was Chompu with the signals. He pointed to himself, twiddled his fingers to suggest walking, and pointed to the external staircase they'd passed on their way in. He indicated for Grandad to take the internal stairs and in seconds he was gone. Grandad remained alone at the foot of the staircase. It was hard to tell what he was thinking at that moment, because he never shared his feelings with anyone. As a lifelong traffic policeman he'd never been in a life or death situation. He'd had a gun during his career but had never fired it in all of those years in uniform. It was unlikely he was as cool and calm as he pretended to be as he climbed the stairs. He reached the top landing, which was pitch black, but he knew his silhouette would still be illuminated from below. An easy target for anyone armed. He flicked the two-way switch at the top of the stairs and instead of seeing everything clearly, the downstairs lights went out and he was once again blind.

'Are you feeling afraid?' came the voice of Coralbank, the music increasing in volume behind it. Grandad had no idea what the voice was saying, so he didn't reply.

'This is how it feels,' Coralbank continued. 'That moment of confusion. What lies inside the darkness? It's the moment when you don't know with any certainty how close to death you are. When you wonder what I am holding here in this invisible void.'

Grandad Jah was actually wondering where the hell his brave policeman colleague had gone. Why Kow didn't answer the phone. Why he was all alone in this raid. Why the rain lashing against the windows sounded so final. Whether the Burmese were here too, lurking in the blackness with their knives. One old man against three assailants. The writer was still babbling on.

'Come in,' he said. 'Take one brave step further into the darkness.'

The only choice Grandad had was to remain silent. He had his gun. All it lacked was bullets. Only he knew this fact. Pistol ammunition could only be sold if you had a certificate from the police. As the gun was unlicensed he'd not had that option.

'Just trust me,' said the writer. 'Follow my voice. Put all your faith in me. Come to me.'

Grandad felt along the upstairs landing for a second switch, one that might end this terror. He crept silently sideways with his back to the wall, away from the voice. All the time feeling for a light switch. He wondered what he might be reincarnated as. A horse? A cockroach? As barely living coral? He wondered whether he'd be given a choice. Wondered whether his unpleasantness in this life might condemn him to misery in the next. If only he'd spent those nights in the coffin.

He was about five paces to the right of the staircase now and decided he had no choice but to attack. To run head first towards the speaker. Perhaps he might barge into him and catch him by surprise. He let out a deep breath and started across the room. After only three steps he was blinded by a battery of spotlights embedded in the ceiling. He looked to his left to see Lieutenant Chompu at the study door with his hand on the main light switch.

In the centre of the room was a two-person dining table, laid to the nines with a candelabrum, several plates with stainless steel covers and a full bottle of wine with two glasses. On the far side of the table, naked apart from a leather waistcoat, thigh-length boots and a black Lone Ranger mask, was the famous author, Conrad Coralbank. His lips formed an almost perfect O.

'It begins,' she'd said, the insipid smile still on her face, 'with a slight catch in the breath, then a heart flutter. Then the room tilts first one way, then the other.'

I was living her description.

'You feel as if your sense of balance has been lost,' she continued. 'As if you couldn't stand even if you wanted to. Then, poof, you're gone.'

Just before I fell head first onto the glass coffee table and made a big bloody crease across my forehead, I thought I'd seen someone – a woman, perhaps – walk into the room. But I had been too preoccupied with my fight against unconsciousness to notice who she was. The bitter Shiraz. The sleight of hand. The overwhelming feeling of stupidity. All this came to me in the seconds before the crash of glass and the swirling pool of nausea.

They sat in the main room of the big glass house. It was something Lieutenant Chompu had dreamed of – a drawing-room denouement. He didn't actually know what a drawing room was, but he and Jimm had watched *Poirot* on illegal BBC downloads. All the murder mysteries ended like this and it gave a clever police-man the chance to bamboozle a confession out of the guilty party.

Seated around the glass coffee table were the author, now dressed in a *yukata*, the maid with her face caked in powder, the man she claimed to be her husband but who was actually her brother, a retired traffic cop, a fisherman, and him, the clever police officer. And he needed to be brilliant that evening because as far as he could see no crime had actually been committed. Not unless you counted trespassing on private property and illegal entry. But the air was thick with potential confessions.

There was, it had to be said, one more flaw in the methodology of this denouement. There was no common language. Coralbank's Thai was only matched in its awfulness by the English of Grandad Jah and Chompu. The latter had a number of memorized phrases but no vocabulary that could be considered 'functional'. Captain Kow happily confessed that Manchester and United were the only two words he knew in English. Jo the gardener spoke nothing but Burmese, which left only A, the maid. Although her English and Thai both sounded like Burmese, she had the vocabulary and was truly the only person who could act as interpreter. Which explains why one of the main suspects in a crime nobody could actually put their finger on was translating.

Chompu walked around the circle of chairs with his hands behind his back.

'So,' he said. 'A . . .'

'Would you like some coffee?' she asked.

'No, I would not. But thank you for asking. I was—'

'Tea?'

'Ms A,' he said. 'Let us just imagine for a moment that you are not a maid. You are merely a member of the household. Do not feel obliged to serve us.'

'Very well, sir.'

'Right,' said Chompu. 'Now we have a number of issues to work through. I'd appreciate it if you could translate for your employer as we proceed. I shall, of course, be checking the accuracy of your English because I am fluent in the language. I'm just a little too shy to speak it.'

'Yes, sir.'

Chompu flipped open his Hello Kitty notepad.

'Ms A, on the evening of the twentieth, your . . . husband was seen in the garden of this house with a machete and a cement bag. Could you tell us what he was doing there?'

'Yes, sir.'

'I mean . . . tell us.'

'It's difficult,' she said.

'Sometimes the truth can be,' said Chompu.

'No, I mean it's difficult to answer your questions and translate at the same time.'

'I understand. Then we'll allow you to translate at the end of each block of questions.'

'Thank you, sir.'

She told Coralbank, who didn't seem to be in the mood for any of this. In fact, since his embarrassing exposure, the renowned writer had been remarkably short of words.

'So, Ms A,' said Chompu.

'Durian, sir.'

'What about it?'

'The master has a dozen durian trees along the edge of his land. He hates the smell. He kindly allows us to sell the fruit we get from those trees but he refuses to let us harvest them during the heat of the day when he's around. He has a very sensitive nose. So Jo cuts them down late at night when it's cool and the master is asleep.'

'A, could you ask the master if that's true?' said Chompu.

'Are you nuts?' asked Grandad. 'Do you honestly think she'd tell us if he said no?'

'I know what I'm doing,' said the policeman.

'You could have fooled me.'

'The master says it's true,' said A, and Chompu felt even more stupid. He returned to his notes.

'On the night of the thirteenth,' he said, 'you hired a motorcycle taxi with a sidecar to take two polystyrene boxes to the bus station.'

'That might be true, sir.'

'Might be?'

'It's something we do often, sir. But I'm not sure whether we sent boxes on that date.'

'What was in the boxes?'

'Why, the durian, sir. We send them to my sister in Chiang Mai. These are very expensive durian. Golden Pillow. The best. They cost a small fortune in the north. My sister sells them at Warorot Market.'

'It all smells pretty fishy to me,' said Grandad.

'It all sounds pretty logical to me,' said Captain Kow, who knew what fishy smelled like.

Captain Kow smiled. Grandad Jah snarled. Chompu realized he was on dodgy legal ground by just being there, interrogating people without a warrant. And still there wasn't a hint of a crime. He knew he'd have to get his questioning done and leave before the owner came to his senses and called his lawyer.

'Ms A,' he said, 'could you ask Mr Coralbank where his wife is?'

'Oh, I know where she is, sir.'

'You do?'

'Yes, sir. She's in Bangkok.'

'Is there any way of verifying that?'

'I have her cell-phone number,' she said. 'We chat often. I was quite close to the mistress.'

'Do you have the number?'

A took her cell phone from her pocket and scrolled

down. She pressed 'connect' and handed the phone to the policeman. There followed a short but friendly conversation in which Chompu asked Coralbank's wife how she was and apologized for the inconvenience. He clicked 'End call' and nodded to his cohorts. The chances of a major crime having taken place at the big glass house were becoming remote. He tried one last ploy.

'Ms A,' he said.

'Yes, sir?'

'Did you, or did you not make threats against Jimm Juree?'

'Threats? No sir.'

'Are you sure?'

'Why would I make threats to her?'

'That's for you to tell me.'

Chompu knew that Poirot would have had a tearful confession out of the girl by now. Fiction was so . . . convenient. She still wasn't near to breaking point. He pushed a little.

'So you didn't write a threatening letter to Jimm Juree or try to poison her dogs?'

'No . . . no, sir. I'm very fond of dogs, and . . .'

'And what?'

'I can't write so well.'

'You were a university graduate.'

'I used to write, sir. I used to write a lot. But then this happened.'

She rolled up her sleeve to reveal a wrist wound.

'What's that?'

'A bullet, sir. We were passing through the no-go zone to get to the camps in Thailand. The Burmese military weren't so strict back then. I imagine I was just unlucky. I was shooting practice for some bored army sentry. He hit me in the right wrist and severed a nerve. I can't use the thumb on my right hand. But I can type.'

'And you expect us to believe the Englishman hired you with a disability like that?' said Grandad.

'I can do all the big jobs,' she said. 'And the master's very kind.'

'Oh, come on,' said Grandad. 'She's got bullshit coming out of every orifice. Let me do this. I'll show you what an interrogation looks like.'

He stepped past Chompu and pointed his index finger in the maid's face.

'Girl,' he said, 'what about your warning to Jimm when she came here. Are you going to tell us that didn't happen either?'

A was shaken. She looked at her boss and her husband/brother.

'I . . . I did warn her,' she said.

'What about?'

'I can't . . . I can't really tell you, sir.'

'See, son,' said Grandad to Chompu. 'That's the way you do it. No need to pussyfoot around with these people. Go for the jugular.'

A was translating, but not for Coralbank. She was

speaking Burmese with her brother. The writer continued to sit deaf and dumbfounded. If anyone looked guilty in that room it was him.

'And while you're at it,' said Grandad, 'you can tell us why you thought it necessary to pretend this little midget here was your husband when in fact he's your brother.'

This really stunned the maid. She blushed and looked fleetingly at Coralbank, who didn't make eye contact with anyone.

'I would like to maintain my right to remain silent,' she said.

Grandad laughed. 'You're Burmese, girl,' he said. 'You don't have any rights.'

'That's not strictly true,' said Chompu, 'but I will take you to the police station if you refuse to answer those questions. And the first thing they'll do is ask to see your papers.'

'It's not . . . I can't, sir,' she said.

'Why not?'

'We'll lose our jobs here,' she said.

'It's that serious?'

'Yes, sir. Please don't make me.'

'It's simple,' said Grandad Jah. 'You talk or you're on the next armoured police truck back to Burma.'

There followed a few minutes of Burmese as A explained the situation to her brother. This gave

Chompu time to glare angrily at the old policeman. Finally, A sat forward on her chair and said, 'All right, sir. I'll tell you everything.'

CHAPTER SIXTEEN

TAKE OFF YOUR HEAD
(parking garage)

I came round, not in a start as if from a bad dream, but in a gentle quandary. It took me some time to work out who I was and longer before I gave any thought at all to where. There were white tiles under my face. The smell of blood. Something sticky on my cheek. Who was I and why was I slumped on the ground like a sack of yams, soaked to the skin? I was woozy and having the worst hangover at the same time. Objects were passing in and out of focus. I couldn't move but I willed myself to concentrate. To match contradictory facts. There was a huge standing air-conditioner but the room was sweaty. I was thinking in Thai but hearing words in English. They were muffled and angry.

But wait, I was me. Jimm. I was on a bicycle in the rain. A truck with no seatbelts. And . . . a glass of quick-acting sedative.

I raised my head and saw only white walls. No windows. It was the bank of eight parallel fluorescent lights on the ceiling that reminded me I'd been here before. The floor tiles had been red then and the equipment was still packed and covered in cellophane. But this was the new Lang Suan Hospital operating theatre. The Medley-sponsored facility with its spacious ante-room with an en-suite shower. The operating table leaned up against the far wall, waiting to be welded on to the four metal studs that protruded from the floor on either side of me. I was tied wrists and ankles to those studs. It was just as well the air-conditioner wasn't functioning because I suppose I should mention I was buck naked and face up. It was odd because one of the early thoughts that entered my head was, when I wrote the screenplay of this, whether I should drape my character in a silk slip to avoid an R18 certification, or whether I should make it Indie and have this whole scene unashamedly nude. Europe would love it. I suppose the drug still had hold of me then. There would be time for terror later.

If any of you are having unclean thoughts at this time, I suggest you move along to the S and M section of your public library and get your thrills there, because there was nothing at all erotic about my predicament. The longer I lay there, once the drug had worn off, the more my mind gave vent to its imagination. You can only pretend to be brave at moments like that and there was nobody to be fooled by my fake courage. The sound effects didn't help. The angry English from not too far away was no encouragement at all. It was mostly 'Bastard', 'You deserve this', 'How do you like that?' A woman's voice accompanied by the thud of metal on metal. I knew something very nasty was going on just a short way away.

I focused on the imaginable. The tangible. I had an itch. A really serious one beneath my left breast and there was nothing I could do about it. Forget waterboarding. Just leave Al Qaeda naked and strapped to a mattress full of bedbugs. I also looked at the positives. There weren't that many, but being flat on a hard floor was really good for my lower back twinges.

Dr June walked into the room wearing green scrubs with a shiny dark red motif. She had a visor pulled down over her face and I couldn't help noticing the axe in her hand. Both the visor and the axe were splattered with the same fresh crimson as the tunic. I didn't think she'd been out playing paintball. With her looming over me and me spreadeagled on the floor, the left-tit itch seemed the least of my problems. She flipped open the visor like a welder pleased with her latest exhaust pipe joint.

'It appears to get better every time,' she said.

She leaned her axe against the white wall tiles and sat on a plastic chair, catching her breath. Still sweating from her last kill.

'It was better before they put the floor tiles down,' she said. 'I didn't have to be careful about breaking

278

them. But they left this sheet of metal that's just the right length for my purposes.'

I'd read somewhere, hopefully not on the internet, that it helped to engage homicidal maniacs in mundane conversations about personal matters that establish you as a human being with an identity.

'Been killing someone?' I asked.

She looked at me as if I'd spoiled her day.

'That's an awful lot of blood,' I continued. 'Be a bugger to get that stain out. My mother, Mair, swears by Fab Extra. She says it can get out even the most stubborn stains.'

I laughed, hoping to get a chuckle out of Dr Doom. She glared.

'Can I ask why you're doing this?' I asked.

She could probably tell I wasn't wearing a wire. She swayed back and forth in her plastic chair.

'You know? It's the strangest thing,' she said. 'I stumbled on it by accident. Murder, I mean. I'd been fascinated by death ever since medical school.'

I hadn't asked her for her résumé, but better yakking than hacking, that's my philosophy. It was at that moment that I realized we were speaking to each other in English. I wondered why.

'I suppose that's why I naturally gravitated to a field that allowed me to study it,' she continued. 'I'm something of an expert in child morbidity, you know. I'm invited to give papers on it. Yet the irony of it is that I never caused a death while I was practising. Patients had died whilst I was treating them but not because of anything I did or did not do. It's really not the same. And really, an injection? An overdose? Where's the thrill in that?'

My strings were tight. She'd used that annoying nylon twine that deteriorated rapidly once exposed to the elements, but was like steel wire when it was fresh. If I had a cigarette lighter on me, I could have melted it in seconds. I wondered if she'd find it suspicious if I asked her for a light. Fortunately I'd somehow pressed a 'Play' button.

'I suppose I'd been taught to prevent it,' she said. 'But I had ... well, not fantasies exactly, more like dreams. They disturbed me at first. What possessed me to have such dreams? Should I seek professional help? But the interesting thing is that I never saw them as nightmares. Do you know what I mean?'

Time to bond.

'I know exactly what you mean,' I said.

'Don't humour me.'

'No, really. I have dreams like that all the time.'

She stared at me doubtfully.

'Describe one to me,' she said.

'Really?'

That put me on a spot. I needed a victim nobody would miss. One that would not be cursed by me telling the story. Someone who was already cursed.

'It's my grandad,' I said. 'He's always in a bathtub. Now that's odd in itself as we've never owned a bathtub. The first time I used one was in Australia and I almost drowned myself because I'd had a few tinnies of Victoria Bitter. That's what they call them over there; tinnies. I never—'

'The dream!'

'Right. So I creep into the bathroom. He should have locked the bathroom door. I always tell him that. So I creep into the bathroom and there he is, submerged. His skeletal frame thankfully concealed beneath a raft of red rose petals. I think that was a subliminal cinematic reference to *American Beauty*, the scene where Kevin Spacey has this erotic fantasy ab—'

She reached for the axe.

'All right. So I approach and I think he's asleep, but when I reach out to him his beady little old man eyes spring open and . . . and I panic. I grab his throat. I force him under the water. His talon-like fingers reach up to pull me on top of him. I mean, *eeuuw*. He tries to wrench my hands from his throat but I'm too strong for him. I push with all my might. The last bubble of air rises to the surface. His wiry corpse is still and lifeless against the porcelain.'

She took the axe in both hands. My story doubled in speed.

'I lean back exhausted. I sigh. I have killed my grandfather. Now, at last, I have peace. Then, to my horror, the dead corpse of Grandad Jah bursts from the water and scratches at my face with his two-month untrimmed fingernails. How many times have I told him to trim those nails? Blood gushes from my cheeks.'

She smiled.

'Pouring from my skin like water through cracks in a dam. Spraying this way and that. Red. Bloody. Gushing. I plunge the knife into his chest, once, twice . . .'

'The knife?'

'It's a dream. Four, five . . . eleven times. Slash, slash, slash. And, finally, he is quiet and completely dead. The bath is a vat of bubbling crimson.'

She shuddered. It might have been an orgasm. She nodded slowly.

'Yes,' she said. 'That's what it's like.'

'We are one,' I said, hopefully.

'No,' she said. 'We are not.'

Bummer.

'I graduated. I moved on to reality. You will never kill your grandfather.'

'I could. Just give me a chance. Give me a couple of hours.'

'A medical doctor with twenty years of experience does not suddenly become a fool in moments of heightened arousal.'

'No?'

'Absolutely not.'

'In that case, can you grant me just one last wish? In fact . . . two.'

'You're hardly in a position to ask, but you have a few minutes to amuse me. I'm still exhausted from my exertions in the next room. This is going to be an enormous night. I'm in no hurry.'

'Good. OK. Second one first. Would you mind scratching below my left breast. Mosquito bite. It's killing me.'

To my surprise she put down the axe, knelt beside me and scratched the red welt. It was heaven until her hand began to wander.

'Better?' she asked, stroking my breast.

'A little, thanks. Although both you and I know only too well that scratching a mosquito bite rarely improves the situation. Much better to leave it alone and imagine it doesn't itch. But I've never been Buddhist enough to get away with that.'

She was at my other breast.

'What is your other desire, my darling?' she asked.

'All right. Things aren't looking that good for me right now,' I said. 'But I'd hate to go without knowing what happened to Dr Somluk.'

She gave me a disgusted look and returned to her chair. That was a relief.

'Your last wish and that's the best you can do?'

'It was my last story. My last case. I'm a journalist. We don't like to leave stones unturned.'

To my utter surprise she stood, carried her chair to the far wall, stepped onto it and started to remove the plastic wrapping from the air conditioner. What a dedicated hospital-administrator-cum-axe-murderer she was.

'She worked here with me, as you know,' said Dr June. 'She was competent, good company, attractive I suppose, more to a woman than to a man, and we became close.'

'Lovers?'

'Don't interrupt.'

'Sorry.'

'As a journalist you probably know already that I have a reputation in the province. I have made things happen. There are royal awards for medicine and I am in line for one. I have been offered senior administrative positions at major hospitals up and down the country. There has been talk of a seat for me on the Thai Medical Council.'

'Congratulations.'

'Thank you. At first, Dr Somluk showed respect both for my work and to me. We were a good team. Partners. Yes, partners. I'm happy to call it that. Given the limited budget we receive from the provincial medical administrators, she was curious as to how I could organize so many conferences, pay so many per diems for special projects. How I could pay . . . for this.'

She swept her hand around to draw my attention to the room just in case I hadn't seen it already. She stepped down from her chair, went to a small cabinet not yet screwed to the wall and took out a scalpel.

'It really is a lovely facility,' I said, fearing I hadn't shown enough enthusiasm. But the doctor returned to the chair and used the scalpel to cut through the tape that held the plastic.

'In this country,' she said, 'you have to balance your government budget with what's available from the private sector. Neither education nor medicine can survive on what we get from the coffers of government after the crooks in parliament have had their share of it. You'd be surprised how many inappropriate sponsors there are lining up to fund worthwhile causes. The sports drinks people. The brewers. My goodness, even the tobacco companies. But not me. I drew my lines. I selected my sponsors ethically.'

'Medley?'

'A great provider of health-giving milk products and a benevolent donor. Without them, medical services for children in the south would be back in the Dark Ages.'

'When women suckled their own children,' I said.

She looked down at me.

'Careful now,' she snarled. 'You're sounding like her.'

'Dr Somluk obviously didn't share your enthusiasm for Medley.'

'She was so blinded by the internet anarchists that she ignored the scientific evidence. She openly insulted rural women by suggesting they couldn't make rational decisions about the health of their own children. Saying they were too stupid to use the product safely.'

'So you fired her.'

'If she'd merely stated her opinion I would certainly have respected it. A relationship thrives on differences. But she started the campaign. She became an internet renegade. She dared to contradict me in public. After all I did for her. All I've done for this province.'

She was shredding the shit out of the plastic.

'So you killed her.'

Dr June stopped slashing and became calm, as a result of my apparently cathartic observation. She looked up at the fluorescent lights as if they were heaven.

'It wasn't quite as . . . cut and dried as that,' she said. 'I'd had instructions from Europe to negate the propaganda Dr Somluk was spreading on the net. To make her less of a threat to the well-being of health care. She had a contract and I couldn't fire her until the Rights Committee saw fair cause for her dismissal. So I put her in a little clinic in the wilds. And still she ranted. She had crossed over from friend to enemy in a comparatively short space of time.'

'So you killed her.'

'She'd pushed me just a wee bit too far,' she said. 'The display in the Novotel was the last straw. I calmed her down that afternoon, convinced her that my car wouldn't start and she drove me back here. I told her that I was prepared to look into the practices of Medley. That her passion had made me think differently about things. In fact, I was about to present her with a folder I'd received from Switzerland. It cited fourteen malpractice complaints made by her former patients. Some leading to death.'

'They were real?'

'Probably not. It didn't matter. The Thai Medical Council would have been obliged to suspend her while they investigated the claims. The TMA isn't the FBI. It would have taken a year at least. And all that time, Dr Somluk would have been unemployable. I thought that was unnecessarily cruel.'

'So you killed her. Not nearly so cruel.'

'We came here. This was just a concrete bunker then, but the ante-room was kitted out with its fancy equipment. There was a cabinet with a hose, and that beauty.' She pointed to the axe. 'We'd had a couple of glasses of wine to make up. I took out the axe and we were playing. She was confident she'd won me over. I promised sincerely that once the operating theatre was complete I would discontinue my relationship with Medley. To cement our reunion and my decision we drank a toast to breastfeeding. Just as in your case, the opiate was already in the glass when I poured the wine. A quick swirl and it was absorbed.'

I felt relieved that even a doctor would fall for it.

'My mistake,' she said, 'was that I killed her when she was unconscious. It was a cowardly thing to do. But she was my first. It was the lowest point on the y axis of my learning curve. My sponsors had asked me to shut her up. It was freeing. It was as if they'd recognized my need to take a life and given me a pass. I had permission to live my dream.'

'How did you dispose of the body?' I asked.

'The simplest thing,' she said. 'There's a system. We have foam boxes that are officially labelled "Hospital Waste". They contain the bits that fall off or are sliced off, the stomach contents. The stomach itself. We send them to a ratified temple where they are blessed and cremated. Nobody thinks to look inside those boxes.'

'And me?' I asked. 'Why am I here?'

'You didn't respond to the warnings, dear. I told you to keep off. I warned you what would happen but you kept on probing.'

'So the cleaver in the kitchen door and the poisoned dogs were you?'

'You failed to read the signs.'

'You should have been more specific. You aren't the only one threatening me, you know?'

'My sponsors suggested I should use whatever method had been successful with Somluk.'

'You do realize they probably weren't aware you were cutting people up with an axe?'

'"Whatever it takes," they said. I am certain they wouldn't have been disappointed.'

'Given what they do for a living, I have to agree with you.'

She stepped down from her chair, checked her blood-spattered watch, and went for the axe. It was apparently time.

'And who was that in the next room?' I asked.

'Ah, no, Aladdin. Your two wishes have already been granted.'

'They usually come in threes.'

'Then let us just say that some nosy parker came looking for you.'

My heart dropped into a sinkhole.

'I said you weren't here,' she continued, 'but some people can't take no for an answer. I had wanted my second kill to be more refined. A little banter, something like this – perhaps a touch more intelligent – and then a dissection without the benefit of anaesthesia.'

I wanted to say something like, 'You heartless bitch', but everything I came up with had been used before. I didn't want my last line to be a cliché. There were so many nosy parkers in my life. Who had she chopped up? Was it somebody I loved like Arny or Mair or Chompu or, yes, even Captain Kow? Or a new friend like Nurse Da or my darling Conrad? Or one of the villagers, or . . .

I hadn't cried for so many years it had occurred to me I might be heartless after all. But there's nothing better than being strung up for the slaughter to bring out the weak girlie in one. It was all so hopeless. And what a way to go. Whoever remembered the names of the victims of serial killers? I certainly didn't. And I didn't want to go without knowing who I'd be meeting in limbo on his or her way to the next life.

'Who was it?' I asked through the embarrassing tears.

'No. Now you're being greedy.'

'Come on. Man? Woman?'

'None of it matters.'

'Not to you it doesn't. You're at the beginning of your notoriety. You'll be going on to have Michelle Yeoh play you in a biopic on HBO in five years. But me? I just vanish. It's worse than death to not have the answer to a riddle. Who's in the next room?'

She took up the axe again and knelt at my feet. I should have been petrified with fear as she started to explain what cuts she'd make in me. What parts might be too large and too long to fit in a foam ice chest. But I firmly believe that finding oneself tied naked to the floor of a deserted operating theatre at the feet of an insane woman with a sharp axe was a defining moment. What I did then . . . that's how I would be remembered. I could tell as I looked into her eyes that my time had come. If you're certain you're about to die you really don't want to waste time begging. You don't scream for help or for forgiveness or mercy or whatever it was that got you in that mess in the first place. You do a knock-knock joke.

'What?' she said.

'I said, "Knock-knock."'

290

'You aren't really taking this seriously, are you?'

'I'm just trying to lighten the mood a little bit.'

'Lighten the . . .? You do understand what I'm saying here, don't you? You do know what's going to happen? Or are you completely stupid?'

'Not completely. I still have a couple of months of the course to go.'

That pushed her over. Nobody likes a smart arse. She got into a position that would make chopping more comfortable.

'What temple?' I asked.

'What?'

'You said you'd be sending my parts to a temple for cremation.'

'It doesn't matter.'

'Of course it matters. I'm fond of this body. I want to know where you're sending it.'

'Shut up.'

'Make me.'

That line works better when the person you're talking to isn't holding an axe over her head. But I did notice her hesitate. There's a difference between butchering a dead body and slicing up a live one. At least I hoped so.

'The tiles,' I said.

'What?'

'You'll crack the tiles.'

'Damn it.'

She threw down the axe and ran into the other room for the sheet of metal she'd been so pleased with. She dragged it into the operating room. It was dripping with blood.

'I hope you're going to wash that down,' I said.

'No. What does it matter?'

'It's disgusting. I'm not lying down on someone else's blood.'

'Just lift up a fraction.'

'No.'

'Please.'

'No.'

'Perhaps you'll cooperate if you have a little incentive.'

Almost before I knew what was happening, she'd grabbed the axe and brought it down on my hand. It grazed my knuckles and made sparks on the tiles. I have no idea how I'd been able to retract my fingers in the split second she'd given me.

'Good reflexes,' she said.

She used her free hand to try to prise open those fingers, but I was as stubborn as she was nuts.

'You know I doubt whether your toes have the same reaction time,' she said, crawling on her knees across the floor.

She was right. My feet were rock bottom on the flexibility chart. I don't mind telling you I was at my maximum level of petrifaction by then. All the knock-

knock jokes on the planet wouldn't have cheered me up at that moment. I was a mess. I had a small bladder accident. She grabbed my shin, raised the axe and there was not a thing I could do about it.

'Stop right there,' came a familiar Thai voice from the direction of the doorway. Dr June and I turned our heads at the same time to see Arny standing there like some comic book hero. Except he was as white as the tiles on the floor. I knew why straight away. He'd seen a sight in the ante-room that probably turned his stomach inside out. I knew that expression on his face. He was about to pass out. He was already swaying.

Dr June got to her feet and charged at him with the axe raised. She let out a frightening scream. She truly was mad. She swung her axe downwards at a forty-five degree angle just as Arny sank to his knees. The blade took off a layer of his scalp and a tuft of hair and the momentum sent the axe all the way round its arc until it sliced through the doctor's left foot just below the ankle. I imagine she'd sharpened the blade beyond what the fire marshal considered necessary to chop down doors. That was evident from the ease with which it severed her foot. Arny, by now face down on the floor, was spared the nightmare of an open faucet of blood pouring from the doctor's leg. At the sight of her own blood, Dr June also passed out. And there they lay, the pair of them, unconscious on the tiles and me tied to the floor. It was what they called 'an awkward predicament'. Should Dr June come to first, she might summon the strength to use her axe on Arny.

I yelled my lungs out, 'Ar-ny! Ar-ny!'

He didn't move. The doctor coughed.

'Ar . . . ny!'

She was conscious already and increasingly aware. She slowly pulled the green scrub jacket up over her head to reveal the largest bra I'd ever seen on a small-breasted woman. With deep controlled breaths she wound the shirt around the remains of her bleeding foot and knotted it tightly with the sleeves.

'ARNY!'

His eyelids fluttered. He needed something to wake him up. There was nothing to hand . . . or foot. If he hadn't interrupted us so soon I could have thrown a toe at him.

'Arn—'

He looked up. Saw the blood. Saw the doctor reach for the axe. Lift it. Lunge. And he smacked her one in the kisser with a magnificent right. She dropped like a bag of suet pudding. I had nothing free to applaud with, so I whooped. I'd never seen him throw a punch before. It was another major breakthrough. Admittedly this was a small, middle-aged woman with one foot but you have to start somewhere.

'Arny,' I said. 'Get over here and untie me.'

'I'm feeling a bit . . .'

'I don't care. Untie me first and you can faint for as long as you want. One wrist would be fine.'

The knots were too tight to untie. All he had was the axe to cut my bonds but it was bloody and he refused to look at it, which made him every bit as dangerous as Dr June. But after a little back-and-forth gentle sawing he had my right hand free and the rest I could do myself.

'Arny, take off your shirt.'

'Why?'

'Because I'm naked.'

'Oh, right.'

His T-shirt was a cocktail dress on me and it was dramatically stained with the blood that ran from my brother's head wound. I tied Dr June's hands behind her back using my own bonds, conscious of the fact she might bleed to death but not really caring that much.

'Who's in the next room?' I asked Arny.

'It's . . . it's a body. I couldn't look.'

'I understand. But I want you to avert your eyes as you walk back through that room and keep going till you find a doctor. This is a hospital so it shouldn't be that difficult. Tell him or her to get over here immediately. And get someone to look at your scalp. Do you have your cell phone with you?'

'It's in the Mighty X.'

'Right. Then I want you to call the Lang Suan Police Station. Tell them we have a murderer here who's bleeding out. If they take their usual sweet time they won't have anyone to beat a confession out of. When you get back here you can tell me how you knew where to find me.'

'OK.'

He started off on wobbly legs, a small piece of skin on his head flapping open like a trapdoor.

'And Arny . . .'

'Yes?'

I walked up to him and squeezed him so tight he might have even felt it through all those muscles. I whispered in his ear. 'In your own usual weird Arny way, you saved my life. Thank you.'

I kissed him. He usually spat when I kissed him, but he accepted this one with good grace. He smiled and headed off through the ante-room. I checked Dr June's pulse and tightened the wadding around her stump. It was odd that all the floor tiles should end up red after all. It was amazing how much blood one person could shed. Her severed part, complete with toes, lay off to one side wanting nothing to do with her. I summoned what little was left of my courage and walked into the ante-room.

The body lay in pieces in front of the coffee vending machine, both human and appliance in a pool of blood. Dr June had stripped her victim and begun the dissection. I recognized her straight away and was embarrassed to feel relief at the sight of a dead body. It was not one of my loved ones. I'd only seen her once. It was the

woman with the wrong initial. Chompu's friend, Dr
Niramon.

A sign at the front of the vending machine said OUT OF
CONTROL.

CHAPTER SEVENTEEN

SNOW WHITE & THE SEVEN PYGMIES
(T-shirt)

The storm was so malicious it seemed to render the events of that night insignificant. Arny and I drove to the Lang Suan police station in a cream and brown highway patrol vehicle so old it could have found a niche in the law enforcement museum at the ministry. The water in some places was deep enough to seep into the cab through the rust holes. We saw people being blown against walls. Umbrellas leaving earth. Power lines draped like spaghetti along the pavements. Zinc roofs flapping. I remember thinking what a relief it would be to finally arrive at a solid concrete structure.

On the way I'd used Arny's phone to let everyone know I was all right. I'd heard snatches of bizarre news from the surveillance team, but I hadn't been in any fit state to take it all in. It wasn't until the horrendous encounter with Dr June was over that the shakes set in. My body had been drained by the effort of being cool.

Arny had hugged me all the way to stop me shuddering completely out of the truck. I could see his reflection in the window. With his head shrouded in a white bandage he looked like a muscle-bound Q-Tip.

'So tell me,' I said from the rock-hard pillow of his chest.

'What?'

'How did you know where to find me?'

'I was driving around looking for you,' he said. 'And I wondered what would possess you to head off on the worst night of the year on a bicycle. I mean, I know you're nutty but that was outrageous even for you.'

'Thank you.'

'You had to have gone somewhere close and most of our village had shut down to prepare for the storm. So I thought about your story of Dr Somluk.'

'You pay attention to my stories?'

'Of course I do. Don't be rude. I listen to all your cases. You're my lifeline to the exciting world I don't live in. I'd been hoping you'd ask me to help find her but you never did.'

'You were always off with Gaew.'

'Only because I didn't have a purpose at the resort. Cleaning rooms that nobody stays in. Sweeping a beach that gets a new batch of garbage every day. But, anyway, I wondered whether your running off had anything to do with Dr Somluk. So I called Nurse Da.'

'You had her number?'

'Yes . . . I . . .'

'I know. I bet you've got a lot of numbers of single women.'

'I don't ask for them.'

'I know you don't, and you're too polite not to key them into your phone when they give them. So, anyway . . .?'

'So, anyway, she told me about your meeting with Dr Somluk. As you've been working on it so hard, I thought that would be a big enough reason to go out in this weather. I went to the health centre and I found your bicycle. Grandma Nida who lives opposite the clinic told me she'd heard an old pick-up truck drive into the car park about five forty-five and then drive out again a few minutes later. This was just before all the power went off. The whole district was blacked out. So, being a nosy old dear, she had her head out the window watching the truck leave. She couldn't see who was in the cab but she did recognize the hospital sticker on the tailgate.

'It was the only clue I had, and Grandad Jah and Chompu had turned off their phones so I took a chance. You'd already mentioned Dr June so I went to her office but it was dark and there was nobody there. The guard said the doctor must be working late in the new complex again. She usually locked the door, he said, but I found it unlocked when I got there and a bunch of keys still in the lock. I suppose . . . she must have opened it. The dead woman.'

'Yes, mate. So it seems.'

I kissed him again and thanked him for being related to me. I promised I'd involve him more closely in future cases. He didn't say anything but I caught the reflection of his smile in the window.

I was wide-eyed conscious of the fact that I should have been dead rather than drinking hot tea in the office of a nice policeman with sideburns. I should have been dead because I'd missed the clues. I should have been dead because I'd allowed myself to select a likely antagonist and ignored everything and everybody else. Really, I should have been dead.

The captain who interviewed me was a bit out of his depth with axe murderers. He was clearly relieved when Major General Suvit arrived, dragged from a reception at the Kangaroo Hotel. I'd heard about the tough, apparently clean policeman they nicknamed Ridgeback, but this was the first time we'd worked together on a case. I mean, him asking questions. Me answering.

'You do know you can't print any of this?' he said once he'd heard the entire, ridiculous story. We had six other senior officers sitting around us with notepads.

'Well, indeed I can,' I told him.

'It's an ongoing case. I can block anything you care to write.'

I smiled at him. He was probably in his fifties but unmarked by time. A good jaw. A trim figure. Kind eyes. Chompu had hinted that he might even be incorruptible, which was a bit like saying dolphins don't necessarily need water.

'What ongoing case?' I said. 'You have a dead body, two eyewitnesses, and a suspect with a self-inflicted amputation. You even have the murder weapon peppered with fingerprints. And I'd be surprised if you didn't find emails on her computer linking her to a missing doctor and a huge disgraceful advertising campaign launched by the true villains in this drama, the Medley Corporation. But, one nutty case at a time, right?'

I wouldn't have been surprised about what they'd find on Dr June's computer because in the car over I'd arranged for Sissi to copy a legible version of all her encrypted messages into her inbox. And I was being particularly disrespectful to a senior policeman, because cheating death allows one a certain level of cockiness. But I was also wondering why the major was being so unenthusiastic about this self-solving case. It would certainly look good in the press.

'This is a police investigation,' he said. 'Not a newspaper exposé. Details of the case will be released by my department as they unfold, after a thorough check of the facts. Any public disclosure of events by a material witness will be considered interference and you would be subject to arrest. Do I make myself clear?'

'Perfectly,' I said. 'And how is the progress going on the new police gymnasium?'

'What on earth has that to do with anything?'

'Well ... Major, when I was doing research on the Medley Corporation's involvement in rural communities, I found the list of projects they're involved in. And what should I discover halfway down the list but the Lang Suan Police Gymnasium, proudly sponsored by Medichoc, Your Family's Favourite Nibble. I could sing you the jingle as well but I'm tone deaf.'

'Jimm.'

I'd forgotten Arny was sitting beside me. That happened often. I could tell he was feeling uncomfortable. He often encouraged me to temper my assaults on public officials. But this was important. I ignored him. The major blushed slightly and laughed unconvincingly.

'Are you suggesting,' he said, 'that a major murder investigation might be influenced by a relationship with a sponsor?'

'Yes. This is Thailand.'

'You are Thai, aren't you?'

'Absolutely. So I have a natural right to insult my country. And you know it's true. Did Dr June have a hand in getting you the deal?'

He smiled at his wall calendar.

'She did, didn't she?' I smiled. 'Well, I think that's called a conflict of interest damning enough to bring in the big boys from Bangkok, don't you?'

'We're perfectly capable of impartially conducting our own investigation.'

'I'm sure you're right. Just as I'm perfectly capable of writing this up in a way that doesn't negatively influence your case. I could even make it a heroic police operation in the sticks rather than, say, a mania triggered by pressure from a demonic multinational organization.'

'Are you blackmailing me?'

'A bit.'

Arny slumped back in his chair. It had been an exhausting night and I wasn't helping him to relax at all. The major stared into my bloodshot eyes.

'You don't want to make an enemy of me, Jimm Juree,' he said.

'Not at all,' I agreed. 'As my readers will learn when I describe the case, you are a conscientious, hard-working ally. A good friend. The country will love you. Never underestimate the power of the press.'

It was a bold speech from an unemployed journalist who made a living correcting bad English. The sign on his wall said, in Thai, THE ROYAL THAI POLICE ARE ALWAYS UPRIGHT AND HONEST. The English translation would have it that THE THAILAND POLICEMAN ALWAYS ERECT AND STRAIGHTFORWARD.

He stood, glared at me once more, and said, 'You can write your damned story.'

And without another word he left the room, trailed by his six silent aides. I had indeed made an enemy and I knew I would come to regret it.

*

Lieutenant Chompu, Captain Kow and Grandad Jah were sitting in the public waiting area when Arny and I emerged. A red beach umbrella flew past the entrance and momentarily distracted me. The police station car park was a pond in which Chompu's SUV floated like a shiny black lotus. There was a lot of touching and feeling with everyone except Grandad. I ignored their questions about me and trauma and whether I'd be all right.

'Is Mair OK?' I asked.

'High and dry,' said Captain Kow. 'Her and the dogs. The local headman came by earlier and evacuated everyone. There's probably nothing to worry about but the surf's high and these storm surges are unpredictable.'

'They're reporting five-metre waves off Chumphon estuary,' said Grandad. 'They're billeting everyone in schools till it's all over. Everyone but your foolish mother, that is.'

'Why except her?' I asked.

'She refused to leave without the dogs and the cows,' said Chompu. 'And the schools aren't accepting any livestock.'

'So, where is she?'

'She's in the hut in my palm garden,' said Kow. 'It's on high ground. Bit cramped but as long as she leaves the cows outside . . .'

'I can't even guarantee she'll do that,' I smiled. 'Thanks, Kow.'

'You're welcome ... my daughter.'

'You poor darling,' said Chompu. 'You've had such an awful night. I heard all about it from the desk sergeant. And I'm afraid I should accept some of the blame for what happened over there at the hospital.'

'Why on earth should you do that?' I asked.

'Dr Niramon was one of the people I phoned when we were trying to get through to you. She lives in a dormitory behind the hospital. She promised to go over to see if Dr June had any idea where you were. She had a spare key to the operating room. She must have walked in on ...'

Chompu shed a tear. He was fragile and I knew the thought that he'd caused someone's death would linger for a long time. I put my arm around him and rested my cheek on his shoulder until his sobs subsided. I looked at my father and grandfather, who were both averting their eyes. I'd rather been hoping to see my Englishman waiting there but it occurred to me he didn't know anything about the night's events. He probably felt he'd been stood up. I'd tried to call him from the police truck but the signal said he wasn't connected.

'I don't suppose any of you have seen Conrad tonight?' I asked.

'Oh ... we've seen him,' said Grandad.

'Pretty much all of him,' Chompu said with a sigh, pleased to be given more pleasant thoughts.

The three men giggled like schoolgirls.

'What?' said I.

'There's a story you need to hear,' said Grandad.

'I'll tell her,' said Chompu.

'What? What is it?' I asked.

'Your boyfriend's a sleaze bucket,' said Grandad.

'That's exactly why I should tell this story,' said Chompu.

'Filth,' said Grandad.

'If somebody doesn't tell me soon, there's a perfectly good axe in the evidence room just back there,' I said. 'I swear . . .'

'All right, here it is . . .' began Chompu, and he told me the whole story, from the surveillance, to the naked dinner, to the Agatha Christie gathering in the living room. It sounded like a fun evening and believe me I wish I could have been there to enjoy it. But nothing they told me made me think any less of my dashing writer. Not, that is, until they got to the part about the maid. They'd asked her why she felt she had to warn me on that first day at his house.

'At first, she wouldn't say,' said Chompu. 'She said she was just making a friendly suggestion from one woman to another. Then I reminded her she didn't have a work permit and that I was a policeman. Thence honesty set in.'

'A scumbag,' said Grandad.

'Your writer seems to be doing the rounds,' said Chompu.

307

'Of what?' I asked.

'Of the local gals.'

'Oh.'

'He's bedded every remotely attractive woman in the district and not a few plain ugly ones,' said Grandad. 'Wouldn't be at all surprised if that's why his wife left him. No-good lump of—'

'The staff are apparently given a lot of nights off,' said Chompu. 'But there are ... how can I put it? Remains. Sometimes in the form of prophylactics ...'

'Eeuw.'

'... or certain ... equipment. As you've been there, I'm sure I don't have to go into any detail. But often, actual young ladies come down for breakfast in various states. A recognized a lot of them as local girls. She'd tried to warn them but they rarely listened.'

Guilty. And, as if it had always been there, waiting for recognition, the nickname Gogo passed into my mind. The Thai pronunciation for Cocoa. Or, Co ... Co. Eighty-six kilos would be overweight for a Thai, but perfectly normal for a tall Westerner. For a tall Westerner like Conrad Coralbank. It wasn't a coincidence that my horny writer and our local nurse had disappeared during the same twenty-four-hour period. Da was another one of his local conquests. A friendly smile cuts through a lot of language barriers. And I bet he charmed them all the same way he'd won me. It wouldn't have surprised me if he had a list somewhere with ticks beside the names.

But, what the heck? I used him, didn't I? And just where did unfaithful men fit in a cosmic chart that included things like almost being chopped up with an axe? What did I care? In a way I felt pleased for all the women he'd bedded politely and respectfully – whom he'd gone out of his way to satisfy so they'd go to the pyre knowing, however briefly, what romance felt like. Goodness knows men in this country didn't bother with any of that unnecessary nonsense. Oh, he was a bastard to all of us, no denying that. But in my case he'd exceeded my expectations and stuck around long enough to give me hope. Hope is a dangerous thing. But still I couldn't hate him. He'd made me dinner, damn it. Tonight would probably have been the most romantic night of my life. Instead I'd had the most frightening. Such is fate.

'So why did she pretend that her brother was her husband?' I asked.

'The only way A could keep his hands off her was by pretending she and Jo were married,' said Chompu. 'Even then it wasn't as if he stopped trying. I suppose some heterosexual men can't keep it locked away.'

CHAPTER EIGHTEEN

WHERE THE SOFT SAND CARESSES THE HORIZON
(beach resort ad)

Just like romance, intrigue and Dr June, who succumbed to her injuries during the night, the storms of Christmas Eve had passed away when the sun came up on Christmas Day.

The conditions had been so awful the night before that when we left the police station we barely made it to the Hibiscus Motel. There, we'd taken the last two rooms. Arny, Chompu and I stayed in one room, me in the middle to spare my brother the accidental creeping hands of our randy policeman. Grandad Jah reluctantly shared the other with Captain Kow. Naturally, none of us got a wink of sleep. When we drove out the next morning, Lang Suan looked as if a hurricane had ploughed through it. Santa had delivered debris. Vendors were mopping water from their shops. Palm fronds were wrapped around road signs far from any coconut trees. The council garbage bins had been thrown through windows and onto roofs.

The bridge over the Ga River had been washed away, so we had to turn around and take a route via Bangladesh to get home. We were in a comparatively jolly mood considering, but all we really needed was a good day's sleep. Or two. In my case they could wake me up at New Year. On the way we slalomed around roof tiles and tree branches. Lost dogs in collars sat beside the road looking for their owners. Bamboo sheds lay flat and signposts were bent over like old ladies. Ignoring all this, the sky was a magnificent crimson, not unlike the floor of the operating theatre the night before.

We drove through six centimetres of mud as we forged up to Kow's palm plantation, although plantation was far too grand a word for the small patch of land he'd carved out of the jungle on the side of a hill. Mair and the dogs came running to greet us with their tongues out. The cows ignored us. My mother had been cut off from the outside world when the nearest cellphone tower slid down the side of the mountain with several hundred rubber trees. So she hadn't slept either. Arny and Grandad travelled in Kow's motorcycle sidecar combo while Chompu and I in the SUV updated Mair on all the fascinating news. The dogs sat on the back seat and, to Chompu's dismay, all threw up within the space of ten minutes. Knowing Chom, I expected him to buy a new car rather than disinfect this one.

We headed to the coast. We crossed the little bridge that forded the stream that had always meandered gently behind the Lovely Resort. But, oddly, like an incomplete memory, the stream, not gentle at all now, meandered at speed directly into the sea. To the west, the house of our neighbour, Guy, usually hidden behind a bank of thick bushes, now had an unrestricted sea view. To the east, a still-snarling surf threw itself onto a ribbon of beach strewn with bamboo and garbage. We all instinctively looked behind us to see whether we'd taken a wrong turn. Had we been so befuddled with fatigue that we might have come to entirely the wrong beach? But there was the end of the bay with its distinctive rock formation. And there was the quaint bridge we'd planned to turn into a tourist attraction for Japanese honeymooners. And there, tossing around on the waves some fifty metres out, was Grandad Jah's coffin.

We were in the right place. Everything else was where it should have been. But the Gulf Bay Lovely Resort and Restaurant was gone.

DISCOVER THE JIMM JUREE SERIES FROM

COLIN COTTERILL

Intrepid crime reporter Jimm Juree and her eccentric family move across Thailand from exotic location to exotic location, all of them seemingly quiet, crime-free and therefore career-destroying.

But you can't keep a good woman down and sooner or later Jimm is on the trail of the most dangerous criminals and killers she has ever had to face...

Crime fiction has never been funnier or weirder.

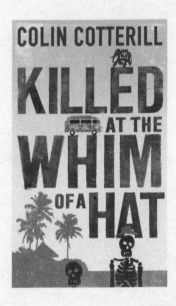

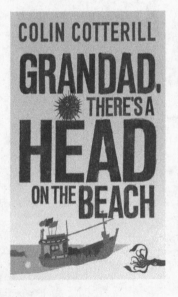

Find out more about Colin Cotterill at
www.colincotterill.com

Sign up for news about other fantastic authors at
www.quercusbooks.co.uk